Where the Cherries End Up

Where the Cherries End Up

Gail Henley

LITTLE, BROWN AND COMPANY

BOSTON   TORONTO

LIBRARY OF CONGRESS CATALOG CARD NO. 79-83703

FIRST AMERICAN EDITION

All of the characters in this book
are fictitious and any resemblance
to actual persons living or dead
is purely coincidental.

BP

PRINTED IN THE UNITED STATES OF AMERICA

To
Florence Chippior Olsheskie
her husband
and their eight children

I

We never missed a wedding. No one in Polackville did. People came from miles around to celebrate. During the day, the men and women sat around on benches and talked. I hated to get stuck on a bench. My feet didn't touch the floor, they just swung in the middle of nowhere and you just knew anybody could catch them and topple you over. I spent most of my time running back and forth. You could find anything you wanted in the kitchen, and if you couldn't reach it, somebody always came by and got it for you. If you were smart, at a wedding you could fill up and it would last for three days.

Everyone was happy. When they were corked up enough, all the grandfathers had a go on the fiddle and accordion. There was more square dancing than you had breath for. The men swung the ladies so hard you could see their panties flying in the air.

But it was really the bride I couldn't keep my eyes off. People lined up two or three times for another chance to kiss her. Tende. sweet kisses. It didn't matter how ugly she was in person, on her wedding day you could always overhear someone say she looked beautiful. I just hoped with all my heart there would be a wedding day for me. Just to know there was one person in the world who loved you. That there was someone, on some bench, who knew you were good looking, even if it was only for one day – it would be worth it.

By the third wedding, I knew exactly when the fighting would start. As soon as it got dark, you could feel things changing. All the drinking the men had done all day settled in their blood. Someone would fall over someone else by mistake and they'd remember a grudge. You could see the poor bride trying to protect her white dress. But none of the men would take pity. Nobody could hear her begging them not to ruin the most important day of her life. Most of the brides just cry.

At the fifth wedding I was at, I think someone tried to pick a fight with my father because Mary Poderskie came running over to tell me he was rolling around in the middle of the dance floor. "Guess what, your father is fighting with someone and he's really getting beat up." Mary was too stupid to know that us Luckoskies were different. "No, he's not in the fight. And anyways, if he was, he'd win." I didn't have a chance to squeeze through the crowd to see for myself because Momma gathered us up and told us to get onto the back of the half-ton, we were going home. Momma drove and Daddy sat all slumped over in the front seat.

I knocked on the window. "Hey, Momma." It was hard to get her attention. "Hey Momma, was Daddy in a fight?"

She didn't answer. She never used to answer half my questions. But it seemed as if he was, because whenever a half-ton passed us going the other way, I could see something wet on his face. When we got back to the farm, I told Momma that there was blood on the new tie she had bought Daddy for the wedding. She just told me to go to bed. But the very next time that Daddy got dressed up in his suit and put his tie on, I saw that the white stripes had turned pink.

Daddy wished I wouldn't be living with them, but I was. And Josef, who was the oldest, thought just like Daddy, only he was trying to figure out a way of getting rid of me. Urek, who was two years younger than me, imitated Josef, and tried to make himself older than me. He treated me like one of the kids and said I was a pest. They all told me that I was lucky, that I was just hanging on by the skin of my teeth. But every time I counted, it always came out the same – Daddy, then Josef, then me, then Urek. I was there, right in the middle, and that made them really furious.

And I wasn't going to move. I liked living on our farm. It isn't really a farm. It's just a big piece of land the government gave our great-grandfather a hundred years ago, and then he gave it to our grandfather and then our grandfather gave it to Daddy and now we're all here. It's just a lot of hill and stone. You can't grow anything on it except purple thistle and dandelions and scotch grass. We've been trying to grow potatoes in one of the fields, but we only get a crop every second year because the stones just take right over whenever they feel like it. Our land is just someplace for us to live. We didn't know what else to call it, so we called it a farm. We don't bother keeping any animals, they couldn't survive here. We have a dog that Daddy calls a mongrel but we have no idea where it came from or what it's doing on our farm. Nobody likes it.

It's good to know exactly where you are in case someone tries to trick you. In Polackville, you might think that everybody's farm is the same as everybody else's – all the houses are black because the weather got into the wood before it was painted, and they all have leaky roofs because you can't get the shingles to stay on, and the clothes lines break down every month because the clothes are so heavy. But if you check it out really carefully you can always spot one or two differences. Our place had something that no other farm had – a straw cross and a rusty horseshoe tacked up on the outside of the house. We don't know who put them there, so no one's dared take them down. They make me feel so good, whenever I see them I always know I'm in the right place.

I wanted to live with Daddy because I knew he was a King. You could catch glimpses of his kingliness, if you knew when and where to look out for them. And I knew. As soon as I saw him circling his half-ton truck, I'd try and jump in with the rest of the kids. We knew he was only going into Hopefield to get himself a supply from the liquor store but it was like driving around heaven. That's why our great-grandfathers named it Jasno Gora. In English it meant shiny hills and blessed earth. "You know kids, we live in God's country." I wanted to clap my hands and bounce up and down. I was so happy that the King knew about his Kingdom.

The cap on the top of his head bounced to one side. Even though it was old and greasy and one of the ear flaps wouldn't stay up, we all knew it was his crown, and that's why he wouldn't go anywhere without it. Underneath, his sharp eyes surveyed the countryside. He could spot a partridge in the thick of any bush. Two minutes later he would quickly turn around in his seat to notice that Madinskie had another cord of pulp on his pile. In the distance he could see that the tractor Poderskie was using had a new tire. In the middle of another bush he would point out a tree and tell us that if there was a tree like that on our farm, we would be rich. "I'm telling you a tree like that could fill three truck loads of pulp." He could see everything. He would slow down, then speed up, look out the side window, then straight ahead.

Then there would be a silence. Nobody ever wanted to talk about it, and nobody ever told anybody anything, so you had to figure it out on your own. Maybe it wasn't an accident that God hadn't given us any decent trees on our farm, maybe we were too good to have ever become farmers. Maybe we were supposed to be different. It might have been a plan. Daddy and Josef and me and Urek had been given blue eyes. And Momma had blue eyes. When my younger sister Krysia opened her eyes we saw that they were blue too. And after that all four little kids, one by one, came with blue eyes. Every single person on our farm had blue eyes. We were meant to do something. I knew that God had brought us together for some reason.

We should have slowed down when we started the drive back up the old gravel road to our farm, but we didn't. Daddy'd speed over those stones and they'd rattle our truck. We hated those stubborn bastards.

"Well here we are, the great Luckoskie farm." He'd throw an

4

empty beer bottle out the window. In revenge. "You couldn't get the edge of a pick axe into the ground." A hundred years ago, one of the Luckoskies must have started to collect the stones because you can see a few stone fences, but the stones grew faster than he could pick them. Nobody's ever figured out a way of making a living out of this place.

Daddy tackled the bush. Every day he went into the bush and cut the trees and logged them. He skidded and peeled the pulp. He lifted every single piece with his bare hands and loaded them onto the half-ton so high your head would spin when you saw the truck squealing and crawling out of the bush. All this hard work. For us.

When you'd watch him get ready for supper, you could see his undershirt soaked with yellow and the muscles of his arms sticking out like round balls, and no matter how long he washed his hands, he could never get them clean. I wanted to go up and touch him, but I couldn't because I had to stay out of his way all the time, so I wouldn't remind him that I was still there. But I could feel how sore his red neck was from the thousands of mosquito bites he had. And I could see how hard it was for him to straighten out his back when he sat down on a chair. I remembered every cut he had on his hands so I knew they had never healed. And to me, there is something very special about a man who's not afraid to see himself bleeding when he works. Every suppertime, I'd run to put a fresh raw onion on the table beside his plate. A treat for someone whose hands show that he has suffered.

From the first day I learned how to pray, I only prayed for one thing. I prayed that one day Daddy would find good drinking water on our farm. Everywhere you look you can spot a half-dug well. Daddy hates our rusty water. He can't get used to drinking it. It turns the tea grey and it smells in your cup and it makes you sick to your stomach. I only wanted God to give us one cup of good water. For Daddy. Then he could stop going to the liquor store to buy something to drink.

As for me, there was only one thing I really didn't like. The outhouses. We have five useless ones. Daddy builds a new one

5

every so often because the old ones start to stink and no one feels like using them. The trouble is that no one ever got around to taking the old ones down. There just never seemed to be enough time – if it wasn't night, it was winter. Daddy said you hardly had a chance to turn around, because before you knew it the day would be gone.

I didn't have very much time myself. Every time I'd sit down to play with my cut-outs, I'd be called back to change another diaper, or find Josef or Urek a pair of socks, or peel the potatoes, or wash the floor. There was always something. But still I managed to get hold of the old catalogue every year and get myself a whole new set of cut-outs. I thought that maybe one day, when I'd have time, I'd play with them. I keep them in a cardboard box which I hide, because it's private.

It was the same with Momma's cedar chest. She used to keep it in the living room but then she moved it into the bedroom because it had her private things and she didn't want us digging through it. Inside are all the wedding presents she got. There's two beautiful embroidered pillow cases and a nice Kenwood blanket and a real silver teapot. She's saving them.

*　　*　　*

We'd practically forgotten about Father Anotskie. He'd gone off to some city somewhere. All the seminaries that anyone had ever heard about were in the cities. When he came back you could see that the pollution had affected him. Everyone said he looked unhealthy. His skin had turned grey. We couldn't figure out what was the matter with him. It was the first time I had ever heard people talk about unhappiness.

He walked around his rectory as if he didn't know where he was. It made everyone in Polackville sad. We could see something terrible was eating him up inside. Whatever it was, he couldn't shake it off. No one had ever seen a man go downhill so fast.

People wanted to pick him up. They brought him homemade bread and chicken-feather pillows. Some said that

6

maybe one night in his seminary, he'd seen God. Others said it was depression from all that studying. Everyone watched patiently as he drove in and out of Hopefield in his rented half-ton truck. They said that in time he would come out of himself and start being a priest. The fresh air in Jasno Gora would cure him.

And they were right.

One year, six months, and three days later he was delivering humorous sermons at mass. Even though you weren't supposed to laugh in church, you couldn't help looking down at your rosary and smiling. Now the talk changed. Everyone was saying how young, friendly, and down-to-earth he was. Some people put an extra ten cents onto the collection plate. In school, religion class became the favourite subject and started to last a whole day. Everyone forgot that Father Anotskie's skin could turn grey.

Father Anotskie had a plan. He wanted to make the parish – the township of Jasno Gora and the town of Hopefield – into a place we would never want to leave. He suggested that all the young from every part of the parish should have a social evening once a month in the church basement. The evening would begin with him giving a talk, followed by a question period in which we could ask anything we felt like, and then end up with sandwiches and dancing to records. All the girls, every one, was for it. But they only backed him up because he was good looking. No one meant it as whole-heartedly as I did. I could see the brilliance behind the idea.

It was at the youth meeting that Father Anotskie showed himself for what he was. He'd let go completely. He spread his legs in front of him so everyone could see his black crotch. He wasn't sincere and he didn't care. He thought he could get away with anything. There was nothing holy about him. Then I saw it – a distant blank look in his eyes. He was having a relapse. The greyness came back to his skin. I could see his failure in the city, his mistake in choosing the priesthood. His greed to pull down everyone with him.

"I'll tell you something. Regardless how educated you get in your lives, or where you end up living . . . ." He was smiling. "It doesn't matter who you marry or how much money you'll make, you will never be able to run away from the fact that you were born in Hopefield. Jasno Gora. Right here." He was pointing to the stupid floor. He crossed his arms, sat back, stretched his crotch out even further and looked up at the ceiling. "In northern Canada."

He was practically laughing now. He knew that you couldn't find Jasno Gora on any map that's ever been printed in the world. "Wherever you go, you will always take the small town with you." He looked straight at me, caught the corner of my eye. I should have got up and left, but I've never had any guts.

None of the others were even thinking of leaving. Mary Poderskie sat there soaking it all up with her white face. You could see she would never amount to much. The Poderskies were probably the stupidest people in all of Polackville. I don't know why Daddy always stood up for them. He said you couldn't ask for better neighbours.

Even my cousin Agata who was always telling me she was going to be a psychologist sat frozen. I had never seen her with such a calm face in my life. Well, I wasn't going to let Father Anotskie get away with it. Maybe I couldn't do anything about it at that very minute, but someday I would prove him wrong.

I looked around again. I really didn't want to be the one to sacrifice my life, but I could see that none of the others would bother. And somebody had to do it. Someone had to prove to him that we were as good as everyone else. I knew in the end it had to be me.

The Hopefield girls didn't even blink an eyelash. I guess they didn't have to. They knew that Father Anotskie wasn't really talking to them. Hopefield only had eleven hundred people but those girls were as up-to-date as anybody in the world. They were all wearing mini skirts and they were always talking about the Beatles or the Rolling Stones. In another two minutes they would be on the floor showing off the latest dances. They never told anybody where they learned them from. I guess they wanted us to think they were geniuses. Maybe they were, but they still had a better chance than the rest of us because most of them had a television in their house and every once in a while someone from some city stopped in Hopefield. No matter how closely I watched them, I knew I wouldn't be able to imitate them. I didn't even bother practising on the farm because by the next youth meeting the style would have changed again anyway.

I knew Hopefield as well as any of them did. I was there every chance I could get. We used to go to school there, and on some Saturdays we'd go shopping to Stedman's store and every Sunday we'd go to church. Everything was in Hopefield – the hockey arena, the liquor store, and the joining corner for two of the biggest highways in Canada, 36 and 38. Anyone who went from Toronto to Ottawa had to pass through Hopefield. But what spoiled Hopefield was Metamonskie's sign. It was painted on the side wall of his hardware store. It stood out so much that every stranger who passed through Hopefield automatically thought he owned the town. But Leonard Metamonskie was really a nobody. In fact, he would never even have the hardware store if old Mr. Metamonskie hadn't given it to him, and already he had drunk half of it away.

Not that many Polish people lived in Hopefield. Most of the town was Irish. We knew them all and they knew us, but you still couldn't get a hello out of them, when you'd meet them in the post office. There was no mixing between the Polish and the Irish. Even the Irish kids at school thought they were better than us. They couldn't pronounce their *th*'s either, but on the whole they spoke better English. They didn't have to go home and listen to someone yelling in Polish all night. They didn't understand one word in Polish. It made them think they were big shots. After all, Irish is English.

Momma told us that if they didn't know any better, we weren't to pay attention. But my mother didn't have a good memory so she'd forgotten the differences that separated me from the Hopefield girls. I had a big black stain in the hollow of my neck. The dirt had started to grow there. It wasn't the same for them because they all had hot running water, so they could wash once a week. For me, it was impossible to wash in the winter and even when I scrubbed away at it in the summer, I could never get rid of it all. It always came back. So I just had to go around pretending it was something I was born with.

But I knew things about the Hopefield girls they didn't know I knew. Momma had asked the manager of Stedman's store if I could babysit their new kid whenever they went out. At least one Saturday night a month I sat on top of Stedman's store, right on the main road, in the centre of Hopefield. No one got a better view than me. As soon as they'd leave, I'd shut off all the lights, pull up a chair to the window, open the curtains just a sliver and watch. The baby cried all night but I never gave in. I wasn't going to miss a thing.

How great Hopefield was at night. Seamus, Tomek, Eileen, everybody – everybody would sit on the post office steps. And they smoked cigarettes. If Father Anotskie wanted me to, I could take one look around the church basement this minute, and tell him everybody who smoked. They'd shout back and forth to each other. They'd walk in the middle of the road. They'd drink Pepsi Cola from the machine outside the Esso station. Every ten minutes the cars would come by, and everyone would cheer them. It was a never-ending contest between Peter Dooley and Stefan Winchevskie. Stefan used to spend all day in the garage lifting the back end of his Chevrolet as far up as he possibly could. But still he couldn't go faster than Peter Dooley. He never gave up and they'd spend all night chasing each other. The louder they screeched their tires on the main road, the more the kids on the post office steps laughed. Upstairs, behind my curtain, I laughed too.

No wonder none of the kids from Hopefield took these youth meetings seriously. It was stopping them from going out on the street and having fun. I hated the youth meetings too. Especially the social part. I could tell from how quickly and easily the guys stacked the chairs that no one would ask me to dance. For a whole month before this meeting, I'd offered up all my masses and did extra penance so that I wouldn't end up sitting all night, but it wasn't enough to save me. It was just my luck that the night before, Josef picked up a really sad song on his transistor radio from Wheeling, West Virginia. It was about a girl who kept going to dances and having to sit all night because no one would ask her to dance. And as she'd be sitting there, everybody would walk back and forth in front of her. Even when she wore a yellow dress, no one noticed her. When she was ninety, they still called her the wallflower of the ball.

On the way to Hopefied in the half-ton, Josef gave me some advice. He told me that whatever happens, even if no one asks me to dance, I'm supposed to look as if I'm having a good time by keeping myself busy. He hated to give me advice but this time he had to, because he didn't want me to make a fool of him. I knew I better take his advice or I'd never hear the end of it, and on the way back to the farm I'd probably get it once over the head for having acted stupid. But what could I find to keep myself busy with?

I looked around.

Father Anotskie was the only other person who wasn't dancing. I thought I'd better go over and start a conversation with him. After all he didn't know I was angry with him, and he was still everybody's favourite, so it might look as if I was doing an interesting thing. Something even more interesting than dancing. If I was lucky, he might even apologize for the blank look in his eyes and tell me why he had a vicious streak. Who knows, we might even become friends. I was going to seriously consider becoming a nun.

He saw me coming. I had to think quickly about what I could ask him. "Father Anotskie, uh . . . why do you think it is, that so many people who don't believe in God and never go to church or ever pray, don't suffer, and end up having a better life than . . . " I wish I would have found a better question to ask. " . . . than those who go to church and pray all the time and never sin?"

He found it difficult to smile at me so he didn't. "I can't think of the word, but there's a word that fits you perfectly."

Eileen Skuce walked by in that tight green-and-grey checked skirt with the frill. He didn't have to pretend to me, I knew he was looking at her ass.

"Eileen's such a nice girl."

I tried to get his attention back. "Come on, Father Anotskie, you can think of the word."

"What word?"

"You know, the word that fits me."

He looked at me with the coldest, smallest eyes he could find. Funny how small his eyes got when he had to speak to me.

"Scrupulous. You're scrupulous."

So that's what was wrong with me. Scrupulous. It sounded exotic. Was it something you could be proud of? Now if someone asked me how I was doing, I would have to shake my head and say sorrowfully that I had my problems because I was scrupulous. If only I knew what it meant?

"Oh wait, Father Anotskie, I don't know what scrupulous means? Can you please tell me?" I wanted to figure out a way of curing it. "Holy Please?"

"Find out for yourself."

He was pretending he wanted to mingle but I knew where he was going. He was going to sit in another part of the room, to look at Eileen from a different angle. God how I prayed she would get pregnant. Then he'd see what a nice girl she was.

I stopped going to the youth meetings altogether. But I couldn't forget that Father Anotskie had turned his back on me. It grated on my mind. Why was he being so critical of me? What had I ever done? And why had he come back to Polackville?

12

2

I got stuck with a pair of glasses because I was short-sighted, and I was so tone deaf people wouldn't let me hum. But I still saw and heard everything. Especially the stories Momma told Daddy in the middle of the night. Not even the wolves crying, nor the crickets singing could drown these sweet stories. Stories about the rich and happy. They floated away from the privacy of their bedroom, up the cold stairs, past the piece of plywood that closed the downstairs from the upstairs, past the clothes on the floor, to our three old beds in our one small bedroom.

Josef couldn't hear them. He had his transistor radio near his pillow and was listening to music and news from Memphis, Tennessee. The four little kids – August, Ignacy, Bernadette and Honey – were sleeping. Their only interest was finding enough room on their bed for all their legs. Since Krysia slept with me, I made her listen.

"You should listen too, Urek."

I promised them they would hear stories about magic. In the night. No one was ever let down.

"Well I'm telling you I've never seen anyone have so much trouble trying to chop wood."

I knew that Daddy looked forward to going to bed at night because Momma kept him laughing for hours about the Montgomery-Joneses.

"It was only a small piece of wood. For the fireplace. I could've split it in two with my hands."

It was strange to hear Daddy laugh. I always wanted to sneak back downstairs to see what he looked like.

"He had nothing better to do than to spend the whole afternoon with that piece of wood. I'm telling you, he had every kind of axe you can think of. For the sake of the Blessed Mary...."

She liked bringing in the Virgin. It was the closest she came to swearing.

" ... Holy Mother of God, he came into the kitchen three times for a glass of water and ice. He was telling me, 'You know, Mrs. Luckoskie, that's really tiring work out there.' I told him to leave it and go down to the beach. I felt sorry for him so I went out there and chopped it up. Well I'm telling you I never saw anything so funny in all my born days."

The stories about how useless Chester Jones was were the funniest, but the ones I liked most were about Honey Montgomery-Jones. Momma changed her voice and put on a phoney accent to imitate Mrs. M-J.

"Oh my goodness but we must have our cocktails before dinner."

It seemed as if Honey was the luckiest woman in the world. Momma said that all the men would hop for her and she never thought twice about bossing anybody around. She was very fussy. She'd shave her legs in the morning before she put on her bathing suit and then half way through the day she'd come up from the beach and shave again. She could never make up her mind about what she should wear for dinner and would come down in three different costumes before she could find one there was nothing wrong with.

"I'm telling you those people really have a hard time trying to have a vacation."

I really wanted to go to the Montgomery-Joneses and see for myself. I couldn't figure out how they lived, but I knew I'd like it.

14

While we were driving to their place Momma wasn't laughing, she wasn't even smiling. She was driving so fast she didn't realise how much noise the half-ton was making on the gravel road. It looked as if she didn't care if all the small children were safe. What was the matter with her? Then in the middle of nowhere she stopped the truck and started parking it.

"What are you doing?"

"We're going to walk the rest of the way."

"Why?" I couldn't stop myself from shouting.

"They want me to park away from the cottage because they said they never know when their friends from the States might show up. They don't want an old truck beside their cars."

I was sick to my stomach, I felt like throwing up. "I've changed my mind, I'm not going."

She was busy loading her arms with more than she could carry. She walked off without saying a word, and three of the four kids ran behind her falling and crying.

I was trying to figure out a way of getting back to the farm as fast as I could. I should never have got this far in the first place. I moved behind the wheel of the half-ton. I would have learned how to drive right there and then, only I still wasn't big enough to reach the gas pedal.

I got out and screamed with all my might. But she was gone. I picked up the rest of the stuff she left behind for me to carry – the fresh strawberries, the newspaper, the milk – and little Bernadette, Momma had forgotten her, and ran to catch up.

We walked for a quarter of a mile.

Then I saw it.

"Oh, my God!"

It was the most beautiful sight I had ever seen in my life.

I couldn't believe that right here in the middle of nowhere there was a sparkling blue lake with clean white cottages dotted all around it. In all our drives around Polackville, Daddy had shown us sawmills, good trees, partridge, but he had never taken us to this beautiful lake with all these wonderful cottages. All this time we'd been so close to it, and I could have lived until I was a hundred and not even suspected that it existed.

All around the cottage was short green grass, real grass without any thistle or rusty nails or broken beer bottles. And there weren't any flies. You could stand up straight right in the open, and there would be nothing that would land on your neck or chew behind your ears.

What a beautiful, beautiful cottage. If you looked straight ahead you couldn't see the entire cottage all in one shot. And the whiteness blinded you. I had to turn my head to the right, to see the end of it. If I hadn't been so excited, I would have counted the windows.

Momma didn't stop. She just kept ploughing straight ahead. That was the difference between us. I would have stopped to admire it every day of my life.

I followed her up the long flight of stairs. Can you imagine, stairs on the outside of a cottage! Who knew where we would end up? I kept looking down and watching my feet because I was worried that I might fall.

At the top stood Honey Montgomery-Jones. Waiting for us. She was tall and blonde and pink and lips and cheeks. Her feet were tanned and her toenails painted. Fresh clothes, brand new, like straight out of the catalogue. Clothes that I cut out and put in my cardboard box. The very first thing she said was Good Morning. My knees were shaking. Imagine someone saying Good Morning! I just stood there. How could God have created anybody so beautiful? If I was a man, I would have hopped for her.

Then Momma spoiled it all.

"This is my daughter, Genia."

Right then and there I knew that something had gone wrong somewhere, because I didn't want to be a Luckoskie. I didn't care how many times the government had changed the spelling of our name. They could take it all back. Something was telling my brain that I should have been Honey Montgomery-Jones. I smiled and looked up at her. I wanted her to see in my eyes that I really wasn't Momma's daughter. But Honey just smiled back. She didn't catch on.

I couldn't keep my eyes off Honey all day. Where did she get her height? She took such long steady steps when she walked around the cottage. She always seemed to know exactly what she was doing. Every time she spoke she seemed to know exactly what she was saying. She used such perfect words and everything she said sounded so nice in her fine American accent. She always knew how to finish her sentences. Everything happened so quickly, you couldn't see the ideas going to her brain. Her lips moved back and forth from the corners. I was embarrassed that she took so much effort to speak to me. I wanted to tell her it was okay if she muttered.

In the afternoon, they all went down to the beach. In between making the beds, mopping, doing the dishes, and washing the windows, I sneaked out onto the verandah to take a look at them. They were really having a good time. They were taking turns water-skiing and then they swam, but mostly they just sat on the beach and talked and laughed. None of the women were afraid to show their bodies, and they paraded back and forth in front of the men in their bathing suits. That would have been the only hard thing for me to do, if I had lived with them. I wouldn't want a man to see me in a bathing suit. Momma kept asking me what I was looking at and reminding me that I couldn't stand around on the verandah all day or I wouldn't get my work done.

"If you want to go down there and take a look at the beach, I'll give you some sandwiches and cold drinks to take down for them."

"No! I don't want to go down there."

I watched my poor mother walk down to the beach balancing two big trays. I felt sorry for her, she didn't know what she was missing.

Then I saw them all heading back to the cottage for dinner. This was the moment I had been waiting for. Finally I would be able to see them mixing their cocktails. It seemed to me it was some sort of quiet dance they all knew and that could only be done once a day, every day, before dinner. Momma had shown me the glass cupboard in the livingroom where they kept all the bottles and cherries and long sticks and spray cans for the cocktails, so I had a pretty good idea how the dance might go. But I wanted to see it just once for myself. I wanted to see exactly what parts of the body shake, and who'd to and fro to who, and where the cherries end up.

Momma and me have heard all the babies cry and we could usually comfort them, but when pesty little Bernadette started, I knew it was more than just a cry. It was bad luck. She screamed and cried and cried and cried. When the Montgomery-Joneses were in the cottage, it was my job to keep the children quiet, any possible way I could. But there was nothing I could do to shut Bernadette up. She cried so much and so hard, I was sure her little mind would never remember what it was like not to cry and she'd be like this for the rest of her life. And on top of everything, Momma had started acting strange again. She wouldn't talk and she made me whisper. I could hardly get her attention.

"Momma! Have they mixed the cocktails yet?" I was desperate. I didn't hear her answer and finally I had to move outside into the yard with Bernadette. I walked up and down, holding her in my arms, up and down until the cocktails were finished, dinner was eaten, and the day was over.

It was dark and sad when we climbed back into the half-ton and headed for the farm. Momma ignored me. She sat stubborn as a stone and stared at the road. The kids were fighting and Bernadette was still crying. The M-J's cottage seemed like such a happy place, I didn't want to leave it. If only I could have figured out a way to be Honey Montgomery-Jones's daughter. How great it would have been to live in their cottage. I don't think I would ever have been able to make up my mind which bedroom I wanted. Lots of food and someone to do the dishes when you're finished eating. No, I think I would have done my own dishes. But the bathrooms, real live bathrooms.

I could just see them all, sitting in front of the fireplace, sipping their cocktails towards the quiet satisfied end of the cocktail hour. My face got hot. Maybe I was sitting in one of those soft armchairs too. I should have stayed behind. They probably wouldn't have noticed. You sank so deeply into those chairs, you couldn't be seen from most angles. After a few days, they would have got used to having me around, and they wouldn't have minded. I would have just fitted in. What difference would one more person make to them?

I looked over at Momma a few times. I wanted to ask her all sorts of questions, but I was afraid I'd start crying. I guess I knew all the answers. Whatever else I didn't know I would find out in the night. They were rich. American. They had come to Jasno Gora for a full summer's vacation. They had been coming here for the past twenty-five years, and they would keep coming forever. They liked it.

At one time there was hope that somehow the cottage would pass from old Mr. Lew Montgomery to Momma, not Honey. Old Mr. Lew Montgomery didn't get along with his daughter Honey, and he really liked Momma because she had been helping them for peanuts all those years since he'd first started coming up. Everyone knew that Momma really deserved it, but Honey got her name down. A few times old Mr. Lew Montgomery threatened to change his will, but Momma said there was little hope. It was the final will. It seems now the last chance for the cottage has gone because Momma said that Honey would certainly never let it out of her hands. Eventually, it will be passed down to Honey's own daughter. I know if we could have got something like that cottage it would have been easier for us. Daddy wouldn't have had a reason to lose his temper so often.

I looked over at Momma again. She had a real ability for turning into stone. She didn't care how much the silence was killing us. No wonder Daddy had it in for her. He wanted her to stop working at the M-J's cottage every summer, he accused her of not doing enough on the farm, he said she was lazy. He couldn't forgive her for being engaged to Franek Rudkowskie before she married him. He called her the dirtiest name in Polish, *corva*, because a year ago when they were drunk together, Franek told him as a joke that he had had her before Daddy did. It wasn't true, she was like the Virgin Mary. It was the biggest sin on earth to call Momma a whore. And she worked even harder than he did.

But when he was drunk, Momma was just as good as dead.

19

He'd throw hot frying pans full of fried potatoes at her. If she'd try and answer back, it would make him even angrier and he would fly at her with his fists in the air. She had a different colour bruise on every part of her body. It made you sick when you looked at her face and arms and legs. Still Momma never left him. She stuck by him, as if he was made of gold. She always pretended that everything was okay. She believed that the future would be better. It was easy to work up a hatred for her. How dare her laugh at the way Honey Montgomery-Jones lived. She should take a lesson from her and try to be more like her. I bet no man ever hit Honey and gave her black eyes.

I knew I'd scream at Momma, but I had to break the silence.
"Will I be coming with you again tomorrow?"
"No."
"Why not?" I could have hit her so hard.
"You'll have to stay at home with the kids."
"We can take them with us again."
"No."
"Why not?"
"Honey doesn't want them at the cottage."
"Why not?"
"She said they can't have a good vacation if they have to listen to kids crying all the time."

Well I don't care. I saw enough. I have a good memory. I know exactly what she's like. I know exactly what sort of woman I'm going to become.

Now that we had finally started talking, I wanted to try and get something across to her. I didn't want the silence to get the best of us again. I took a deep breath. I wanted to sound as mature as possible. It was about time that Momma and I started telling each other how we felt.

"Look, I feel sorry for the hard life that Daddy's had, but you shouldn't have married him in the first place."

God did she get angry! She nearly swerved off the road. She's really unpredictable. You never know what to expect from her. Those eyes looked at me as intently as they had been watching the road.

"I'll tell you when Daddy's not drinking, he's the best and most honest man in the world. And you better not count your chickens before they're hatched, because you might end up with a far worse man."

I didn't look back into her eyes. They were too blood-shot for my liking. "Never."

Even though I said *never*, Momma's words had frightened me. What if her predictions came true?

3

From what I could see it didn't matter where you lived if you had a good body. Eileen Skuce seemed to be as happy as Honey Montgomery-Jones. Every single boy, man, and priest in Jasno Gora and Hopefield, in all the surrounding towns and townships, had their eye on Eileen. She got whistles every time she moved. Cars stopped and honked. Pepsi Cola had to be ordered twice a week. Old men at the Post Office nudged each other and nodded. Eileen wouldn't have changed her name for all the white cottages in the world.

Just the idea of her flirting around in that tight green-and-grey checked skirt with the frill made me sick. She had let her early puberty go to her head. I couldn't stand the way she told everybody at school that Peter Dooley thought she had the nicest eyes and the nicest smile he'd ever seen on any girl.

I knew I had to do something. If I waited for time to make me into a woman, I'd wait forever. And by then there wouldn't be anybody left.

I knew I had to take it into my own hands. Anyway, I had my eye on Paddy O'Hagan. He sat beside me at school and I suffered every time he looked at me. My heart ached for him so much. I had to get him before Eileen noticed how much his eyes sparkled when he laughed.

There wasn't a chance in hell to get Paddy in the summer. You can't hide your body in the summer. Everyone can see as plain as day what's inside your nylon stockings. The Winter was the best time for me. Anyway, it's winter three-quarters of the year in Polackville so I knew I was thinking along the right track.

During the week, the Hopefield Hounds played in Brudmar, Halfway or Long Post, but on Sundays their games were always on home ice. I've always wanted to go to a hockey game but Josef and Urek never let me go with them. They said it cost too much to get in and they weren't going to fork out for me. They said it was better to stay at home and be warm. What did I want to pay money to freeze for? But everybody went. All of Hopefield. Eileen. I knew as a fact that Paddy O'Hagan never missed a game in his life. I wanted to go. I didn't care if I was going to freeze and I was going to use my own money from babysitting.

I wasn't going to ask them again. I'd just get ready and slip onto the back of the half-ton when I saw them leaving.

On Saturday, in Hopefield, I went into Stedman's store to buy myself a package of hair dye. I didn't have time to make much of a choice because I could see the manager watching me from his mezzanine office. I know he was thinking that I must be a fool and don't know what to do with my babysitting money. Next time I babysit, I bet he'll give me less because it probably annoys him to see how his money is being wasted. I had to pick up the first package that I could get my hands on and move away from the hair goods counter. Everybody in the damn store was watching me. I walked down the aisle by the aluminium pots and pans because I wanted to see if I had the right colour before I paid for it. It was black, I didn't want it. Carefully, I weaved my way back to the hair goods counter. I put that one back and picked up another package. I couldn't fool around any longer because I felt any minute now the manager would come down and say something to me, so I decided to take it regardless what colour it was. I would have to leave it to chance. Even if it was another package of black dye it wouldn't really be the end of the world, I guess. Elizabeth Taylor has black hair.

I headed straight for the cash register. It would be just my luck that Mrs. Yakaruskie, the biggest gossip in Hopefield, was working this Saturday. I quickly put down the package of dye and looked up and around. I smiled and got out my money. I was pretending I didn't know what I was buying. When I gave her the babysitting money, she smiled back at me with that I-know-what-you're-going-to-do smile. She was such a hateful person. You never knew if she was on your side or not, but if there was a vicious story of you going around, you knew you weren't. She really was having fun taking her time with me. She tried two different sizes of bags, and put in the bill, and stapled it in four places. I would like to have punched her in the face but finally when she gave me my package all I said was, "It's for my mother."

I didn't want to dye my hair red either, but that's what was in the package that was stapled in four places. Couldn't God get it into his head that I wanted to be a blonde?

I tried to talk myself out of being disappointed. It seemed sensible to dye my hair red. Red hair would look more natural. Who knows, maybe I wouldn't have had enough guts to be a blonde. Maybe not, but somehow I feel that if that package just happened to have been blonde dye, my whole life would have been completely different. If only I would have had the courage to take one more step.

Very little effect. By suppertime, the kids had lost interest because my hair hadn't turned pink, Momma was too busy with her work to bother, and Daddy, Joe and Urek never suspected that I'd done anything at all. I could have got away with anything. Nobody cared.

Well I saw the difference. Especially if I stood under the light long enough.

My next step was to go to bed early, get eight hours solid sleep, because Sunday was going to be a big day for me and I didn't want to be tired. But I've never been able to get sleep when I've needed it most. Daddy was on an all-night rampage. When he was drunk like that he wouldn't let anybody sleep at night. He was banging around the rusty water pail in the kitchen. He wouldn't let the dog in and it cried outside the door all night. He cursed at Momma for having been engaged to Franek. He yelled upstairs to us and told us to get up and go to work and stop sleeping our lives away. I was just praying that Josef and Urek wouldn't go downstairs and try to make him shut up, because there would have been such a fist fight it might have ended in a death and I would never have got to the first hockey game of my life.

First thing after church Sunday morning, I got busy. I didn't want to waste a minute in case Josef and Urek would go early and I'd miss my ride into town.

I got Momma's boots and stuffed the toes with paper and put two inches of stone in the bottom. I knew you never got anyplace if you were short. I put on three pairs of slacks, so my legs wouldn't look so skinny. I put on three sweaters, so it would look as if I had my puberty already. Then I put on my jacket. I left it unbuttoned because in the winter everyone walked around that way. I knew that. I smiled to myself. Eileen Skuce didn't realise that I spent all those nights when we weren't allowed to sleep figuring out how to flirt. I was a bit afraid of catching pneumonia, but I decided it was more important to look desirable than anything else. I wasn't going to wear mitts. None of them did. If they didn't die there was no reason why I should.

The only make-up I could find for myself in the whole house was Momma's orange lipstick. I was really hoping that someplace she might have some eye make-up hidden that she was saving, but she didn't. After five tries, I got it on perfect. My hand was a bit shaky because I didn't really know if Paddy liked orange lipstick. Then to top everything off, I put my brand-new white toque on my bright new red hair. I had ordered the toque a month ago from the catalogue and I was saving it for a great occasion.

I looked beautiful. For the first time in my life, I could see how beautiful I looked. I couldn't stop staring at myself in the mirror. It seemed as if my blue eyes were singing. And I thought of Paddy. I wondered what it would be like to have someone following me around trying to get my attention? It's too bad we didn't own a camera, because I really would have liked someone to take a picture of me.

I was ready two hours early but I didn't want to take any

chances, so I decided to stay in my clothes until it was time to go. Daddy, Joe, Urek, nobody said a word about the way I looked. They just asked me why I was walking around the house with my coat on. I knew they would have to know sooner or later, so I told them. "I'm going with yous to the hockey game."

"We're not going anywhere."

I didn't believe them. They went to the hockey game every Sunday. Why wouldn't they be going today? Nobody was going to trick me. I kept my eyes on them.

One-thirty. Nobody budged. I knew we were going to be late but I couldn't yell and scream or they'd never take me. I depended on them. Hopefield was twelve miles away. There was no other way I could get into town. Two o'clock came. I knew now the game had started. Maybe they were waiting to go for the second period. I've always heard the second period is more exciting than the first. Three o'clock came and still nobody was bothering to make a move. I went to Josef.

"Come on, aren't yous going to the hockey game?"

"No."

"Why not?"

"Don't feel like it."

I went upstairs and said a prayer. Maybe they'd change their mind and decide to go for the third period. It was almost four o'clock.

"Daddy can Momma have your truck for five minutes to take me to Hopefield for the hockey game?"

"The truck won't start."

He was a liar.

"How come it started for Mass this morning?"

"I took the battery out so it won't go down on me."

He didn't fool me. He took it out so no one could use the half-ton. How right Momma was, when she said we lived with really sarcastic people. They would go out of their way not to help you. Five o'clock. There was no chance now. The game was over. I got out of my clothes. They had won today, but my turn would come. I had learned that if you want to get someplace, you walk.

The very next Sunday, I got dressed in my sexy outfit and

left. I didn't say a word to anyone. I wasn't going to hang around waiting for them to make up their minds whether they were going or not. I headed for Uncle Bronek's place. It was only a three-mile walk down the road from our farm. The stones at the bottom of Momma's boots hurt, but I didn't cry. After the first mile I started to like them, they reminded me of Paddy O'Hagan. I decided when I married Paddy I would tell him about the stones. If we became very rich, we could have a fireplace like the Montgomery-Joneses and I would have the stones enshrined in it forever. We would sit with our cocktails in front of the fire and look at the stones. I would smile and Paddy's eyes would sparkle. I walked faster. I knew if I lived to be five thousand and walked to the ends of the earth, I would never find another man who had such sparkling eyes.

Uncle Bronek was sleeping when I got to his place so I had to wake him up and coax him into going to the hockey game. He was a single man, a bachelor, there was no reason why he shouldn't be at the hockey game. He told me not to bother him but I wasn't afraid of Bronek. Nobody was afraid of Bronek. He'd do practically anything for anybody. I sat on the edge of his bed. I told him I wouldn't move and I wouldn't stop bothering him until he took me to the hockey game. Every time he dozed off, I woke him up. He got really angry but finally he got up, got dressed, and jumped into his truck. I jumped in too. He couldn't understand what I wanted to go to the hockey game for. He told me that I should have been bothering my father and not him. I wasn't listening. I was just happy we'd get to the arena before the second period would be over.

I couldn't find Paddy. I refused to wear my glasses and everything was a goddamn blur.

Everyone crowded into the canteen for a hot chocolate at intermission. It's easier to find someone if they're all in one spot and two inches away.

There he was. In a corner with some other guys. Perfect chance. I got close up beside them and then walked straight past him, as if I didn't have a care in the world and as if I was really looking hard for someone else. I stopped. Near him. By accident. I had my head in the air pretending that someone was going to show up with a hot chocolate for me. Paddy sort of leaned my way. I knew he was going to speak to me.

"Hello Genia."

"Hi."

I was really busy putting my hands in my pockets and shifting my weight from one foot to another. Paddy came closer to me. Our shoulders were practically rubbing.

"Hey, I didn't know you were this tall."

I hardly looked at him when I answered.

"Ya. Well you just can't stop yourself from growing, you know."

Then the stupid, stupid bell rang. Paddy rushed back into the rink to see the third period. If only I would have had five more minutes with him, I would have got him. Or I wondered if I wasn't playing too hard to get? I never goddamn knew the right thing to do at the right time. Maybe I should have told him right then and there that I loved him. It did seem like he was interested in me. I almost had him.

I bumped into Joe and Urek. So they had decided to come this Sunday. I asked them if I could go back home with them. Just before we left, I looked around to see where Paddy was. He was in the middle of a crowd from Hopefield. There were always lots of people around him. No, I'll never get him. He kept looking straight down into his second cup of hot chocolate. He was laughing at something. The cold had made his cheeks as red as his fingers. Where did he get that beautiful sparkle? I was hoping he'd see me walking out on him. Maybe I should have waited until he finished his hot chocolate? But I knew that Joe and Urek would drive away on me. They were in such a hurry to take off. As it was, I just got to the truck in time.

"Come on, get in. What do you want at a hockey game anyway? You should stay at home where you belong."

Even if they would never have said anything, I would still have come to the same conclusion. That was it for hockey games for me.

In fact, I wish Joe and Urek would have kept their big mouths shut. It was their fault I was so skinny and small. If they wanted me to look like Eileen Skuce they should have let me have my fair share of the food at suppertime. They always emptied the pots well before I'd finished setting the table. They never realized that after they were finished stacking their plates, there were still eight more mouths to feed. Momma never said anything. She was on their side. She treated them as if they were going to become kings.

On the days when we'd have our meat stew, I got so excited about my three cubes of beef I never knew how to eat them. I'd always put them on the side of my plate and save them for the end. When I wasn't looking Urek would steal one of them, and then I'd eat one and the last one I always gave to Momma. I wanted her to have it as a treat because she looked so worn out and she never gave herself any. But even that one she'd give to Josef or Urek. She said they needed it. I don't know what was the matter with her? They were already over six feet tall and weighed one hundred and seventy pounds. I was the one who needed it. I was short. I was skinny. I wasn't growing. I'm the one that everyone called anaemic. I needed it more than anybody else in the world. But she never stuck up for me and I always went away from the table starving.

I was just glad I wasn't the dog. Every night he followed me back and forth from the table to the sink as I cleared the table and washed the dishes. I'd scraped the pots as hard as I could but still there was never anything to give him. He never whimpered. He just kept following me around with his hungry eyes. He must have thought I was hiding the food and that I was mean. He must have dreamt that one day I would fill up a bowl for him. Stupid dog. I felt like kicking him and telling him that I was hungry too. I don't know why we had a dog anyway. It just got in everybody's way.

I knew exactly what there was to eat in the house. In one of the drawers there was a few loaves of homemade bread. In the cupboard there was margarine and cold potatoes. We never ran out of cold potatoes. In Daddy's hiding place there was a jar of homemade pickled herrings and onions. He loved onions. Just before I finished doing the dishes I would check all the cupboards to see if I was right. I was. There was nothing else. Maybe I should have given up trying to find something to eat. It was getting pretty boring, looking into the same empty cupboards day after day. But I lived in hope. I hoped that someday, just by miracle, I would open the cupboard and there would be a package of cookies or a dozen oranges. My God, that would have made me happy.

I never had any peace doing the dishes. Daddy kept coming into the kitchen and telling me to hurry up. He accused me of hanging around purposely. "Probably looking for some more food, you stinking frog."

I hated being called a *smierdzaca zaba*. It sounded so terrible in Polish. I thought he was calling me a rat. "I'm not."

I wasn't looking forward to having another piece of bread and margarine. I lived on bread and margarine and there was nothing I hated more in the world. I could hardly swallow it. It had no taste at all. But in the end I knew I would have to try for it, otherwise how would I survive?

"You're the slowest fool in Jasno Gora." He acted out *tak pomalu*, with his wrists hanging loosely and his chin sticking out, so that I would see that slow also meant stupid. "We should get Agata or Mary Poderskie over here to show you a thing or two. Those girls know how to work. It doesn't take them all night to do a few dishes."

He wanted me out. Maybe he thought I was eating his pickled herring on the sly. He had no way of checking when I was right there in the kitchen.

It was hard to get away with the bread and margarine. If I cut it before I'd finished doing the dishes he would see it when he came in to criticise me, and if I waited until I was finished there wasn't enough time before he'd come in to stay. If he caught me, I'd have to run for my life. He'd notice the half-sliced bread and start cursing. "Stupid kids, always wasting food."

I could hear him from under my bed upstairs. When he'd ease off, I'd sneak back downstairs and peek around the corner. There he was sitting at the table with his pickled herrings and cold potatoes and freshly peeled onion. From where I was standing, I could see my piece of bread on the cupboard.

I hung on to my cut-outs because I knew I was going to be little for a long time. Year after year, I lugged around my cardboard box looking for new hiding spots. It was getting so difficult to keep my cut-outs private. Josef and Urek had eyes like hawks and they were always suspicious. They would run around the farm waving the tattered catalogues and the dulled barber scissors, complaining that there was something wrong with my mind.

"Probably still playing with her toys when we're not looking."

"No, I'm not."

These weren't toys to me. These were pictures of real men and women, upper class families who had lots of clothes to wear every time a new catalogue came out. And they just sat around in my cardboard box and looked beautiful and every once in a while I heard one of them say to another one, I love you. These were the people who knew that I was more than just Genia Luckoskie.

And if I was playing with dolls, so what. I was trying to catch up on my childhood.

4

Nobody knew that there was one more reason why I would always be little.

It goes all the way back to my baptism. If Aunt Tessie hadn't been my godmother I know it would have happened to someone else and not me. But it was me. I was the unlucky little baby they were holding in their hands. I wish I would have been old enough to open my eyes. I would like to have seen them all standing there, smiling, thinking about the good start they were giving me. They didn't know there wasn't enough clean water in all of Polackville to get God on my side.

So many things they didn't know. That Aunt Tessie was going to marry an ugly Scotsman.

I guess even if they had known it wouldn't have made any difference because right from the day Angus Mauldoon married my godmother he had the wool tight over everybody's eyes. He laughed and talked so loud everyone thought he was happy. He had a job in the city, so everyone thought he was brilliant. Mostly Momma. She thought the world of him. I know she wished she had married him. He was the only person we knew who drank coffee. Momma had so many stars in her eyes, she didn't have time to say no when he told her his plans. "If it's all right with you, we'll take Genia to stay with us in the summers. She's too young to be much help to you yet, so we'll take her off your hands. We can always manage for a few weeks since she's Tessie's godchild." I don't know why they spent their time thinking about me, they had their own child every year.

Mauldoon put himself in charge of taking his children to the bathroom in the middle of the night. The very first night I was at his place he came for me. Woke me up.

"It's your turn to go to the potty."

"I don't need to go."

I was five. I was much older than he realised. If I needed to go, I could find my own way.

"Well at least let your uncle kiss you good night."

I was glad he was going to kiss me good night. I had always wanted to be kissed good night. It would be something you'd remember for your entire life. It didn't matter that I'd already been sleeping and it was the middle of the night, I was still going to count it as a good night kiss.

He kissed me ten times. I thought he was making up for all the good night kisses I missed since I was born. Then he said he was too tired to go back to his bed and wanted to rest in my bed for a few minutes.

"Let your uncle give you a little hug." I fell asleep during the hugging so I didn't hear him go back to his own bedroom.

Would he come again? The next night I lay in bed awake, waiting. I could see his shadow bouncing around on the door. He was telling Aunt Tessie that he was going to check on the children. Only I knew what he was coming for. For more kissing, more hugging. My body jumped underneath my blankets. He tiptoed in, came up close to me, and whispered. "I came to say good night to you Genia." I kept my eyes closed and pretended I was sleeping. We both knew that this was sex. He laid down on the bed beside me, and cuddled me up into the cavity of his chest. While he was kissing me and squeezing me tight I pretended I was still asleep. I didn't want him to know I liked it.

But then he went completely crazy. He couldn't stop. He'd come into the bathroom when I was sitting on the toilet so he could wipe me, he'd stretch his long arm under the table and touch me inside my panties all during supper, in the car he'd make me sit on top of him when Tessie'd go in to do the shopping. He always found a corner that I'd never seen before. He could close a door quieter than anybody I knew. He never wasted one shadow. Every single minute of the day, every day, in all those corners, behind all those doors, hidden in all those shadows, he'd pick me up and slide me up and down his body, he'd draw my head to his thighs and hug me with two arms and one leg, he'd stick his tongue in my mouth and tell me he was French kissing me. I knew it wasn't right, because I got as scared as he did if Tessie came back sooner than he expected, or if one of his kids opened the door by accident, or if the sun started to shine in our eyes.

Every year it got worse. I know I hated it more than Aunt Tessie did. In the days I could put up with it because it only lasted a minute or two minutes or five minutes. But in the middle of the night, he stayed with me for fifteen minutes or a half hour or sometimes an hour. It was pure hell. He rubbed me between my legs until it burnt. Up and down with his hand until my skin started peeling away. It was so sore I couldn't stand it. I wanted to stop, but I couldn't see a way out, I was in so deep. How could I ever have liked it? If only I would have known. Five, six, seven, eight, nine, ten, eleven, twelve years old and I was still in it.

Twelve years old and I had to get out of it, once and for all. Over the winter my nipples had pricked up a little bit and under them was a slight swelling. And I had grown a tiny, tiny bit of pubic hair. I was getting too old to go away for the summers. Nobody could force me now. How much did they want out of me anyway? Seven years was enough time to give anyone. Not even your godmother could expect you to keep going all your life.

This summer when they came for me, his evil eye could scan the whole farm back and forth, and get worried, and scan the farm again, but it wasn't going to see me. He was never going to see my precious nipples and my private hair.

The minute I heard him coming into the house, I hid under

the bed upstairs. I wasn't going to come out for a whole day and a whole night, just to make doubly sure he wasn't lingering around somewhere to catch me. I could hear Momma fussing in the kitchen, getting the coffee ready. I could hear Mauldoon's laughter. It shook the house.

"Where's Genia? Where's Genia?" He asked for me about one hundred times.

Josef found me, and Urek tried to drag me to the steps but I held onto the leg of the bed so he gave up. Then Momma came upstairs and begged me to come and at least say hello. I knew I was spoiling things so I decided that, just for her, I'd bring myself to say hello to this dirty man but that was as far as I was going.

"Here she is. Well come over here. Aren't you going to kiss your uncle hello?"

"No."

His eyes were working ferociously. He was looking for something.

"Genia's becoming a big girl. Come over here and tell your uncle all about school."

His legs were stretched wide apart and he was holding out his big hands.

"What's the matter?"

He knew damn well what the matter was. I hated his stinking guts.

"You're not shy of your Uncle Angus?"

His voice was getting louder and he was laughing like a maniac. Everyone joined in, especially Josef.

"Go on. What are you afraid of?"

I wish my family would stop coaxing me. They didn't know what sort of man he was. Then Urek started coaxing, too. "Stop being so bold. Go on." It was easy for them to talk. All they had to worry about was how to make their coffee tasty enough to drink.

Okay, to please them, I decided to go to Mauldoon and say hello. But I wanted him to see, by my eyes, that I was doing it for my family and not for him. He wasn't going to trick me any longer, this was as far as I was going. I let him kiss me hello. He tightened his grip on me.

35

"What are you running away for? Stay and talk to your Uncle Angus for a few minutes."

He got me up on his lap, clamped his hands around my waist and started bouncing me up and down on his knee. He was roaring with laughter and I could feel his slimy hands weasling their way up to my new breasts. I couldn't believe it. I was doing him a favour sitting on his knee so he would stop begging. Maybe his hands slipped up by accident. From all that bouncing.

"Your hands."

"Shhh. Keep looking straight ahead. No one will know."

How did he expect to get away with it, right here in front of everybody? What if all at once, Daddy, Momma, Joe, Urek, Krysia, the four little kids, what if everyone in the room, stopped talking, stopped sipping their coffee, stopped being so trusting, and turned to look at us?

"Mmmmmm . . . you're becoming a big girl. Starting to fill out, eh?"

Big? They would never be big now. He was pinching them, squeezing them, wringing them. I sat riding up and down on his knee and I knew now I would always be little. I knew that in these five minutes he would take away my whole lifetime of wonderful large soft delicate woman's breasts.

"This year we're going camping to Lake Ontario for a week. That'll be a nice change won't it Genia?"

"I'm not going."

I didn't even have to think twice about it. I didn't care if it was Lake Ontario. I would get to see it another time.

"But we need you. Tessie might need you for something."

I didn't say anything. Nothing was going to change my mind.

"Come on, go get your things. We'll want to be going soon."

He had already got the breasts, but I was going to try and save the pubic hair. "I'm not going."

Joe told me I was crazy. "Oh stop it. You should consider yourself lucky."

Then Urek chimed in. "What other girl from Jasno Gora has the same chance as you?"

I never cried, especially in front of people but now I didn't care. I wanted everyone to see how unhappy I was. I wanted them to feel sorry for not standing up for me. I stood in front of everybody and cried out loud. But no one paid attention to me. They went ahead talking about Mauldoon's plans. How long it would take him to get to Lake Ontario, where he would camp, and how much it would cost. Momma slipped away. I started screaming and crying louder. My lungs were bursting, the tears were rolling down my face, the whole front of my shirt was getting completely wet. What was the matter with them? Couldn't they smell his fingers? Did I have to spell it out for them?

Momma came back with a brown paper bag and handed it to Tessie. I knew my clothes were in it. I howled even louder now. I knocked over the coffee pot. I watched as the coffee spilled all over the table. The poor kids were so shocked. Then I lifted up Momma's china cup that she got as a wedding present and had taken out of her cedar chest especially for today, and I let it dangle from my finger tips and then I let it drop to the floor and watched it smash to a thousand pieces. Joe came over and hit me in the head and Urek punched me in the stomach. I didn't care.

Mauldoon came over and picked me up. I was in his hands again. He was rocking me back and forth. "Shhhh . . . there's nothing to cry about. We're going to have a good time, you'll see. We're going to swim and go for rides in the car and I'm going to buy you ice cream every day."

He started carrying me out to his car. I used all the strength I had to fight him. I kicked my heels into his stomach. I dug my nails into his hands. I bit his neck. The more I tried to get away the more he tightened his grip. Above my screaming, I could hear him tell Momma that I was probably getting homesick and that once we left the farm I would be okay. Momma and the kids were the only ones that stayed on the verandah to wave good-bye. It looked as if she cared, maybe it wasn't too late to get her on my side. I cried out to her from the car window.

"Momma, I don't want to go."

"Genia, there's nothing to stay at home for anyway. You'll just have to work and Joe and Urek will be fighting."

I felt sorry for her. She didn't know what was going on and yet she had such a good heart. I didn't care if I had to work, I wanted to stay home. I wanted to be with Joe and Urek and Daddy. Maybe they were violent, but at least they were clean men.

After we left the farm I shut up. I didn't mutter one sound. I hated Mauldoon and Tessie. They did nothing but argue for the four hundred miles to Lake Ontario. I was freezing in the back seat because Mauldoon kept his window open all the way. By the time we arrived I had a cold and had lost my voice. And I didn't see anything. Nothing. We were on the freeway all the way so we bypassed everything. Then I got really gyped. Tessie said it was too expensive to rent a camping space on the lake so we would pitch our tents at Marek's place in Cleckheaton.

"It's only five miles from the lake so it's just as good, and it won't cost us anything so we'll be able to save a lot of money. It would be a crying shame not to make use of his place especially since he's not even there."

Uncle Marek was laid off from his job at the General Motors factory in Oshawa and had gone to live in a homemade trailer on Bronek's property in Jasno Gora. Now I knew why he never wanted to talk about his house in the city. It was a dump. I would have left a place like this too. Momma was right, it wasn't even worth putting up for sale. It was worse than any house I had seen in Polackville. I was ashamed when we turned into his driveway.

The people next door stopped the mower, closed the newspaper, put down their lemonade glasses, and watched us. What were they thinking? I really felt like cursing at Marek. He did a good job of ruining the Luckoskie name. I looked back at the people on their lawnchairs, behind the mower, beside the water hose. I wanted to apologize. I knew it wasn't right to leave so much mess in a city. But I felt sad too. Once it must have been a nice house.

You could see that a city family could have lived here. It was quite big and it had been painted white and there was a cement sidewalk right up to the front door. How could he have let it go to ruin like this? The windows were broken, the paint was peeling off, one part of the roof was missing, the door had fallen down. There was nothing at all inside and most of the floors were gone, so grass was growing all over. The yard was completely covered by weeds and small shrubs and prickly stuff. Everywhere you stepped there were old corks, broken wine bottles, and rusty beer cans. I wish I didn't have to stay.

But they were already starting to put up the tents. Thank God there were two. I was going to sleep with the kids in one and Tessie and Mauldoon were going to sleep in the other. Their stupid kids were all excited about getting up early and going and looking for Lake Ontario. Well they could go. I was going to sleep in late. I figured I should try and get something out of this stupid vacation.

I didn't hear the kids get up and leave the tent, but when I heard Mauldoon come in, I knew I was alone. I turned around in my sleeping bag and pretended I was asleep.

"You're not going to go to sleep on me are you?"

"I'm tired."

"Well I am too, so I'm going to join you."

"Well why don't you go back to your own tent?"

"Because Tessie's sleeping."

Lucky her. Mauldoon stood up at the back of the tent and started to take off his clothes. This time he was going further than he ever had before. Completely undressed. In two minutes, he was standing stark naked in front of me. Where did he get the guts to do it? Then he touched himself.

"Look here Genia. This is my penis."

Well I wasn't interested in what it looked like.

"Some people call it a cock."

"No, they don't."

He brought it up closer for me.

"You can touch it if you want."

"I don't want to touch it."

"I'll help you."

He took my hand in his and held it around his penis and squeezed it. I hated the ugly thing. It felt so meaty. I was ashamed that he owned it.

"Well, aren't you going to ask me into your sleeping bag?"

"There's not enough room."

That should have stopped him. He was over six feet tall and I was in a very small child's sleeping bag.

"Of course there's room."

"No, there isn't."

He practically ripped it apart when he got in.

"See, if we stay close together there's enough room."

I was hoping that now that he had gone through so much bother to get in, he would try and fall asleep. And why weren't his stupid kids running back and forth into the tent? What were they doing anyway? And why was Tessie sleeping in so late?

"Here open your legs."

He shoved his penis in between them.

"Now put them together. Squeeze them. Hard."

I was getting so many instructions.

"Squeeze harder."

I was squeezing as hard as I could.

"Harder. Harder."

I couldn't squeeze my legs any harder. I was using all the strength I had. But I kept trying because I wanted to keep his mind off the new things.

"Ohhh . . . you've got pubic hair this year."

Now there was nothing left.

I knew that Eileen Skuce didn't have any Scottish uncles. You could bet your boots no one was dragging her off to Lake Ontario to stunt her growth. I had hardly had a chance to get any of it started, and there he was feeling it all, rubbing it all, squeezing, pinching, making holes. Okay, maybe now nothing was going to grow, but I knew one thing for sure, if there is a hell, and I'm pretty sure there is, he'll be the first one to go.

I was so sick of his big fat tongue in my mouth.

"Look Uncle Angus, I'm telling you I'm going to choke."

"I thought you liked French kissing."

"No, I don't."

I was so tired out. I just wanted to get some sleep. That's all I was hoping for now. I wanted to save my forehead. I could just imagine how worn out I must be getting. By the time this vacation would be over I would look as if I was seventy. I started crying.

"Please Uncle Angus, can you go now?"

"What's the matter? Don't you like it?"

"No."

"What don't you like? Come on tell me."

"My legs are sore from the squeezing and I don't like the French kissing."

"Don't you like anything I'm doing?"

"Well, I like some things."

"I'll only do what you like. Tell me what you like best."

"I like . . . the hugging."

But I didn't mean it that way. I hated everything. I hated him. I didn't want to be here. And I certainly didn't want any more hugging. All I was saying was, that if I had to have a choice, it would be the hugging. He didn't see what I meant.

Suddenly without any warning at all he jumped up and got dressed. It was so quick.

"Don't you get up Genia. I want you to sleep in."

He came over to kiss me good-bye. I turned my face away from him.

"You see, we're going to have a good vacation. Come on, give your uncle a good morning kiss."

He practically broke my jaw, turning my head to him.

"Now what was all that crying and fuss about when we left Jasno Gora?"

I should have spit at him but I didn't think of it.

The next morning my mind was ticking much faster and I got up early enough with the kids so that I avoided him. God he was shocked when he snuck into the tent and found I wasn't there. Two minutes later he was out among the thistle trying to corner me.

"You cheated on me this morning."

I pretended I didn't know what he was talking about, and

ran off after one of his kids. I hated his ugly weak-kidneyed children but I needed to stay close to them so I would be safe. I laughed to myself. I had won. I had really won. I decided I would catch up on my sleep when I was Tessie's age.

We probably would have gone through the whole week without even seeing Lake Ontario, but his kids screamed about going swimming so much, that Mauldoon finally had to take them. Tessie said she wasn't going. I figured maybe I shouldn't go either, but then the more I thought about it, the more I convinced myself that I should. He won't try anything because all his kids will be with us. And I really wanted to see Lake Ontario. I wanted to be able to tell Mary Poderskie that I had seen it with my own eyes. Besides, if I stayed behind, Tessie would make me help her clean up Marek's yard some more. I was sick of picking up broken glass. I decided to go.

The lake was dirty and big and it frightened me. His kids were running all over and no one was looking after them. Mauldoon didn't care. I had a feeling that maybe one of them was going to drown. This was the perfect chance for God to punish Mauldoon. But Mauldoon wasn't worried about God. He was too busy following me around. He came up to me in the lake and grabbed me. He tried to get his penis inside my bathing suit but it just wouldn't stay in. Then when he used both hands, I slipped away. He got really angry and told all his kids that we were going back. I didn't care. I was glad. I wanted to go back. But his kids were screaming, they wanted to stay longer. Mauldoon had to promise to buy them an ice cream on the way back or they wouldn't have come. Now we'd see. I really wondered if I'd get the ice cream I had been promised?

Mauldoon came back with enough ice creams for everyone including me and him. I felt proud sitting in his car, eating his ice cream. I had got something for nothing. And it was really good ice cream. Maple walnut. Mauldoon stretched out his long arm across the back of the seat and with his skinny finger lifted the strap of my bathing suit and started tugging it.

"You take this bathing suit off tonight."

I smiled at him. He had given me another idea.

"Well I've treated you well haven't I? Ice cream. Lake Ontario."

Poor Mauldoon. I started to feel sorry for him. I never did anything he asked me to. For the rest of the week, I wore my one piece elastic bathing suit under all my clothes and got up at the crack of dawn.

The last day. I walked around with a smile on my face. I didn't even bother to help them take down the tents. They could talk all they wanted about next year because I knew I had taken my last vacation with them. I knew that as well as I knew that we were finally going home. Mauldoon had cornered me for the last time.

"I hope you're not going to go and tell Tessie what happened."

"No."

"It wouldn't be too nice if Tessie found out?"

"Well, I'm not going to tell her."

"I don't know what I'm going to do if anyone finds out?"

"No one will."

I was ready and willing to give him his miserable wish because that was the last thing he would ever get from me. And I knew something else. I already had my revenge. I would never ever forgive him for what he had done, and I would hate him for the rest of my life.

I was looking forward to Jasno Gora so much. No place in the world seemed sweeter to me. Who would have ever guessed that there would have been absolutely nobody at home? The screen door was open but the winter door was locked. I didn't even know we had a key to that door. There wasn't anybody anywhere. Down the road I could see the dust swarming after Mauldoon's car. Thank God they were gone. Even if my whole family had died I still wouldn't want to call that car back.

But where were they? They must have died. I decided to sit on the verandah and wait. The dog crept up to me. He wanted to sit with me. It figured that he would be the only one left.

"Get out of here." I batted it with my hand and pushed it away from me. But it kept coming back to me and sitting near me. It was so skinny and weak. I felt sorry for it and started to pet it. It moved as close as it could to me and leaned right against my arm. I promised I would never shove it around again and every time Daddy kicked it, I would go over and pet its head, so that it wouldn't feel so bad.

I waited and it got dark. No one came. Where were they? I could hear the crickets and I knew that an hour after the crickets get started the wolves begin howling. If there aren't any lights to stop them, they come straight up to the house. I was getting scared.

I opened the screen door and hid between it and the winter door. I couldn't close it on top of me so it sort of stayed half open. It got even darker. I could hear things walking all around me, but I didn't cry. I wanted to stay as quiet as I could so the animals wouldn't know I was there.

I was asleep when Daddy's truck lights shone on me. The little kids thought I was dead. Joe and Urek said I was stupid, I could have got into the house through the basement window. Momma felt sorry for me because I was cold. I was glad everyone was yelling at me. I was so happy to see them.

"Where were you?"

All four kids answered me.

"We went for a picnic to Tekawanee Park."

"And we saw an old steam engine."

"And we fed turtles that were over one hundred years old."

"And guess what Genia? Daddy bought a quart of chocolate milk for our picnic."

I ran over to Momma. There were tears in my eyes. "Why didn't you tell me you were going for a picnic? I wanted to go with you. You knew I didn't want to go with Angus and Tessie. You knew."

"We didn't know we were going to go. The kids were complaining because you could go camping and they couldn't, so we took a drive for a day. Stop crying you've been away for a week."

That was tricky of her. They never took anybody anywhere

and then when they decide to do it, they do it when I'm not there.

"I borrowed a camera from Aunt Zosia to take a few pictures so you'll be able to see the turtles."

Funny how she thought of everything when I wasn't around, even a camera.

When the pictures were developed and sent back to us, I was the one that looked at them the most. They were the only pictures we had of our family. I couldn't stop looking at them. They were huge and glossy. Everyone looked so nice. You could see Josef's black hair and Momma cutting the bread. And there was Daddy sitting at the picnic table. He was smiling. In every picture I could see the quart of chocolate milk. Dairy chocolate milk. Everybody was there, Urek, Krysia, August, Ignacy, Bernadette, and baby Honey. I couldn't stop looking at them. To me, the pictures were proof that God knew how to make people happy. I wish with all my heart I could have seen myself in just one of them.

5

I had a solution. Stick together. I don't know why I hadn't thought of it sooner. It was common knowledge, anybody who had ever stuck together made it – the Kennedys, the Rockefellers, the Bronfmans. We even heard it in church every Sunday – the family that prays together, stays together. I was convinced that if we all worked together, we would get ahead. I wasn't even surprised when the golden opportunity knocked on our farm door. I was ready for it.

The two men in heavy black overcoats told Momma they were important people from the Government in Toronto. Momma tried to push me and the kids back into the house but none of us wanted to go.

"We only want information. As you know, there is going to be another Provincial Election soon. The former constituencies have all been reorganized and subdivided so that more people will have direct representation."

The other black coat spoke for a while.

"You will now be a part of the County of Sterling. The County of Sterling will consist of all the farming communities around here, Jasno Gora, Halfway, Long Post and the towns and townships of Hopefield, Brudmar and Gungrog."

It was the first man's turn again.

"We need an MPP for the County of Sterling, and preferably someone from around here. We're going around to all the farms, talking to people and asking them to nominate someone."

The other man gave us a hint about who the other people they had spoken to, were thinking of nominating.

"We have had the following suggestions – Sean O'Grady, Franek Rudkowskie and Boris Weickmann."

Momma and I practically stepped back into the house. We certainly didn't want a German from Brudmar ruling us and we were sick of the Irish getting first chance at everything.

"Would you give your vote to any one of these and if not who would you nominate?"

I looked at Momma. I knew who I'd nominate. She started smiling and getting nervous. But she looked pretty.

"I haven't had a chance to think and I'm in the middle of my washing."

"We'll leave you this form, you can fill out who your nominee will be, sign it and leave it at the Post Office."

Momma headed back for the washing machine. I followed her.

"Why did you have to wait? Why didn't you say Daddy right away? You know he's better than all the others they mentioned. It'd be good for Daddy, you know."

She spoke so gently.

"We'll see."

When I left her, she was still smiling.

We didn't know what exactly was the job of an MP. Nobody in Polackville knew. But we had a pretty good idea. Besides your own home in your county, you have an apartment in Toronto so you can go to meetings in Parliament. The tricky part was, you never knew how long your job would last. But who cares. Even if Daddy was an MP for only four years, he could always go back to logging. Nothing would be lost. We knew that an MP had to give speeches. But Daddy wouldn't have to worry about that. We were going to look after that for him. Josef would write them, and I would teach Daddy how to say them.

I know he'd be a good speaker once he got going. And there was an extra bonus. Momma was a good cook and she said she would be willing to bake fresh cakes and pies for all the people that voted for Daddy. The best thing about being an MP was that you were always dressed in a suit and tie, your hands were clean and uncut, and you had to be sober. If Daddy was nominated for MP, he'd have to stop drinking. I would have been proud to be an MP's daughter. My bad start would be lost forever. Nobody would question my background. People would automatically assume I was well brought up. What would it be like to have someone jealous of me? I would be kind and I would tell them that if they stuck together, they could do it too.

It was all very disappointing. Daddy wouldn't let us nominate him. He said it would be too much trouble. None of us could talk him into it. He didn't want to be bothered. He couldn't see that he didn't have to do practically anything. All he had to do was say yes. We were going to make sure he got elected. He wasn't careful about his decision, he didn't consider what he was letting slip through his fingers. Why was he being so stubborn? He was intelligent and a hard worker and now here was the chance he had always been waiting for. I could kill myself every time I think about him passing it up.

And you know who got nominated in the end – Leonard Metamonskie! The biggest drunk in Polackville! Every Sunday morning without fail you could find him at the bootleggers. His wife and children tried to cover up their shame, but they weren't fooling anyone. No one in Polackville had a good opinion of Leonard Metamonskie. Everyone said that old Mr. Metamonskie would walk out of his grave and ask to be cremated if he knew how Leonard was drinking away the Hardware Store. Still, nothing stopped Leonard from accepting his nomination.

His official acceptance day was the biggest celebration day we've ever had in the County of Sterling. Even the Premier of Ontario came. It was such an important occasion no one was allowed to stay at home. We were all told to gather outside in the church parking lot in Hopefield. Someone had hired a military band from somewhere. As we were standing in the church parking lot they marched around and played music. It was so loud you couldn't hear yourself talk. Someone was passing around streamers and balloons, free candy, and chewing gum.

Then Leonard and the Premier rode up to the door of the church hall, got out of the car, waved at everybody and went in. We followed them into the hall. There was going to be more music, then speeches, then free food for everyone.

Leonard and the Premier were already sitting on the stage. They were completely surrounded by all sorts of coloured flags and banners. The Premier looked impatient. I could tell he was waiting for everyone to take their chairs and settle down, so he could begin. When he stood up, Leonard and everyone started clapping. But the Premier stopped us so he could say his speech. He told us how lucky we were to have a chance to have our own MPP. It was important to have your own MPP because your own MPP takes only your concerns with him to Parliament. He can ask for and bring about changes and improvements for us, the people of the County of Sterling. He told us that now, whenever we wanted anything, we should tell Leonard. Come election day, he was going to be our MPP and he would make every effort to meet any of our wishes. He told us that no wish was too small or too silly and we should trust Leonard to help us. Then he turned to look at Leonard, shook his hand, and said we got a good man.

Now it was Leonard's turn to give his speech. He stood up. It was hard to see because everyone was leaning forward, but he looked different. He was wearing a suit and tie. In his hand he was holding the speech his children had written for him. I overheard Momma whisper to Auntie Zosia that he had a nice manner about him. He was so sober it shocked everybody. Everyone was hoping to see that drunk look in his eyes, or to see his hands shake a bit, or to hear him slur a little. But Leonard never once let on that he was a drunkard. He did everything very seriously. He first thanked the Premier for his kind words, but he told him quite honestly that he didn't deserve them. Then he looked at us and said yes, he would try and do anything we would ask him.

"I know you all very well. I've been visiting at your farms . . ." A few people laughed. They knew he used to come around looking for drinks, when he ran out. " . . . or you've come into my Hardware Store to buy nails, so I don't want anybody to be afraid to come up to me about anything. I already know one of the things I can help you with – education. Canada is a nation where everybody has a fair chance and doesn't matter where you come from or how much money you have, everyone can go to University if they want to. I'm a poor man but I'm hoping my kids will go to University and so can yours."

Everyone clapped for an hour. The band played. There was no shortage of food and drinks. The balloons and streamers floated around.

Leonard and the Premier left right away because the Premier had to go somewhere else. I wanted to follow them. I would have ran behind their car if they would have let me, but no one else was allowed to leave the church hall. We were supposed to stay and celebrate for the rest of the night. All of a sudden it seemd as if Leonard was everybody's best friend. Everybody said that it was about time a Polish boy from Jasno Gora was a member of Parliament. Everyone wondered if Leonard had really stopped drinking or if he was just being careful not to be caught drunk. If it wasn't for his wife and kids, he would never have got anywhere, and they said he was still a real bastard to them. Everyone was looking forward to election day except Momma and me.

Election day was the biggest drinking day of the half-decade. Every single man and boy in the County of Sterling was drunk. I could smell election day. It smelt different than any other day of the year. The people from around Polackville only drank beer, except for the hard-core alcoholics who drank cheap Jordan wine. But on election day there was everything you could think of – vodka, gin, whiskey, beer, and wine. And it was all free.

You could smell it everywhere. It was in people's houses, on their clothes, in their half-tons, on their food. What I hated most is that it was even in the air. You couldn't get away from it. This was one day of the year the men didn't have to go looking for it. It was there for the asking. Leonard had hired men with cars to go around to all the farms and pick up everybody of voting age and drive them down to the Church Hall to cast their vote. If they voted for Leonard they were given a drink.

The people of Polackville disgusted me. Just for a free ride to the church and a free drink afterwards, they took off a whole day's work and dressed in their Sunday clothes and acted as if this was something that happened once in a lifetime, like a wedding. In the end, Leonard and his family were the only ones that came out of it happy. The rest of us had to put up with it for the next three months. You can't give a man everything he wants to drink in one day, and expect him to go to work the next.

I hated election day. I decided I'd never vote in my life. Momma said she wouldn't either. We had nothing to gain by it.

6

It seemed as if there were a million opportunities around and soon everyone would be talking about the ones I missed. I just knew that in the end, it would be me that would be the failure. I worried myself sick when the girls at school talked about their summer jobs at Sutcliffe Lodge. Even stupid Mary Poderskie made it sound as if it was so easy to get a job there.

"Well he comes around every year, looking for girls to work there."

"Ya I know, but how do you get the job?"

"I don't know. You just go up there and work."

I was hoping that no one at home would notice and that the summer would just come and go. But Josef and Urek started in on me, at the first sign of spring.

"You should be out working, like every other decent girl."

"You won't catch Agata or Mary Poderskie at home in the summer."

"If you weren't so lazy maybe someone would hire you."

Everyone wanted me to get a job so badly. But the more Josef and Urek looked at me, the more hopeless they knew it was. They saw my skinny legs and my skinny arms. They knew I was the last person anyone would hire. They called me a *maly biedak*, a little weakling, for getting tired after hanging out the wash. They didn't know I felt as worn out as the old clothes I put on and took off the clothes line every week.

Momma told me how important it was for me to have a summer job, now that I was close to puberty.

"There's going to be things now that you're going to have to buy for yourself. Things you need."

It looked as if she was starting to back me.

Momma was the first one to spot Mr. Sutcliffe. She stopped him on the Post Office steps and told him that she had a daughter grown-up enough to work. She persuaded him to come out to the farm to see me. I was glad he told Momma he'd come after he finished all his other business because that gave me enough time to get ready to make a good impression on him. I got some of the small kids to go and sit on the fence at the bottom of the farm. With them as my look-out, I could work right up until the time he arrived. There was so much to do. I had to wash and wax the kitchen floor. I had to do all the windows. The kids' fingermarks were all over, so I had to wash every archway and the best part of every wall. I picked up the men's clothes and put them away. The more I worked, the more excited I got. A clean house would be proof that I was a good worker.

I had done everything I could think of and still there wasn't any sign of him. I was hoping he'd come before Daddy'd get back from the bush and start cursing for supper. I could have killed Momma, she probably hadn't given him good enough directions. He was probably at someone else's farm hiring the wrong person. She wouldn't talk to me anymore, so I couldn't find out if he'd actually promised to come or if he just said maybe. I was just starting to scream at Momma again when one of the kids came running back to the house.

"He's driving a really long shiny blue car. It's got a silver statue sticking up on the front hood."

"Okay, I want all the kids away from the door. It looks really dirty to have everyone peaking out the windows."

They weren't listening to me. I couldn't get them away. They were fighting and stepping over each other to get a better view. I wish someone had taught them some manners.

That was an expensive car he had. Momma said it was American. It had silver chrome all over it. I felt embarrassed because he drove it right up to the verandah steps. Nobody had ever come that close before. Two steps later and he was knocking on the screen door. I didn't expect him to knock. It sounded as if he was going to give me the job.

"Hurry up Momma, answer the door."

"You answer it."

"No, you."

I ran and got a chair for him to sit on.

He was gigantic. He filled the whole chair and went a bit over on the sides. I wondered if he would be able to cross his legs. He didn't try. He sat with both feet spread apart and firmly planted on the floor. What sort of women married men like him?

"Is this the one?"

He was wearing a pair of glasses. And so many clothes. A shirt, a tie, a sweater, a jacket and on top of everything a coat.

"Yes, this is my oldest girl, Genia."

He took something out of the pocket of his coat, looked at it, then put in into the pocket of his jacket. I was afraid that after he left, my name would get lost in one of his pockets. He had so many, and his hand could only reach half of them. He stood up. You could tell he was a very busy man.

"I have to go now. I think you're a bit too small for us."

Thank God, Momma spoke up. "She looks small, but I'm telling you she's a good strong worker."

He looked at me again. I was afraid he was going to laugh in my face. Who could tell what sort of things men like him did? But he was very matter of fact.

"Can you wash floors?"

Well it had paid off. I could afford to smile now.

"Yes of course I can. I did this one just today."

He didn't really look it over well. Maybe he didn't think it was clean enough. Too bad he hadn't seen it before I washed it. I think I should have told him I had done it on my hands and knees. He headed for the verandah. We all followed him out. He stopped for a minute.

"Okay, we'll let you come up for a week."

54

He slammed the car door shut. When he tried to back up, I noticed that he was so big he couldn't turn around in the front seat to see out the back window. It was lucky that all the children were standing around the door, otherwise he probably would have run over one of them without realizing.

Now it was all happening at once. Getting a job, buying a bra, having a spot of puberty, fainting in church. Having a job at Sutcliffe Lodge was just the thing I needed to help me to grow. Ann Landers said in the *Ottawa Journal* that you're usually as big as your friends. At Sutcliffe Lodge, I'd be with all the girls from Hopefield, day in and day out, plus I'd have fresh milk and three full meals a day. My chances for finally growing were good. By the end of the summer, I could probably be as big as Eileen Skuce, if not bigger.

Josef and Urek didn't believe that someone had hired me.

"Well when you see me leave, you'll believe me."

"Ah, you won't last more than a day."

I didn't care what they said to me now, or what I said back. Actions speak louder than words, and I would be working this summer at Sutcliffe Lodge and for every other summer for as long as I wanted. What could they say about Agata or Mary Poderskie to me now?

Everything was changing. Every day I was one step closer to what life should have been like for someone who is the oldest girl in the family. I was standing on the verandah, taking the clothes off the line. My arms weren't tired. I could hear Josef coming up the steps behind me. I didn't bother to pull down my skirt, to hide my legs. He stopped and just looked at me. I turned around and looked back at him. I couldn't help smiling. He didn't say anything. He walked straight past me into the house. I could hear him through the screen door.

"Momma, is Genia wearing a bra now?"

Poor Josef, what if they grew to be as big as battleships. I jumped for joy. How differently he would treat me now. I got so optimistic, I was sure that even my hair would turn blonde overnight. It was only a small bra. There weren't any cups in it at all, but doesn't matter what angle you looked at it from, you knew it was a bra. It was Momma, she had it ordered from the catalogue for me.

"Now that you'll be working, it will be too hot and not so nice for you to go around with an undershirt under your blouse. All the other girls will have bras so you shouldn't even bother taking your undershirt."

I didn't say anything because I had screamed at her so much in the past, but now I knew for sure we were on the same side. At last.

I was in such a big dream when I got to Sutcliffe Lodge, I couldn't see anything except the guy who worked in the boat-house. Someone said that he was from Toronto and they thought he was Italian. That's all I could find out. No one was interested in giving you the time of day. It was as if all of a sudden everybody stopped talking to each other. They all acted like strangers. Nobody even told me what I was sup-posed to do. I was forced to talk to Mary Poderskie even though I had vowed to myself that I wouldn't associate with any of the farm girls and once and for all try and make friends with one or two of the girls from Hopefield.

"Well I guess if you didn't get a uniform, you're probably in the cabins."

"But if he hasn't told me anything, do you think he might be planning on using me in the dining room?"

"I don't know. Why don't you ask Eileen or Jane or one of them. They'd know."

I didn't feel like asking Eileen or Jane. Everytime they passed me in the yard they acted as if they had never seen me before in their lives, especially when that guy from Toronto was looking.

"Well how do I know which cabins have to be cleaned?"

"They all have to be cleaned. We split them all between us."

The girls from Hopefield thought they were big shots be-cause all of them had the fancy waitress jobs. All the farm girls had to clean cabins. I was going to have to figure out a way of getting the pails from cabin to cabin without anyone noticing. I didn't want everyone to automatically think I was a farm girl because I carried a pail. Not like Mary. She walked around in full view. I couldn't figure her out. She'd worked here two summers already and wasn't even worried about when in the hell they were going to promote her to the dining room. Well, okay, I'd work as a cabin girl for the first week because everything was so new and I couldn't figure a lot of things out, but I knew that soon I would be a waitress. Maybe by the second week. First, I would have to prove that I was a good hard worker and meant for jobs as nice as waiting on tables in a fancy dining room. In a few days' time it would dawn on Mr. Sutcliffe that I was meant for the better things in life. I smiled to myself. I could just see him getting angry at me, giving me hell for working in the cabins. I had the feeling that he would tell me I should have known he expected me to work in the dining room. I think I must have been letting him down by following Mary Poderskie around.

Everything happened so fast I had no choice but to clean cabins. By Monday morning, even Mary was acting funny.

"Mary can you show me what I have to do?"

"I haven't got time."

"Why not?"

"Because they all have to be done by four o'clock or else."

"Or else what?"

"Or else Mrs. Sutcliffe sees to you."

"Well it's my first day, so she wouldn't mind you showing me what I have to do."

"You wanna bet?"

She took off on me. What a stupid girl. I decided I could do without her, until I took one good look around. I tried to catch up with her. Where else would I get any information?

"Mary!"

She wouldn't wait. "Just get a bucket over there and start cleaning."

"Over where?"

"There."

When I turned to look, she disappeared. I decided to go back to the staff cabin and sit all morning. If nobody was going to tell me what to do or where things were, how would they even know if I didn't do anything? But I got really scared sitting in the cabin. I was afraid that any minute sneaky Mrs. Sutcliffe would come along and find me here. I felt like crying. Why don't people ever tell you anything?

I left the cabin and came out into the yard. I looked left and right but there wasn't a soul in sight. I heard some hammering in the boat shed. I knew that the guy from Toronto was there. He must like me because he's never turned his head away when I've walked past the boat shed. I walked up to the door. He was so good looking. No wonder all the girls from Hopefield were crazy about him.

"I'm sorry to bother you but I wonder if you could tell me a few things. You see I'm new here and I'm supposed to wait on tables but they've asked me to clean cabins just for today. I can't find the buckets, do you have any idea where they are?"

"Everyone is given their own bucket and mop for the entire summer."

"Well, do you know where there might be some spare ones?"

"There might be some left over from last summer outside the storage shed."

"Thank you."

I didn't want to bother him anymore. He sounded rich and educated. I knew I'd never find the damn storage shed. All the buildings looked the same with their red and white trimmings.

"Hey! You go this way. Around the back."

"Oh, thank you."

At least I had manners. I hope he noticed that.

Ya, there they were, last year's supplies waiting to be taken to the dump. I had to use them, now that I had found them or I'd spend the rest of the day looking for the real thing. I took off for the first cabin I could see. It was Mary's and she was half way through it.

"You'd better hurry or Mrs. Sutcliffe will see how long it's taking you."

"How many have you done already?"

"Two. You're not supposed to take longer than a half hour on each cabin."

"Which ones haven't been done yet?"

"Go over and do number ten."

"Does that guy in the boathouse have a girlfriend?"

"Antonio? I think he likes Jane."

Mary was meant to be a farm girl. Farm girls only think about the two inches in front of their mop. They don't realise that all around them people are falling in love.

Cabin ten was the biggest cabin at the lodge, and I got stuck with it. I'd have to work quickly now. Run to the lake for the water, thank God the bucket doesn't leak. Oh hell, I picked up a dirty mop. Ran back to get another one, but there weren't any more. Hurry and get back to wash the floor anyway. Damn, it's leaving dirty marks all over. Rushed down to the lake for a clean pail of water. Do the floor quickly again. Should have left it alone in the first place, it didn't need washing. Goddamit, it's still leaving dirty marks. Oh, stop crying, you don't have time. Just do the job. Take the old mop down the lake, rinse it out once and for all. I'd have to work fast in the lake, in case Mrs. Sutcliffe or anyone else sees me. You're probably not allowed to put dirty mops in the lake. I didn't have the strength to leave the lake and go back up to the cabin, I was tired out already. I wanted to drown with last year's mop, teach them all a lesson. There goes Mary, finished with another cabin. She would have a laugh if I got fired. Come on, get back, if she can do it, you can. Wash the floor again, slowly, carefully,

"Hello Mary."

"Make sure you get every corner, even the ones under the bed because she comes around checking."

"Come on, she doesn't check every corner."

"I'm telling you she does. She runs her little finger anywhere she feels like and if she finds one speck of dust on it, you're fired on the spot."

I didn't want to believe Mary, but I knew she was probably right. She was stupid but she knew how to keep a job.

The huge muddy streaks were still there. Go away you bastards. No time to make two trips to the lake. Risk getting a hernia, do it all in one go – mop, pail, lake. My poor feet were getting cold and water-logged. What was Jane walking by the

cabins for? She's a waitress. She doesn't belong out here. Her
mini skirt never used to be that short. She's hiked it up. And
Antonio. What's he coming this way for? Hide the mop and
pail, please don't float away. Try and look elegant. Smile. I
bet he knew Jane had come this way. I took the mop and pail
and washed the floor for the last time. I blessed myself and
said a Hail Mary.

"I'm leaving the cabin now God. Please let the floor be clean
when it dries. One small, miracle, just for me. I don't ask you
for much, do I?"

I didn't turn around. I was going to put my faith in Him.

The rest of the week was better. Out of nowhere, a clean mop
mop and pail appeared for me. I cleaned my cabins to perfec-
tion. I pushed out every bed and I got into every corner. There
wasn't an inch of my cabins that I didn't clean. I knew I was a
a good worker. Probably better than Mary when I come to
think of it. Even though she talked big, I knew she didn't get
into every corner. Not like me. If someone tells me to do corners, I do corners. My beds didn't have creases in them and
my windows sparkled. Mrs. Sutcliffe could run her little finger
anywhere she pleased in my cabins and it would come back
shiny.

Still when payday came, at the end of the week, I was sure
my name wasn't on the list. The Sutcliffes probably don't
know I'm working for them yet. Maybe they're expecting me
next week. Everyone was rushing to the list posted in the staff
dining room. They were all laughing when they checked off
their names. They probably realised my name wasn't on the
list. I guess I couldn't blame the Sutcliffes for not bothering to
pay me, I had messed up Monday pretty bad. Mary had no
fear in her at all. She came back from checking her name with
real joy.

"Mary, is my name on the list too?"

"I don't know, I didn't look."

"Do you think she checks the cabins every day?"

"No, not every day."

"Well, how does she know about the corners and things?"

"I don't know, but she has a way of finding out everything."

"Naw, she couldn't find out everything."

"Suit yourself, but everyone says that if you can get past the old woman, you can get past anyone."

I wish my name was on the list. I wanted to get paid. But maybe it wasn't worth getting paid because you had to go to the office individually at the appointed time to collect it. Who would notice they hadn't paid me anyway? I better get away before everyone starts to wonder why I'm hovering around. I didn't mean to bump into Jane. I could tell from the dirty looks she gave me all week that she thought I was spying on her and trying to get close to her. But this time her eyes softened and she smiled.

"Genia, yours is the only name on the list that hasn't been checked off yet."

She had spoken to me. I could jump for joy. I was so happy. That was going to be the start of our friendship. How great the summer at Sutcliffe Lodge was going to be. I was Jane's friend. I would be popular. Jane was the best person to have as a friend. Everything happens if you just wait long enough. Jane and Genia. Genia and Jane. Soon people wouldn't be able to tell us apart. No one will even realise I'm a cabin girl. They'll automatically assume I'm a waitress. I wanted to scream with joy but I thought I better control myself. I didn't want to do anything that would make her take her friendship away.

"Thank you Jane. I'll go now." I was so nervous. I wonder if she saw the tears in my eyes.

I knew the whole world was watching me as I stepped up to the list. Maybe it was a trick. They were all waiting to see me not find my name so they could have a good laugh when they knew I didn't have anyplace to put my tick. Please God, let my name be somewhere here, because I've already picked up the pencil. Yes! There it was. Genia Luckoskie, 10.30 a.m. My heart was beating loudly. My hand was shaking. I was so proud my name was on the list. I made my tick. I must have pressed the pencil too deeply, my tick stood out from everyone else's. Now I had really given them something to laugh at. But it didn't matter. Regardless how much they laughed, I was still going to the office at 10.30 a.m. to collect my pay.

Maybe I shouldn't bother going to the office at all. Let them keep the money they might owe me. But at 10.30 a.m. I started to panic and before I could catch up with what I was doing I realized I was standing in Mr. Sutcliffe's office. She was in there with him. I knew it was her. I couldn't make up my mind if what I had heard about her was true or not. Her eyes were too painted for me to see what they were really like. But I gave her the benefit of the doubt. She was too well dressed and had on too much make-up to be mean. And she had a smile on her face. I had courage to stand in front of her because I was thinking that she might see how much I had to offer, and might promote me there and then to the waitress job. What would everyone say if I walked out of the office after a week at Sutcliffe Lodge with a promotion? I would smile from ear to ear, and I would walk around with my lips shut, and Mary's hands could fall off from carrying the wash pails, and I wouldn't tell anybody the secret of my success. Let them come begging me. I smiled back at the old lady. I guess I could afford to smile.

"Is this the little girl you brought up for the week?" She had a thin shrill voice. Sharp. It didn't sound like a woman talking to her husband.

"Yes."

He didn't look up at her when he muttered his answer. He was sitting at the desk writing something. Then he lifted one eye, focused on me and motioned for me to come to his desk. He handed me an envelope.

"You'll be able to go."

I don't know why I was stupid enough to answer because I didn't quite hear what he said. "You mean, I can't stay?"

I kept my eyes on him. I wanted this to be a private conversation.

"Apparently you spent two and a half hours in cabin ten on Monday and the floor was so dirty when you finished, my wife said she had to send another girl in after you to clean it."

I looked back at his wife. I was sure she was going to tell her husband he was exaggerating and that it really wasn't that bad, and to stop making such a fuss. Maybe she was going to tell him that he had already proved he was a marvelous husband and that winning this battle wasn't important. But she just sat there and kept smiling and didn't say a word. If only they would know the truth. It wasn't my fault.

Why did she check on Monday anyway? That was my first day. It wasn't right of her to pounce on me so quickly. If I had been her, I would have waited at least a day. Anyway I had proof now that I was a good worker. She could go right this minute to any one of my cabins and see how spotless they are. Any corner she felt like. In fact, we should all go down together, her, him, me.

How could I make her believe me? Doesn't matter what I said to her now, she wouldn't have changed her mind. She had decided on the first day I wasn't a good worker, and even if I took her on fifty inspection tours she was going to stand firm. She was proud of her decision.

No, I could see the best thing to do, was to apologise for the trouble I've put his wife through, and refuse to accept the money for this week's work. I'll tell them I'll work another week free of charge and the next and the next. I'll work all summer and they don't have to pay me at all.

If at the end of the summer they feel I did my share of good work they could give me a little something, but only if they felt like it. I wanted to tell them what I had decided. I looked at the old lady. She was still sitting there, smiling. I was afraid she might get angry at me for having taken so long to make up my mind. Maybe she was ready to explode. Would she ask her husband to set the dogs on me? I couldn't tell what was behind her smile.

I could see myself running to her, falling on my knees, taking hold of her hands, and begging her to please let me stay for just one more week. One more week. But my feet wouldn't move, so I never got a chance to say all the things I was going to say.

He was doing all the talking. "Go get your things. There's a car waiting to take you back."

I took one last look at her. Yes, she definitely was the meanest woman in the world. The girls were right. She deserved her reputation. It didn't matter how much make-up and bright red lipstick she had on, I could still see she looked uglier than her husband. She looked well over a hundred years old. She had no breasts at all. The whole front of her looked saggy and hollowed out. Her skin fell loosely all over her face and hands. She was so skinny that when she crossed her legs, the crossed leg weaved around the other leg and touched the floor on the other side. She knew how to keep a smile on her face so maybe she had a friend or two, but it didn't fool me. Not now. I don't trust smiling women. As I left, out of the corner of my eye I could see him still sitting at his desk crouching behind his glasses. My hand turned the door knob. My poor small weak hands. I turned around. "Thank you."

It was meant for him, not her. I felt sorry for him because he had taken a chance and brought me here for a week. I knew it was his wife that had forced him to get rid of me.

They all looked at me as I got into the car. The Hopefield girls on their way to the dining room, the farm girls on their way to the cabins. Even Antonio stopped his hammering and looked up for one minute. I didn't tell anybody where I was going. Who was it that went into cabin ten after me and cleaned it? Why hadn't they told me? I might have been able to do something about it. The answer was as clear as their cold stares. Nobody cared. I knew that tonight they wouldn't even waste their time gossiping about me. There were too many preparations to be made for the precious nights to come. They would organise barbecues and dances on the beach, and as the summer would roll on, more and more men would find their way to Sutcliffe Lodge. Soon there would be enough Antonios to go around. In between all the loving, nobody would stop for five minutes and remember that I could have been there with them too. And at the end of the summer the Hopefield girls would have made enough money to buy a life-time supply of mini skirts.

It was such a long, sad ride back to the farm.

"Why are you leaving the lodge now?"

I didn't feel like having a discussion with the driver.

"At this time of the year, I'm bringing girls not taking them away." He paused to make sure I heard him. "No I don't take them away till September, sometimes even October."

I had to be brave and not show him that I was ready to cry.

"Well you see, I only came up to Sutcliffe Lodge for a week to give them a helping hand, until all the girls actually got there."

I didn't know and I didn't care what he had heard from Mr. Sutcliffe. Nothing was going to stop me from lying.

"I mean, they asked me to stay longer, for the whole summer, but I told them I couldn't because I had promised my mother I'd give her help this summer on the farm because she isn't feeling too well."

He wasn't concentrating on what I was saying.

"I thought that it was the least I could do for all she's done for me."

Finally, he lost interest in me altogether. I looked at the envelope in my hands. I wanted to tear it up and throw it out the window. That would be the only way I could get any pleasure from it. Once anyone in the family knew I had a little bit of money, they would keep asking for it and stealing it, until it would all be gone. I would love to have seen it floating out of my hands and flying around in the air. But I couldn't let myself, because it was all the money I'd make this summer. I had to hold on to it, hide it, save it, use it for buying those things Momma said I needed.

I didn't say a word when I walked in the door. They just guessed it.

"She's been fired. Genia's been fired."

First Joe and then Urek took one detestful look at me and said I was a good for nothing.

"Genia's the only girl in Jasno Gora that can't keep a job for more than a week."

"How do you ever expect to get anywhere?"

The small kids looked up at me with sad eyes. Everyone was sure there was no hope for me, and Joe and Urek were still at it.

"You lazy arse."

"They showed you fast enough what they thought about you."

65

I wanted to tell them they weren't so hot themselves. I wanted to say that I wasn't the only failure in the family. But I didn't say anything. How could I? What had I proved?

My brothers gave me no peace. All summer they made me run around for them, cleaning, cooking their meals, washing their clothes. The harder I worked to please them, the more they complained. Every time they came into a room, they'd chase me out so they wouldn't have to look at me. They hit me in the head, punched me in the stomach, slapped me across the face if I spoke. They told me that I was just lucky they were putting up with me. But they wouldn't forgive me because I was a bum.

7

I knew my life was being wasted but there wasn't anything I could do about it. And I had started to decay. The tears were eroding the skin under my eyes. Every day I was aging five years. Every time I scrubbed the kitchen floor, my hands became more red and veiny. Every time I peeled the potatoes, my skin became rough and scaly. If I was married it wouldn't have bothered me so much, my husband wouldn't have noticed me getting old. At night, he would have given me my hugs and kisses for the hard work I did. But I couldn't stop worrying about my sore black hands. I knew that soon nobody would be able to shove a wedding ring on them.

I hung around Momma's and Daddy's bedroom as if it was the last place on earth. I couldn't keep away from there. I always found some excuse to go to the bedroom as soon as I knew Momma was getting ready for bed. Every night I was there, ready to see her take her bra off. She would sit at the edge of the bed. Daddy was already in the bed, propped up. We were both waiting for the same thing. She'd snap the back of her bra. We'd be watching. Me at the door, and Daddy through the mirror. Then her breasts would come out. Lovely, round, big, soft breasts that fell like quiet bubbles on her body. Such beautiful breasts. I wished the whole world knew what nice breasts my mother had. I wanted to run to her, kiss and hug her, say good night, and tell her that I loved her. But how could I do it? How could I explain where I'd learned about love? Then she'd put on her nightie. I was still standing at the door. She always waited until the very end, before she'd look up at me.

"Genia, say your prayers now and go to bed."

During the day when Momma was at Montgomery-Joneses, and Daddy, Josef and Urek were in the bush, and the young kids were out collecting bottles, I'd sneak back into the bedroom and go through Momma's dresser. I tried on her bras and panties and girdles and nylon stockings. My body ached to be like hers. But everything was too big. If only God would have remembered that I was her child.

Then I found something I bet He didn't even know was there. Dirty books. Daddy's. In the bottom drawer. Three. They were yellow and old but I knew they had lasted because they were good. The paper scratched my fingers and the covers didn't want to stay shut, but I knew now I'd never pass another lonely day in the house. I ran to the bedroom every chance I could get to read them. From cover to cover and back. Over and over again. When I knew the story inside out, I would go straight to the juicy sections. I could find them with my eyes closed.

My favourite section started on page 76 of *Sex for Sinners*. The married man was sitting in a bar having one last drink before going home for dinner. Just before he finished, out of the blue, a luscious lady in a green dress walked in. He said she glided in. Her golden-blonde hair touched her bare shoulders teasingly. Her skimpy dress clung to her body desperately. He said his head spun around so fast he almost fell off the bar stool. He completely forgot who he was, where he was going. He said her hips begged you to follow her, her lips kissed you when she spoke. Her breasts panted. Her legs itched. He said he had to take her right there and then, he had to peel off her slinky dress, he had to press her naked god-given flesh into his throbbing soul. I was breathing as quickly as I was reading. My cheeks started to boil just thinking about the precious time

they had together. But every few minutes I had to keep looking up in case someone would come in. I was worried that if I
got caught they would take the books away and I would be left
with nothing again. I always put them away carefully, exactly
the way I found them. Every day when I opened the bottom
drawer my heart stopped beating for a split second. What if
they wouldn't be there today? But they were. They really
cheered me up. I was trying to get as much excitement out of
life as I could.

Next, I wanted to go to the Hogwrastle – the dance hall on the
far side of Hopefield. It was the wildest place in Hopefield and
everyone knew that more god-given flesh melted there than
anywhere else in the world. Everyone went from miles around.
The Germans from Brudmar, the Protestants from Halfway,
the drunks from Long Post, the Gungrog bunch led by Gerald
Chuffart who put his fist through anybody if they stepped in
his way, the big shots from Hopefield and the Polacks from Polackville. Every Saturday night, right after supper, Joe and
Urek would be at the kitchen sink, shaving, getting ready.

But Joe and Urek wouldn't let me go with them.

"What do you want to go for? Nobody's going to ask you to
dance anyway."

"I guess she wants to knock around the parking lots."

The parking lot was as big as the church parking lot and
more action took place out there than inside the dance hall.
Everyone brought their own booze with them and in between
the dances, people kept going back and forth to their cars and
half-tons to drink. It was in the parking lot of the Hogwrastle
that every girl we knew got pregnant. If you didn't get pregnant, you ended up with a hickey.

I had to stay at home and say the rosary with Momma and
the kids. We prayed that Josef and Urek would get back home
alive. We knew the chances were only fifty-fifty. Saturday
night seemed to be created for those who could drink the most
and drive the fastest. The men just used to go completely crazy. They never learned from all the accidents. Horrible accidents. Head-on car crashes. So many, many young people got

killed on a Saturday night – Adam Kaszubowskie and Barbra Izerskie and Victor Kulas and Ivan O'Donnell. Every Saturday the list got longer. Those that didn't get killed got badly maimed for the rest of their life. But still the Hogwrastle was the most popular place on a Saturday night. Not even death could stop anyone from going there.

Even after we'd go to bed, Momma'd stay up for the rest of the night. I don't think there's a Saturday night in her life that she's slept. She'd pray until the early hours of the morning. But it didn't help. One Saturday night, Urek rolled his car. The car was completely demolished but Urek and his seven friends walked away alive. Mind you, Tomek still complains that every once in a while a piece of glass comes out of his skin, and a year later Walter lost his hearing.

Joe managed to stay out of trouble. But not Urek. He made up for both of them. He had little scraps every second Saturday and then one night he was in the biggest fight the Hogwrastle had ever seen. He took on one of the Gungrog bunch, Gary Letchford. Poor Urek was so drunk he didn't have his usual strength that night. And Gary was a dirty fighter. He fought like a cat. He kept going for Urek's face. He cut Urek above the eye with a broken beer bottle and then, when Urek was blinded by the blood, Gary kicked out six of his front teeth.

Urek leaves his false teeth in a pickle jar on the shelf in the kitchen because they don't fit properly and he hates wearing them. They remind everybody in the house that there's still one more fight to come. Every time I see them I curse at Gary Letchford. I hope the hell Urek really gets him. I hope the hell Urek still carries the grudge somewhere inside him. I want Gary to get paid back for every one of those teeth.

I had my night for the Hogwrastle all arranged with Ursula. I met her in Stedman's store on Saturday afternoon and she promised me that if I'd be at the crossroads at nine o'clock, they'd stop and pick me up, so that I'd have a ride to the Hogwrastle. I made her cross her heart and promise me three times.

I climbed into three sweaters and three pairs of slacks and

two inches of stone in the bottom of Momma's boots. It was summer, but the winter wasn't very far behind us and it was night so I thought no one would notice. I found some powder and tried to powder the wrinkle out of my forehead. Momma begged me not to go. The children looked at me, as if they were seeing me for the last time.

It only took me an hour and a half to walk to the crossroads, and I'd left at five o'clock so I knew I was there in plenty of time. I don't have a watch, so I don't know how long I waited but I know damn well that after the sixth car passed me and it was so dark that you couldn't tell if it was me or a dead tree, I knew that I'd been waiting half the night. I thought back to all six cars. Three were half-tons so I knew that wasn't Ursula. She had to have been in one of those three cars. I'm pretty sure she was in the car that speeded by at a hundred miles an hour and flashed their lights off and on and someone shouted out the window. I'm sure that was the car that was supposed to stop for me. Or maybe it wasn't. You don't promise someone something with all your heart and then leave them standing in the wind. But it had to have been her. They must have passed me already. Time doesn't stand still for anybody, and she's probably been dancing half the night already.

I wasn't going to go back home. The very next car that came by, I waved and hollered and pretended I was lost and sick. They stopped for me about five hundred yards down the road.

I don't know who they were but they let me climb into the back seat and said that they were on their way to the Hogwrastle too. I slid from one corner of the back seat to the other, trying to keep the doors closed because every time they took a bend one of the doors would fly open. They ran into a ditch and I had to get out and shove for half an hour. The last headlight on the car blew out and the driver had to stick one hand out the window to hold a flashlight. They got a flat tire and the car rocked from side to side on the metal rim. This made them the happiest. They thought that sure as hell now they could kill me. But I got to the Hogwrastle alive.

Ursula was there. So were Joe and Urek. But I didn't want

to tell any of them that they had pulled one over on me. I bought myself a Pepsi Cola and went to sit down at one of the tables. The Cembalskie Band played a little bit of everything, country and western music, square dances, the polka, a few fast modern dances and nice long slow dances. I wanted to buy myself a ham and cheese sandwich, they looked so damn good, but I didn't dare. If Joe or Urek would have spotted me with one, I would never have heard the end of it. They would think that the only reason I came to the Hogwrastle was to eat. Anyway I had already spent most of my babysitting money getting into the dance hall and the rest I had to save so I could spread the Pepsi Colas throughout the rest of the night. It would probably take too much time to eat one of those ham and cheese sandwiches and in that time I might have risked the chance of losing a dance. I didn't want anything to stand in the way of anyone asking me to dance. So much opportunity, so little results.

As soon as I saw Josef and Urek heading for the door to have a drink in the truck, I stopped pretending I was having a good time. I looked at every guy straight in the eye. I waited for them to look back at me. Then I smiled. If I saw someone coming in my direction, I'd sit up straight and try and look as sexy as possible. I even laughed a little bit as if I remembered a funny joke. But every time, just when I knew they were heading for me because I was the only one available, someone else sneaked up beside me. Every goddamn time there was always a girl behind me, or on my right side, or on my left side, or at the next table, or near the wall, or someone just walking past by mistake. All night my stomach and my heart and my hopes kept rising and falling. And I couldn't stop burping because I'd drunk seven bottles of Pepsi Cola. I wanted to cry when Dominik Cembalskie announced the last dance of the night.

A tap. On my shoulder.

Leaning over me was Felix Hunsicker. Smiling. Did he want to dance with me? Where did he come from? He was right here tapping me on my shoulder and I hadn't even seen him coming. I stood up. He was still there. I hope it wasn't a mistake. I hope it was my shoulder he was tapping. I walked to the dance floor. He was behind me. Then he took me in his arms. I couldn't believe that my luck had changed. My night at the Hogwrastle wasn't a failure. At least I got one dance. The most important one.

"What's this song they're playing?"

I hadn't really heard any of the music until this moment and anyway I never knew one song from the other.

"The House of the Rising Sun."

"It's so nice isn't it?"

"This is the last song they play every Saturday night."

It was so long and so slow and so beautiful. Felix held me close to him, and sang parts of the song while we danced.

It's been the ruin of many a poor boy . . .

I closed my eyes for a minute.

And God, I know I'm one.

He felt so hot and lovely and he smelled so nice. Who would have guessed that hot breath in the ear felt so good.

Even when the song was finished, Felix kept holding me closely and hugging me. He wouldn't stop. Why was the evening over just when I was getting started? Felix took me by the hand and was walking towards the door.

"Where're we going?"

"Home. The dance is over."

"Oh . . . I came with my two brothers and I've got to go back with them."

"I can't see them anywhere. I'll make sure you get home all right."

"Oh no, I better go with my brothers. They're here someplace."

"You won't find them now."

He was right. There wasn't a soul left in the dance hall.

"Look, you need a ride don't you?"

He was so logical about it, I would have sounded stupid arguing.

Felix and I got into the backseat of Stefan's Chevrolet. One of Felix's hands was firmly planted on my shoulder.

"Don't worry, Stefan will be here any minute."

"Of course I'm not worried."

I pretended I wasn't, but I was. I could see what was happening. I had walked right into the trap that Momma, Joe and Urek had warned me about. I was sitting with a man, in the back seat of a car, on Saturday night, outside the Hogwrastle. I almost had a heart attack when it finally dawned on me that I was with Felix Hunsicker. Felix had the worst reputation of anyone in the County of Sterling. He had already made three girls pregnant and it looked to me as if I was going to be number four.

I tried not to panic. It was time I counted my chickens. I was just starting off. If I acted like a child and gave him a bad impression, he could ruin it for me by going around and telling everyone that I'm as boring as I look. There was so much to take into consideration, I didn't know what to concentrate on first.

I decided I'd pretend I was giving in. Only I'd make him do it slowly. Letting him have a little bit more every time to keep him happy. That way I could stall for time, and before anything too drastic had a chance to happen, we'd be back at the farm and I'd be home free.

He kissed me. God, it was wonderful. He had both his arms around me, and he was squeezing me as tight as he could and someone else's half-ton lights were shining on us and I thought I'd die it was so good. Lips that were the same size as mine. And when I opened my eyes, there was a young boy my age. I was happy he wanted to kiss me again after that. I wanted to remember what it was like to be kissed this way. I wanted to know how good it must have felt for his three other girls, and every other girl who got it right here in the parking lot of the Hogwrastle. Stefan came to the car, got into the front seat, and started the engine.

"God, that's a good fight tonight."

I wanted to go out there and see. Maybe Urek was breaking Gary Letchford's neck and I was missing it.

Felix was getting more persistent, more passionate. But I was raring to ask Stefan all about the fight. It was the most brilliant thing to start talking about, because all three of us could talk and drive and talk and then I'd be at the farm.

My mind went completely blank. Felix pushed me down on the back seat and got on top of me as much as he could. He was smiling. A funny little conqueror's smile. And his hands were moving in circles around my breasts.

"They feel nice."

I wanted to tell him, all he was feeling was layers and layers of sweaters but I knew he'd find out soon enough.

Stefan came to such a halt that I thought we'd hit another car. I jumped up. Who knew where we were? Some side road, I'd never seen before.

Both of them got out of the car, to have a conference. I was hoping they'd never come back.

When I saw Stefan heading back to the car alone, I knew that I'd have more babies than I could count. I knew that we were going to sit in this bush until one of them got me pregnant. I could see they were ready to spend all night if that's how long it took. All night, they'd take turns coming back and forth to the car, until I was completely undressed, completely tired out, and completely pregnant.

"Where's Felix?"

"He's taking a leak."

Stefan got into the back seat with me.

"Aren't you driving?"

"It all depends."

He leaned over and started to kiss me. He could try and blow all the hot air in my ear he wanted, but I wasn't going to let myself get pregnant. Not on my very first night.

I reached for the handle of the car door and opened it and fell out.

"Where're you going?"

"Home."

He got so mad he hopped into the front seat, started the car, made three circles, almost hit a tree and burled off. I heard Felix yell at him to wait up. Then I heard the car door slam and I knew both of them were gone.

I didn't worry now about the bears and the wolves and the crickets. I knew something had to get me in the end.

I waited until the very first sign of greyness so that I could figure out the right direction. Then I started walking. I didn't get back to the farm until eight o'clock Sunday morning.

Everyone was raging. Joe and Urek called me a slut for having gone off with Felix Hunsicker and spending the night with him.

"You're worse than the dog. Chase after anything you would."

"Damn good that he got the best of you."

Daddy was too drunk to know that I'd even been anywhere, he was having enough trouble trying to find his pickled herrings. Momma looked at me with red eyes. The small kids thought I'd gone to the devil. It seemed as if everybody expected me to be pregnant. I yelled at them with all the strength I had left. I yelled so hard I could feel the veins sticking out in my neck.

"I'm glad I did it. It serves you right. Now you'll have another mouth to feed."

But I didn't mean it for Momma because I knew she had cried all night for me. And I didn't mean it for the small children. I was yelling at those tall lanky bastards. I was yelling at all the men of Polackville.

8

I had to think, plot, plan.

It seemed to me that there must have been a reason I didn't fit into Jasno Gora.

Why was it that Father Anotskie defied my worthiness? Why did I see Honey Montgomery-Jones's easy life? Why did I remember Leonard Metamonskie's speech? Bad luck with God, a cardboard box come real, and the prospect of an education. All these were little suspicions that I might do something drastic soon.

I decided to keep my thoughts to myself. Everyone would laugh at me if I told them maybe what I'd do is go and get educated. No one knew anyone who had ever gone to University.

I had to think it through carefully.

If I was a Poderskie, I knew it would be stupid for me to think about going to University. But I was a Luckoskie. We were different. There was always something just a little bit different about our farm.

For instance, we received an up-to-date newspaper once a week. Josef was a paper boy. No one knows where he got the job, but every Saturday he'd be standing at the crossroads. Even in the winter. He was always there, even when the bus driver couldn't spot him because the weather was so bad. That was a hardship because the driver would miss the target when he'd throw the newspapers out, and Josef would have to spend up to an hour looking for his small bundle in the snow. There was always an extra paper in the bunch in case the top one got torn. Most of the time, Josef didn't have to use it, so he'd bring it home. Joe read every one of those *Ottawa Journals* from beginning to end. If you just counted the number of times the bus travelled from Ottawa to Toronto in ten years you could figure out how much he's read. He had the biggest vocabulary of anyone in Polackville. Everyone used to say that when he went into the bush he took a dictionary in his lunchpail. It wasn't true. He learned his words from those newspapers. Every day he made a practice of finding one big word and using it. He didn't want anyone to know he was doing it. I just guessed. I knew you didn't learn how to speak and use big words at school, so where else could he have learned them? I would have been ready to bet my babysitting money that it was the newspapers.

I think he didn't want anyone to know so that he could hold one over on us. He just wanted to pretend that he was born smart. For a long time he had me fooled. I believed his theories that some people have more grey matter than other people. I believed he was smarter than me. But the more I thought about it, the more it angered me. I had already been deprived of everything that every girl in Hopefield had. I wasn't going to be left out when it came to intelligence too. I couldn't accept the fact that God would have been mean enough to give me less grey matter than my brother. And anyway how did we know who had more grey matter? You couldn't see it. Not like my skinny legs and my tiny breasts. No, the more I thought about it, the more I came to the conclusion that he couldn't be all that much smarter than me. We both had the same parents.

I listened very hard. I heard the words he used. I looked them up in the dictionary at school and then started using them myself – if I could find a sentence that they would fit into.

I liked trying them out on my cousin Agata because she

wanted to be a psychologist so I knew with her I could get away with it. I practised them everywhere, when I was peeling the potatoes, when I walked to the outhouse, when I bumped into the dog. I decided I'd had enough practice and was ready to show Josef.

"When I do my homework tonight, it's going to be impeccable."

I thought he was just angry because he didn't like me speaking to him. "What are you using words like that for?"

He was getting angrier. "I don't know what you're trying to prove."

The extra blood made his nose red and I sensed that this was more than just his regular hatred of me.

"You think you're smart or something?"

I knew he was going to hit me.

"Stupid, you don't even know what it means?"

"I do so know what it means. It means without any faults, so there! And if I want to use big words I can. You don't own them. And I even use them more impeccable than you. You always get your meanings all mixed up."

Now I had to run for all I was worth. But what I said was true. The more I listened, the more I realised that he made mistakes. I mean, I wasn't listening to catch him out, I could just hear them that's all. I didn't want to hurt Josef. I would have loved if he didn't make any mistakes. Nobody else noticed because they never knew what anything meant anyway. If you just said, "I beg your pardon?" instead of "eh?" they thought you were too high and mighty and educated for them. It was easy to fool the people around Polackville. But Joe didn't fool me any longer. And I didn't even cry when he caught me and tried to knock my brains out with his fist. Nothing was going to stop me from building up my vocabulary.

Too bad I didn't tell Josef that he was still the smartest person I knew. Joe could tell you the name of every country in the world, its capital, its population, its leader and what sort of government it had, when its elections were, and who won them. He remembered everything he read. Every month he'd buy a second-hand book from someone in Hopefield. He could tell you about anything – how to build a bomb shelter, why microscopes were important, and what martial arts meant. When election day came to Canada, he knew who was running for which riding, who had run in the last election, who won and who was defeated and by how much. Joe never showed his knowledge to anyone. The only person he ever used to talk to about these things was Daddy when he wasn't drunk. I know, because I was standing around the corner listening. When Daddy was sober and Josef started talking, there wasn't a conversation in the world that could compare to it.

I wanted to learn everything but I didn't have a good memory and I kept getting mixed up with which capital belonged to which place. I kept forgetting which party the different MPs represented. I was fighting hard to keep it straight but there was always months between these overheard conversations and I lost so much. I couldn't pull myself out of my ignorance. How would I ever be able to prove to them that I had a brain in my head? When would I ever be able to participate in their conversations? It was only the facts that were holding me back.

Then I decided it didn't matter if I knew who was the leader of what country. I really had nothing to do with them and I didn't even find it an important thing to know. I figured if one in the family knew, that was enough. I figured if I just kept getting the right marks in school, I'd be okay. I didn't get the highest marks. Only the Bleganskies got them, because they were all going to be priests and nuns. I didn't get the lowest marks, because I wasn't a Poderskie. They could hardly read or write. They had animals on their farm so they had to spend all their time looking after them. But my marks were good enough to get into university. They were the same marks as Leonard Metamonskie's children.

I liked comparing myself to the Metamonskie children. I knew I was one step ahead of them, their father's success had spoiled them.

"Dorota what are you going to do when Grade Thirteen is over?"

"I don't know."

"Do you think you'll go to university?"

"Are you kidding? I'm sick of school. I don't want to see another book as long as I live."

I didn't bother asking her brother Janusz what he was going to do. I knew all he wanted to do was buy a car so he would have somewhere to hide his booze on a Saturday night. He was going to be a greater alcoholic than his father had ever been. Poor Leonard Metamonskie. He expected his kids to go to university on his behalf. Everything was turning out the other way round. Now it would be he who would be shamed out of his seat in Parliament by his children. Momma said it was a crying shame that his kids were becoming such bums. Secretly, I was glad. They didn't expect to have everything did they? It was about time they had some bad luck.

Everyone at school was getting fed up with me asking them what they were going to do when Grade Thirteen was over. I never stopped. It was the only thing on my mind, morning, noon and night.

"What are you going to do, Martha?"

"You've already asked me."

"Oh, I must have forgot."

There would be a long silence. I looked at them as if this moment would never happen again. What was I looking for? Not one of them could help me with my future.

"Out of interest, what was it you said you were going to do again?"

"I might go to Greenford and look for a job. Later on I might take some night courses in nursing or something."

"Oh yes, now I remember."

They were all going to Greenford. It was bigger than Hopefield and smaller than Ottawa. They had dreams of becoming nurses or teachers, mechanics or salesmen. But I knew what would happen. I could see it like a vision. Everyone of them would get to Greenford and take the first job they could find. Every week-end, they would come back to Polackville to visit. Some would say they had been laid off or that the potatoes needed hoeing so they were going to stay behind. Some would admit that there was nothing for them in

Greenford and the others would pretend they just plain forgot to go back.

One by one, they'd all filter back.

At the end of one year of ordinary week-ends, every one of them would be right back in Polackville. And then it would just be one wedding right after another. Agata would marry Tomek Domanskie. Ursula would marry Stefan Winchevskie. Momma would have so many weddings presents to buy. And then they'd be settled once and for all. Nobody would pretend anymore about their ambitions. There wasn't a hospital in Polackville so they didn't have to worry at all about the nursing, and as long as there were nuns there'd be plenty of teachers. And of course, everyone knew how to be a mechanic so it would have been useless to take a course in it. There was nothing at all to feel guilty about. Even Agata would have completely forgotten that once she had wanted to be a psychologist. Nobody wanted to leave Polackville in the first place.

I envied them. They would all be part of a group. Sort of like friends. They would be watching out for each other in church on Sundays, they'd bump into each other at the Post Office, they'd take each other home-made quilts when their houses burned down. Oh, there might be a few hardships like trying to make payments on the second-hand half-ton or trying to live with an alcoholic if he was drunk all the time, but there was always something to keep you going. Once during the day, your husband would give you a tight hard pinch on your ass and at night you'd both hop into the same bed, you'd be close enough to get excited by the smell, and then later on in the night there would be twice as much pinching.

And the news. The news kept everyone busy. Something important was always happening. The bells would ring if someone died and doesn't matter where you were you'd stop and you'd try and get home as fast as you could to make sure it wasn't one of your family. Or if some woman spotted some girl was pregnant, then there'd be electricity. It would travel in one straight line shocking everyone. She would tell so-and-so, and so-and-so would tell someone else, up and down, from one house to another, in and out, in and out, until the whole town would know and everybody in every house would be talking about it.

But not about me. If I moved to the city and went to university, news about me would have trouble getting started in the first house.

"Do you remember, oh you know . . . ." Poorer reception than on a dead transistor radio. "Wait a minute, her name will come to me yet." One small dull flash. "Genia."

"Oh, you mean that Luckoskie girl."

"Ya her, I wonder what happened to her?"

Two minutes.

"I don't know. She just sort of disappeared."

And that would be it for me. Nobody followed up a shadow. I could be out there having fifty babies or having my legs amputated or having visitations from God and nobody would talk. Nobody would care. When you left Polackville, it seemed as if you were lost forever.

And the real joke is that I would have been the best wife out of the whole bunch of them. I was pretty sure that if I got a husband I could make a good man out of him.

But the hardest thing was finding a goddamn husband. I made a list of every man that I knew in Jasno Gora and Hopefield. I even made a separate list of all the men from Halfway and Long Post, Brudmar and Gungrog, but I hid that one in case Josef or Urek found it and beat me up because they thought I had secret passions.

I went over and over my lists everyday for a year. There was someone there for Eileen Skuce and her bouncy ass, and there was someone there for Agata with her cannon breasts, and there was someone there for Mary Poderskie with her strong arms. I had to stroke off everybody until I didn't even have a list left.

I had forgotten to put John Doyle's name on my list because he was so tall and ugly and old that it didn't occur to me that he was a human being. Even Josef and Urek could see that John was a bad match for me.

"John couldn't bend down far enough to reach Genia."

"Oh ya, he'd step on her before he saw her."

I felt like going up to John. I had a feeling there might be a small heart inside all that flesh. I wanted to tell him I'd do anything for him. If he'd sort of smile out of his big lips, I would persuade him to marry me by telling him I was the best housekeeper of all the girls I knew. I'd come over every Saturday for a trial run if he wanted me to.

"You can laugh all you want, but I might just end up marrying John."

"You won't marry anybody."

"You'll be lucky if the two maids will let you come and live with them."

That's what I was dreading. I didn't want to end up in the old maids' home. Nobody talked to them, and as the years passed they stopped coming out of their house altogether. It was hard to find out what you'd do inside that house all day long if you had to move in there. I figured I should rap on their door one day, and ask them if I could come for a visit. But I was too frightened. And all I could find out from others was that everything in there smelled because they didn't know the first thing about running a house, and they had stopped going to church, and they probably had a strange disease because every year they were becoming like goats – white, with stray whiskers on their chins, and unpredictable. As soon as I heard about the fumes I knew that, regardless how much I'd try and change the place, it would get the best of me. I had a powerful feeling that a year after I move in, the house would burn down with me inside.

I had to go to university.

What I hated about having to decide to leave Polackville was that it would look as if I had no loyalty, when I knew in principle I was one of the most loyal people alive. It was just the facts pushing me out.

You have to go looking for a husband if he doesn't come looking for you. Even if you have to run to a city, to a world full of strangers.

It might be worth taking the risk. I might find some place, somewhere, where small skinny women with blue eyes are accepted. Who knows I might even find someone who would realise if things hadn't gone wrong I could probably have been a princess. And if he would really feel like giving me back everything I should have had, I might even end up in a big white cottage on a hidden lake right here in the middle of Polackville. There'll be some little girl yet, from one of their farms, who'll look up at me with scared eyes. She'll wonder at my greatness. I'll stand tall in my blonde hair and painted toe nails. I might tell her I was standing in her shoes one day a long time ago. I might tell her the secret, but only for her tiny blue-eyed ears. *Go, little girl and find yourself the right man. That's all there's to it.* Funny that no one around here could see that there was this alternative. You don't always have to settle for what you're born with. Why didn't they want more?

You've got to want things or you never get them. I'll come back. I'll come back with things. I'll make them jealous of me yet. Jealousy is the first step to get anyone started thinking. If only there would be joy in giving yourself to a stranger.

I didn't know anybody anywhere so it didn't matter where I went. The whole world was open to me. I picked Montreal. I liked the name, it sounded special. People's ears pricked up a little when you said Montreal. It would be a city I would be proud to say I was from. The more I thought about living there the more excited I got.

I started another round of questioning. This time about Montreal. Nobody had ever been there and all I could find out was that Montreal was a big city. I started looking in the *Ottawa Journal* every Saturday for news about Montreal. Momma found out from Honey Montgomery-Jones that Montreal was beautiful. That settled it once and for all for me. I knew I'd like it. I would fit in better there.

Now I had to move fast. I had to find out from Leonard how I could get into university and where I could get the money he talked about. Thank God, Mother's Day was just around the corner. It gave me a good excuse to go into the Hardware Store. I said extra prayers for a week that the day I had fixed up to go into his hardware store he wouldn't be in Toronto at a meeting for Parliament. But according to the talk I overheard at church that Sunday, he was with us.

"My God, he's become such a big shot. He stands at the door and watches everyone come in and holds the door open for them. He talks to everybody."

"He's trying to get more votes for the next election."

"Well he's got everybody fooled. Mrs. Yakaruskie saw him talking to Old Martin the other day. There was a time when Old Martin wouldn't have bought a screw from Metamonskie's."

I hoped my plan was good enough.

It was time for me to make my move.

I got into the Hardware Store without too much notice. So far, so good. Leonard was there. Walking around. I thought that I should go straight up to him and tell him I was going to vote for him when I was old enough. Get on his good side. No, I decided to look around first, so that I could calm my nerves. I headed for the china section. I didn't look in his direction but I could feel him coming towards me. What if he found out I only had a dollar to spend? I wish I would have picked a busier time to come into the store.

"Can I help you?"

"Oh no. I'm just looking for a present for my mother."

I was in the wrong goddamn section. I wanted to get her a new dustpan.

"Well these Pyrex dishes make very nice presents."

They did look nice. They were white with a yellow painted wheat stock on one side. I was getting confused. The one for a dollar was too small for Momma to do anything with. I knew it would be a waste of money to buy it. But I wanted to get her a present so badly, and I couldn't figure out a way of how to get to the section with the dustpans. Leonard kept standing there holding the Pyrex dish. I couldn't very well have said no.

"Do you think my mother would like that?"

"Oh, I'm sure it'll make her very happy."

He didn't know that she didn't use Pyrex dishes.

"Well if you think so, I'll buy that small one there." We walked to the counter and he gave it to his son to put into a bag for me. "I mean, it is quite a pretty dish anyway isn't it?"

"I think any mother would be pleased to own one of these."

Leonard handed me the bag.

"Oh, thank you."

"Goodbye. Come again."

I started to panic. I knew in two seconds he would be holding the door open for me and I would have no choice but to go and how long would I have to wait before I had another excuse to come into the Hardware Store? This was my only chance to speak up.

"Mr. Metamonskie, uh . . . ."

I was so nervous I wanted to give him back the Pyrex dish and run.

"Yes."

"Can I please speak to you?"

"Yes . . . well what is it you want?"

I could see that his son behind him was trying to catch every word I had to say. He had no manners.

"Well, I mean it's private."

I really was afraid Leonard was going to kick me out of the store.

"Come over here then."

We went over to stand beside the hammers and saws. I felt like Old Martin. We might not have had much to say but when we stood with Leonard we looked important.

"I know maybe this will sound stupid, but I'm going to be finished Grade Thirteen soon and I thought if it was possible I would like to go to university, but I don't know how it could be possible."

I thought I already heard him say, Yes, you know it really is pretty difficult so if I were you I wouldn't think about it too much. But he didn't. He stood there strong and serious. He had a nice straight nose. I moved my feet a little to make sure I was as steady as I could be. He didn't laugh. He didn't even smile.

"Which university?"

"McGill in Montreal."

He crossed his arms and with the finger of one hand flicked his nose.

"Genia, if you really want to go, you get Sister St. Jerome to write to McGill for the application forms. You fill them out and send them back right away. If they accept you, I'll arrange a student loan for you to cover the expenses of going to university."

"Oh, thank you."

I was smiling so much, the saliva was coming out everywhere.

"But you must know this, Genia. The student loans aren't very big and there is just enough money to pay the tuition, and a little bit extra for books. You'll have to save money from your summer job to meet the expenses of living in Montreal."

"Well that's okay, I don't need lots of money to live on. As long as it pays for the university and things."

"I know but you still need a place to live and it has to be paid for so you have to find some money on your own. And you must remember that the money from the government is just a loan and when you leave university it has to be paid back. But don't worry about that now."

"Thank you."

I was in a complete daze. I didn't even wait for Leonard to open the door for me. A grown up man had never spoken so seriously to me before. I bumped straight into Mrs. Yakaruski who was coming into the store. I'm sure she must have figured out what we had been talking about. It was wonderful to think that someone really listened to what you asked them. He really had taken me seriously. I wanted to look back and wave to him through the window but maybe he had seen how I skipped out the door and had decided I was just a little bit foolish. He had given me real down-to-earth practical advice. I couldn't believe it. I was so lightheaded I thought I'd go crazy. Beautiful Montreal. I stopped walking for a minute. I took a breath. I felt the Pyrex dish through the paper bag. It always pays off to buy somebody a gift. Now it looked as if I really might get there.

I could tell that Sister St. Jerome didn't want to write away for the application form for me. I knew what that hateful look in her eye meant: Why Genia? Why not Eileen Skuce or Tadeusz Bleganskie? Genia is the last person I would have picked. She could wish all she wanted for the others, but in the meantime she wasn't going to stop me. Just to make sure, I told her that Leonard Metamonskie was waiting for the application form because he was going to help me fill it out. She wouldn't dare doublecross him. How can a nun be so mean? If there was anything she could have done to stop me from going she would have done it. And she did try. She started giving me poor marks. The very next paper I got back I couldn't believe that she had actually pulled that stunt on me. I went to her because I wanted her to realise what she was doing.

"Sister St. Jerome, you've given me a bad mark on this paper. I'll never get into university if you give me marks like this."

She didn't see that there were tears in my eyes, because she didn't bother looking up at me. She was busy putting a big fat A on someone else's paper.

"You got what you deserved."

I went back to my seat. I'll show her what I deserve, wait until the next paper. It's going to be so good she won't be able to find a mark high enough for it. I'll show her who's got brains and who hasn't.

And next time round, I knew I'd done it. Even Sister St. Jerome looked pleased as she stood in front of the class, passing the papers back.

"I must say this time, there were some very good papers. I gave a few very high marks this time."

I smiled too. I looked around in my seat. I was proud. At last. Even though Daddy had raged about the electricity and kept turning the lights off on me, I had worked long into the nights on it. Even though Urek had burnt the first copy because he got mad at me and I had to start from scratch at the last moment. Even though I still peeled the potatoes and did the dishes and cleaned the house, I had done it. I looked around in my seat just one more time. Who in the whole class could have written a better paper than me?

A small C at the bottom of the last page. In red. Come off it. This must really be a joke. I went back through all the other pages. Looking for the real mark. I turned the pages over five times but all I could find was the small C on the last page. That was it. There were going to be no tears now. I stood up, got out of my seat and walked right up to the front of the class, to her desk.

"Sister St. Jerome, you gave me a C!"

"Go back to your seat."

"But I didn't deserve that mark."

I think my voice must have got a bit loud, because all of a sudden I could feel everyone watching me.

"If you didn't deserve it, you wouldn't have got it."

I could tell that she was being really unco-operative. Now I was yelling. I was waving it around like crazy. "I'll take it to anybody to read. They'll tell you it's a good paper. You didn't give me a good mark, because it was my name that was on the paper. If I would have handed in this same paper with Tadeusz Bleganskie's name on it, you would have given it fifty A's. I deserve a better mark. I'm going to university and I need good marks to get in. Why are you giving good marks to people that don't need them? They're never going to look at another book in their lives. They're never even going to bother picking up a pencil. They're going to get married and settle down on a farm."

I didn't care how many more enemies I was making now. I hated them all anyway. They were safe. They knew I would be revenged. I had done the unthinkable. I had yelled back at a teacher. And a nun. On top of being kicked out of school forever, I was probably committing a mortal sin.

I stood and waited to see what she was going to do. The eczema on her hands was getting worse. I would go straight to Leonard Metamonskie if she kicked me out. She had time to read my mind as she scratched her hands. She knew I wasn't afraid. Her hands were driving her crazy.

"Don't you ever speak to me like that again in your life."

She grabbed the paper from me, stroked out the *C* and put in an *A*. I took the paper back and went to my seat. But she still had the final word.

"Class, what you have all just seen with our loud mouth Genia, is that a little knowledge is a very bad thing."

It wouldn't have been so bad if she hadn't told everybody it was a quote from a very famous person. God, I couldn't wait to get out of this small schoolhouse with its mean nuns. Maybe I only had a little knowledge now, but what the hell do you think I was screaming about? I wanted more. That was the whole point. But you couldn't tell her that. She was too interested in teaching Eileen Skuce how to make a conjunctive clause. She really must have thought it would come in handy some day.

I worked on my application form for over two months. I didn't want to make any mistakes. I wanted them to know how important it was that I went to university. In one section, they asked me to explain in seventy-five words or less why I wanted to go to McGill University. I had the perfect answer. When I mailed off the application form I was certain they would never reject me. It was only the three words too many that bothered me.

> *Dear sir;*
>
> *I want to go to McGill because I want to get educated.*
>
> *Even though I've gone to school for thirteen years and I know quite a lot, I feel I still have quite a lot to learn.*
>
> *McGill is my choice because I want to go to the best university.*
>
> *In the end, I hope to bring back my education to Jasno Gora and teach all the people around here because they'll never have the opportunity I have.*
>
>

Yours truely,

Genia Luckoskie
>

9

Money. That's all I needed was some money. Somehow, someway I would have to find it. I thought about it in the day and I dreamt about it at night. I snuck into church at recesses and asked God to help. Every time I finished my work in the house I'd go out into the fields and think some more.

I passed our five outhouses for the one millioneth time, and for the one millioneth time I thought we should do something about them. Get rid of them. What a waste of boards it was to burn an outhouse. But what could you do with an outhouse that no one used anymore? Josef and Urek had never compared me to one of them yet, but I knew they were as useless as me. I put two and two together. If they're useless and I'm useless then it wouldn't hurt if I tried to do something with them. That's when it hit me.

I ran as fast as I could to find one of the kids. One of them would listen to me. I would convince them to help me with my new idea.

"August come outside, I want to talk to you." I made him come with me down to the big double outhouse at the bottom of the hill. "August, do you think if I asked Daddy he'd let me have this outhouse?"

"I don't know, maybe he's saving it for something."

I took a long careful look at August. I could trust August because he was one of the children and I had watched him grow. He'd grown so fast. Soon he would be a man, but he would be fair and gentle. He wouldn't laugh at me. He would take my idea seriously.

"August, I have a plan on how I'm going to make some money so I can go to university and I want you to be my partner. But I'm only going to tell you my plan if you promise beforehand that you'll be my partner, that you'll help me work on it and that nothing will stop us. I'm really serious, and if I make any money I'll give you some."

"What're you going to do?"

He didn't ask with any enthusiasm at all. Too bad he was only nine. He would really be a great help to me if he was just a bit older so he would understand that life isn't all fighting and shouting and struggling and hating. But still he was the only one of my brothers who would even talk to me so he was better than nothing. I decided to put my faith in him always.

"I'm going to make a chip stand out of this outhouse. Listen, all we have to do is wash it out completely, paint it, draw a few *Chips For Sale* signs on it, cut a window out of the back wall and use the boards for closing it up at nights, buy a fryer, dig the potatoes, cut them, fry them, and sell them."

"No one would buy french fries out of an outhouse."

"No one will know it's an outhouse. We'll wash it and paint it so well they'll never guess. I'm telling you, it's a good idea. People love french fries and I know we'll make money. We can charge ten cents for a small bag of chips and twenty cents for a big bag."

I was afraid I'd lose his interest. "Look, come on. There're no restaurants in Hopefield and when people drive around at nights or when they're coming home from the Hogwrastle or when the tourists come into town and stop for gas, they want to have something to eat and everybody's favourite food is french fries. Right now, tonight wouldn't you like to have a bag of good homemade french fries for ten cents."

Just the idea of it made our mouths water.

"I'm telling you with french fries you can't go wrong – the whole world likes french fries!"

93

"But where will we get a fryer and where will we put the chip stand?"

"I'll look after that. All I want you to do is help me wash it, and then I want you to very carefully saw a hole in the back wall and build a selling counter for me."

August was the right person for this. He wasn't the best carpenter in the family but he was careful, and I knew he wouldn't start, make a mess of it, and then leave it. August would do it right. Now I was really glad I told him. You've got to tell people things. August wasn't as excited as me, but that was because he was young, and he wasn't getting ready to go to university, and he didn't know what it meant to make money. I was happy because I was killing fifty birds with one stone. I had found a way of giving myself a job when no one else wanted to.

It took me two days to corner Daddy. I wanted to get him alone. That way he would have to face me and consider my question without running to anyone and shouting about how stupid I was.

There he was sitting at the table. No one else was in the house. It was only eleven o'clock in the morning but he looked tired. He was resting his head on one hand and scribbling something on a piece of paper with the other. The pencil was broken so he couldn't write much but I could tell he was either thinking about going into Hopefield to buy a bottle of wine or feeling bad because he had practically killed Momma last night. I felt sorry for him. Maybe he was thinking about how hard it was to make any money. Poor Daddy, nobody would believe he had worked so hard in his life because he had nothing to show for it. Well, I knew he had worked hard, and now he must let me do a little bit. Maybe I'd be luckier than him. I hope he won't be jealous of me and try to stop me. No, I know he'll really try and help me. Maybe he'll hope that somebody will do some good in the family.

I was really nervous. I had never spoken alone to Daddy before. He would really think I was crazy to speak to him. But I had to be brave. There's always a first time for everything. I had to forget about all those times he beat Momma and how mean he was when he got drunk, and just think about trying to save myself and the family. I would have to pretend that I was his daughter and he was my father and that daughters go to their fathers when they need help. He never really thought about me as his daughter, but I would have to give it a try. I had no other father to turn to.

I walked very slowly and cautiously to the table. He looked up right away. He was like a scared rabbit, he'd look up at anything. But he didn't have a chance to get up and run away because he knew I was going to ask him something. There was a feeling of importance in the air, and I knew he could sense it. This is the first time I saw his eyes so close. How blue they were. He really looked like a human being. Too human. I didn't want him to look so lonely and helpless. But I had to forget about that now. I needed his help. Genia, think. If he can afford to buy alcohol everyday, he can afford to buy you a fryer.

"Daddy."

God it felt hard to say that.

"Can you loan me some money?"

"Eh?"

He looked more afraid than me, so I continued.

"I want to open a chip stand in Hopefield and I can do everything and look after everything on my own and August will help me, but I need about two hundred dollars to buy a fryer. I know I'll make enough money to pay you back. I'll even pay you back before the summer is over. And even if the chip stand doesn't make any money, I'll pay you back every cent you loan me by going out to work somewhere else. You'll get your money back regardless what happens. I don't want to ask you for your money but I have to."

I don't know where he was looking, but he wasn't looking at me.

"Go ask Bronek or somebody. He has lots of money."

Okay, I'll ask him. I'll ask anybody. I'm going to find the money even if I have to go begging on the church steps or steal the collection tray on Sunday.

I left him and went back to finish the dishes. I knew he was thinking about it because he started scratching his head, and

95

for the first time he noticed his pencil was broken and he started cursing to himself because there was never anything to write with in our house.

All of a sudden, all over our farm, word was out that I was making a chip stand out of our big double outhouse. Josef and Urek were on the warpath. They came into the house so mad at me I had to be careful I didn't say a word or they would have killed me on the spot. I put the meal carefully on the table and made sure they had plenty of fresh raw onions and then went to sit on the verandah till they finished their supper. I decided it was better not to eat.

"Are you stupid or something? Cutting a hole in the outhouse! What do you think you're doing?"

"Who do you think is going to buy french fries?"

"You couldn't make a french fry if you tried. You can't even peel a potato!"

God I really hated them. What the hell were they talking about? Who the hell has been peeling their potatoes for supper every night of the week for the past fifteen years? I figured I had enough practice to last me a lifetime. I had a brown worn-out finger as proof. But I couldn't tell them that, I couldn't tell them anything. I had to keep my mouth shut and pay no attention and prove to them that they were all wrong about me. Now more than ever, I was ambitious to see my idea completed. But more than ever it seemed like it would never happen. Maybe they were right. Who would buy my chips?

Uncle Bronek said he didn't have time to talk to me.

"Stop bothering me. Go ask your father."

"I asked Daddy and he told me to ask you."

"I haven't got any money."

"Yes you do. You're not married and you haven't got any children. It's easy for you."

I had to follow him around because he never stayed in one spot more than two minutes.

"I'm only asking you for a loan and I'll pay you back."

He got into his half-ton and drove away.

I had to go and see him, every day for a week until I could

get anywhere with him. He was my only hope, so I kept trying. Finally I got through to him.

"Okay, I'll give you the money, but I don't want you to bother me anymore in your life. I want it back before the summer is over and I want you to put it all down on paper for me. I want to have it all in writing."

"Yes, I'll put it all in writing."

I was so happy that I wasn't afraid. I didn't know how, but it would all get back to him because he had helped me. In fact, I decided right then and there that when I pay him back I would give him fifty dollars extra for having been so good to me. I was luckier than most people because I had an uncle you could melt down if you pestered him enough. When he handed over the money to me, he looked straight into my eyes and smiled.

"I hope I'll be able to get a few free french fries from you."

I hope I had time to smile back.

I made Momma take me around to all the hotels and restaurants within fifty miles of Hopefield. We went to places I didn't even know existed. Finally, we ended up in Greenford. Momma was so good. She asked everyone she could think of and we stopped at everyplace that might look as if they sold french fries. If they did, we'd buy a pack of their chips and start a conversation. We'd ask them what oil they used and if they had a fryer they could sell us. At last we found a hotel that sold us a second hand one and with the rest of the money we bought cartons and salt and grease and ketchup and toothpicks.

Momma helped me even more than August, and finally our stand was finished. We went to the Esso Service Station right in the centre of Hopefield and asked them if we could put our stand at the side of the station, D.P. Sneath didn't like the idea. We had to promise to pay him so much a week and he said that he'd only let us get away with it for one summer.

Daddy got dead drunk the day we were going to move the chip stand into Hopefield because he couldn't stand it. No one had ever seen him so bad before. He was screaming blue murder because Momma was helping me. I knew he was going to ruin it for us. He kept yelling at us for throwing our money away.

"If you've got so much money, you should go out and buy a few groceries."

When he saw Momma and I bringing around the truck to get the stand on the back, he loaded up his shotgun. He swore he would kill us if we made one more move. "Do you want us to be the laughing stock of the town?"

Momma was the first one he was going to get, so she had to run into the bush and hide. I didn't care if he shot me. I walked right up to him and tried to yank the gun out of his hands.

"Doesn't matter what you're going to do, you're not going to stop us from going ahead with it."

He took the end of the gun and swung it across my face so hard I started bleeding. I crawled under the woodshed and hid for the rest of the day. I cried and cried. But not because my face hurt. I cried because he was making it so hard on us. He couldn't understand that no one would give me a summer job and this was the only thing I could do to make money. I hated him. I couldn't wait to make enough money so I could leave him for good. As soon as I could get ahead and pay back my bills, I would never step foot on his farm again. My only mistake was having asked him for a loan in the first place. I should have known I could do it without him. He was the biggest nuisance alive. He had ruined the happiest day of my life.

Momma had walked to three other farms and got four women to come out and help us. Late at night, when the stars were shining, and Daddy was asleep, we moved like weasels. We loaded the chip stand on the back of the truck. Then we released the clutch and pushed the truck all the way to the main road. We didn't want to take any risks. When we were far enough away from the farm, we started up and off we went. We unloaded the chip stand in Hopefield and then dropped all the women off on their farms.

Momma, August and I headed back to the farm for the rest of the stuff. In the darkness of the night, the three of us peeled and diced our potatoes and headed back to Hopefield. August and I screamed and laughed and talked about juicy home-made french fries. Momma just smiled. She looked like such a beautiful woman, behind the wheel of the truck. I was going to give her some money as soon as I made some so she could buy something nice for herself from the catalogue.

There it was. A bit of Luckoskie in the centre of town. We couldn't stop looking at it. The morning sun came up, and our chip stand sparkled like gold. We were going to sleep for an hour to get some more energy, but we couldn't. We waited and talked about how good the french fries would taste.

I was a bit embarrassed standing up in the chip stand with my white apron. I was afraid everyone would see that I was the happiest girl in the world. When I put on the first fryer of chips, I was sure you could hear the sizzling for miles. And then came that beautiful french fry smell. It was going every-where and I knew that everyone else would be able to smell it too. What if I'd get kicked out of Hopefield for making the whole town smell of french fries? But there wasn't any way I could stop the smell. August and Momma were right there be-hind me.

"Okay let's taste those french fries."

I got three packets ready and salt and vinegared them. And we ate. Who would ever have believed that fresh french fries could taste so good? August and Momma were smiling. We licked our fingers for ten minutes and we couldn't forget the taste in our mouths. I went back to the fryer and made up three more bags. Momma said she had never tasted anything better.

Then Seamus and Silas and Tomek Domanskie sidled up to the chip stand.

"What're you making?"

"French fries."

"Give us three packs. Let's have a taste."

I was worried because I thought that since I knew them, I had to give them the fries for free. I wasn't quite sure what to do. I decided I'd make up the packages for them and I wouldn't ask them for any money. In all that rushing around

I'd forgotten to practise how to ask for money for my chips. I could see I wouldn't make any money at all. Everyone in Hopefield knew me and they'd all expect free french fries. I handed them the first three bags.

"How much?"

It was Silas. Nobody coaxed him. He offered to pay. It was easy.

"Ten cents each."

Every one of them gave me ten cents. They didn't seem to mind giving me the money. I showed it to August.

"Look at that, thirty cents! Now if I can sell ten bags of chips I'll make a dollar and if I sell a hundred, I'll make ten dollars."

We laughed out loud. I counted all the money every time I sold a bag of chips. I wanted to make sure it was all there. By supper time I had run out of potatoes and I had made twenty-five dollars.

Week-ends were good for us, that's when people didn't mind spending their money. I opened a bank account and every Monday I went there with one hundred and fifty dollars. I felt big and important. There I was standing in the bank with Archibald Prosser from Stedman's Store and D.P. Sneath from the Esso station and Mr. Hubbard from the liquor store. A lot of money passed through my hands. People gave me five- and ten-dollar bills and once I got a twenty-dollar bill. They ordered bags at ten cents each, twenty cents each and sometimes I had to make up huge cartons for seventy-five cents.

But all the money I put in, couldn't stay in and it broke my heart when I had to take half of it out every month to pay for more potatoes and salt and packages and oil. And then I had to pay Bronek back for the fryer and D.P. Sneath for the parking space. At the end of the summer, I had paid everybody and there was only five hundred dollars left. But I knew when I finished my first year of university I could come back and make some more. I only wish someone had thought of this a hundred years ago.

IO

No more cutting out clothes from the catalogue and putting them in a cardboard box. This time I was finding them, writing down the description, sending away for them. And as soon as something came, I ran upstairs and packed it into my new green suitcase I had hidden under the bed.

Even after I'd packed everything as well as anyone could, I kept opening it up to touch my stuff. I felt my black winter coat with the antique silver buttons and silver buckle. The grey skirt with the frill. I wanted to get grey-and-green checked material, but if Eileen Skuce had found out she would have accused me of copying her. I made another mini skirt too, a lighter one for spring, in navy blue. I felt the shiny hard paisley blouse I had bought. And the underwear. I was a bit ashamed for having bought the underwear. I didn't really need it. No one sees what you're wearing underneath. Even after I'd memorized all the sayings on the panties, it seemed like such a waste of money. I tucked them into a plastic bag and hid them in a corner of my suitcase. I decided I'd end up saving them. And then the last thing to touch, my alarm clock. It slipped around in my hands like a new born baby, so little and fragile. It felt as if it had always belonged to me. I put it back carefully. I think I was happy because I realised I had everything in the world I needed. And I also knew I was the luckiest person in the family. No one else owned a suitcase full of their own things.

Sometimes I'd just sit upstairs and think. What if I really did turn into a tall blonde-haired woman? What if I did get so educated that thoughts would come so quickly to my head and out my mouth that it would make little girls dizzy? If you go for an education, you're bound to get educated. I might be able to explain things, answer questions, make people listen.

I might have worked myself into a state of expectant ecstasy but I had Momma's eyes haunting me. They watched me as I went up the stairs every day. They knew I was going to look through my suitcase again. They were strange, shy eyes. Why didn't she say anything to me? She was wishing I wouldn't go away. She should have said something because then I could have told her that I was trying to figure out a way I could take her with me. But it didn't matter how many times I checked the suitcase, I couldn't find her in it. If only I could think of a way of repacking it so there would be room for Momma. And the four kids. And just a corner of the farm. Really when I thought about it they were the only things I wanted to take with me. Leaving Polackville would be the most tragic thing I would have to do in my life. I knew that it would never be the same for me if I ever came back. Why is it that the only things you can take with you are a suitcase and an alarm clock? Poor, poor Momma. If only she knew that I was as sad upstairs as she was downstairs. At least she had Josef and Urek and Krysia and August and Ignacy and Bernadette and baby Honey. I would have no one.

I wanted to go downstairs, put my arms around Momma and tell her it was all a joke and that I would never go away. I had bought the suitcase to play with. To open and close. Pack and repack.

I got to the bottom step but I couldn't go any further. I sat down on the step and started to think again. If only I could talk to Momma. I wanted to tell her so many things: I have to go because I have no choice. It's like that summer you made me go away with Angus Mauldoon. You said I had to go so I could see a little bit of Canada, and that there was nothing to stay home for because all I would end up doing is working hard and having to listen to the kids crying and having to put up with Daddy's drinking and Josef's and Urek's fighting. You said that was no life for me and if I had the chance to go away I should take it. So you see Momma, this is just the same as that, only more lasting. This is for good. And everybody needs a boyfriend and the men around Jasno Gora don't like me, so I have to go away to find somebody. You don't want me to be an old maid, do you? I really want to get married. And in order to find a boyfriend in the city I have to have an education or they won't look at me. All the men there want their wives to be well dressed, to talk smartly and to know about a lot of things. It's not that I want to change because I don't like Jasno Gora, I have to change for those men. That's the only way they'll want me. You see Momma, my choice has been narrowed down, and there's nothing I can do about it. You know what Ann Landers always writes in the *Ottawa Journal* – if you're stuck with a lemon the best thing you can do is make lemonade.

Up and down the stairs, until the time had run out.

Everybody had forgotten I was going away except her.

She heard me coming down the stairs with the suitcase, even though I was trying to make as little noise as possible.

"Well Momma, I guess you better take me to Hopefield to catch the bus."

Just as we finished putting the suitcase on the back of the half-ton, Daddy came out of the shed and told me to hold on one minute.

"Where're you going?"

"I told you already, I'm going to Montreal to university."

"Don't be so stupid, stay at home where you belong." He couldn't figure out why I wanted to go to university. "What do you want an education for anyway?"

"I don't know." I knew but I couldn't tell him. I said good-bye to half of them and the other half I couldn't find. No one's ever around when you want to say good-bye.

Momma drove and I sat in the seat beside her. I wanted to slump over and pretend there was blood on my face. I wanted her to save me. But I was stupid. I sat up like a stubborn stone and she just kept driving. Then all at once, for five minutes on the last bend to Hopefield, she told me everything she could think of. She told me to be careful in Montreal because it seemed like too big a city and that I would probably get run over or kidnapped or murdered. She said there were a lot of bank robberies in Montreal. She told me not to talk to strangers because you could never tell what they'd do to you. I loved when she talked to me.

Then she parked the truck and we got the suitcase off the back. She told me to come into the dairy with her, she wanted to buy me an ice cream.

"No Momma, save your money. Please."

But I could see she had it all planned because she had brought her brown leather wallet with her. It was so worn out she could hardly find the twenty cents. I felt sad when she handed me the ice cream cone. We ate it in silence. She didn't know what else to say to me and the bus was waiting.

"I better go now."

"Okay, well good-bye and take care of yourself and don't forget to say your prayers every night."

Her good eyes had turned weak with water. She bowed her head and pretended she had to close her purse. I didn't want her to cry. She had so much unhappiness in her life I didn't want to be the cause of any more. I wanted to kiss her good-bye. But I didn't know how. I wish someone had kissed someone just once in our family. Then it would have looked natural for me. The doors of the bus were closing and I was standing on the first step and all I kept thinking about was how much I wanted to kiss her. I didn't care how stupid or embarrassing it was going to be.

I quickly bent down and tried it. She looked up. I missed her cheek. Thank God I was going away for a long time. Maybe by the time I got back she would have forgotten that I had tried to kiss her.

I started praying right then and there on the bus. To make

her happy. In between every decade of the rosary, I put in a special request. Please God make sure I don't get into trouble, and help me find someone who won't be an alcoholic. And please Dear God, take care of Momma and the family. If you have to make a choice, I would rather you looked after them than me.

The further I got away from Jasno Gora and the closer I got to Montreal, that feeling of expectant ecstasy finally came to me. I got my list out of my purse. As soon as we pulled into the Montreal bus station I would have to be smart and do everything the way I had planned it, so I would get safely to the Royal Victoria College room that was assigned to me.

✓ – *Get off the bus.*

✓ – *Don't speak to anyone.*

✓ – *Get the suitcase.*

– *Get a taxi just outside the door.*

– *Get in and ask him to take me straight to RVC.*

It wasn't until I was actually in the back seat of the taxi that I had a chance to take a look at Montreal. You couldn't see the city, all you could see were people. I kept hoping they'd get out of the way so I could see what Montreal was like, but there were just too many of them. Then I realised that my taxi was only going about five miles an hour. We were caught in the centre of Montreal and we couldn't move. I had never seen so many people all at once in my whole life. They were walking down the street four or five abreast, one after another, in the same direction, in a hurry. They crossed everywhere. Cars were honking, but the people kept walking. They didn't look at anything. They just kept walking straight ahead. The funny thing is, the cars didn't run them over. They just waited. Every once in a while my taxi would squeeze through the people and keep going, but before you knew it we came to another crowd of people and would have to wait until we had another chance to squeeze through.

I kept staring out the window. I couldn't believe my eyes. It was a mess. I didn't know how we got into it and I didn't know how we'd get out of it. Then I got really scared because the taxi driver started cursing under his breath. I was afraid that he was going to abandon the car and leave me alone in the middle of all this. What would I do? I felt sick in my stomach. I wished I was back in Polackville. Momma was right. Too many people. Who were they? Where were they going? I thought there must be a special celebration further down the street. This wasn't normal. I wanted to ask the taxi driver if he knew where they were going but I didn't dare. I didn't want to remind him of our problem. So I just sat back and tried not to show anybody I was surprised.

I didn't like the room they gave me in the residence. It was big and empty and dusty. I had to tiptoe because you could hear every movement I made.

I unpacked my clothes. Even they felt strange now. They didn't feel as nice as they did when I touched them upstairs in Jasno Gora.

I couldn't breathe, the dust was everywhere. I knew I was going to get lung cancer from all that dust.

I knelt down by the bed to pray, but the bed seemed bigger and higher up than our bed on the farm and I couldn't reach the sides to lean my arms on it. I tried not to let that bother me, but still I just couldn't pray. It didn't seem as if I could reach God from Montreal.

I didn't go down to supper because I was afraid to meet the other girls and I didn't know what to wear. I was going to try and figure out a way of surviving without food.

When it was dark enough, I shut off the lights, pulled a chair up to the window, opened the curtains just a sliver and then watched. All I could see was cement and roads and sidewalks and tall high buildings. Who was it that said Montreal was a beautiful city? I looked and looked and I couldn't see anything beautiful about it. In fact, to me it looked really ugly. Every ten minutes the sirens would go. You could just catch something speeding up and down the streets, faster and faster. But you couldn't see a fire blazing in the sky. All you could hear was the noise. Maybe it was ambulances for people near death. But I couldn't imagine that so many people died in one night. I finally decided it was the bank robberies the sirens were chasing. There was something moving behind the curtains of the building across the street. I thought it might be a kidnapper. Once, my stupid foot touched my other foot by mistake and I almost had a nervous breakdown. I stiffened my muscles so that nothing would move again for the rest of the night. I didn't want anyone to know I was there.

II

I needed to have a talk with God. He needed to know that even though I'd come all the way to Montreal, I hadn't forsaken Him. Maybe this was the proof that God had been waiting for. Maybe this was the time and place He was waiting for, to help me. Maybe now He'd see that I really needed Him.

It made sense that the first time I left my room, the first thing I did in Montreal was to go out and look for God. Yes. I'll start with God. It's best to start at the top and work down.

But I had a problem with my door. I didn't know if I should lock it or not. I stood there looking at the door. Wondering. Feeling the key in my suspicious hands. No, I decided I wouldn't lock it. For Him. But why had they given me a key if they didn't expect me to lock the door? Maybe the right thing to do is lock the door. But just as I finished locking the door a girl came out of the bathroom in a nightie and a towel on her head. She looked at me, said hello, and walked away. She was so friendly. It made me nervous that she had caught me locking the door. Was I never going to trust anyone? I unlocked the door. I wanted to go back into the room and cry. If only I could figure out what was the wrong thing and what was the right thing to do? Maybe I shouldn't even close the door, leave it slightly ajar. That would show real trust wouldn't it? I got one of my shoes to hold the door open, and left.

On the street I was afraid I'd get lost so I only went as far as I could see. I came across three churches, but I couldn't tell if they were Protestant or Catholic. I kept running back and forth comparing them. The more I kept crossing the street trying to make up my mind, the more I ran the risk of getting run over. I gave up. My conscience was still burning but I didn't want to end up in a Protestant church. How is somebody supposed to know which is which?

The whole city looked the same. Ugly. The same tall cement buildings that felt as if they were going to fall down on you. I felt I should get off the streets before it happened. You just can't predict these sort of things.

I was getting really hungry now. The starvation diet wasn't working. Nothing was working. It was hard to get back into the residence without bumping into someone. It was hard to be alone. Every five minutes somebody would come up to me to say hello. Girls. Girls that were bigger and fatter than I had ever seen. Girls that were skinnier and smaller than me. Girls that had brown hair. Girls that were nervous. Not all of them could have been born in a city and be rich and educated. There must be somebody who's trying to make a go as I am.

Then it all started clicking. I remembered that everything depends on the start you get. If you start off on a good foot you can't go wrong, so I pretended I was a snob. I knew people would envy the great things I was trying to protect and want to be my friend because I probably had something they wanted. Judy asked me where I was from, I said Toronto.

"Oh, so am I. What street do you live on?"

I wish I was a quick thinker. I couldn't think of the name of any street and I stammered and sputtered. "My God, I've only been here a day and I've already forgotten what street I live on." My cheeks were hot and my eyes were blinking and I was having trouble with my *th*s. I wanted to run as far as I could. Just when you think you might get your feet on the ground, something small and stupid like this would have to happen. I didn't know if she knew I was lying, but she certainly must have thought I was a fool. I felt like one.

"Well what school did you go to?"

God, I really felt like throwing up. I could feel myself drowning. Why do people always have to cross-examine you?

"I've forgotten that too, isn't that funny?"

I didn't want to become friends with Judy anyway, I'm glad she walked away on me.

When Wendy came to talk to me, I had my background all straightened out in my head.

"Oh, I was born and brought up in Toronto, but when it was time for school my parents sent me to St. Paul's School in northern Canada. You wouldn't have heard of it, it's quite small, but a very expensive boarding school. It was a year round school, even summers, so I never got to know Toronto. I haven't seen my house in Toronto since I was five, and my parents have moved to three different streets since then."

All I kept praying, is that nobody would tell anybody else what I'd told them or I'd really be in a mess.

It was giving me a headache. I longed for Polackville. Life was so simple there. I wasn't going to be able to put up with all this lying and pretended snobbery.

What would I tell in my first letter home? I knew they were all waiting to hear from me about how I was getting on in Montreal. Should I tell them I love Montreal and that it is a beautiful city? That McGill is an excellent school and I was learning a lot. That I had met a lot of nice people and made good friends. No, because then they would all think I was having such a good life and envy me. They would think I was never coming back and think what an ungrateful daughter I was for making it look as if dreams could come true.

Or should I tell them that Montreal is an ugly city and that I had nothing to do and nowhere to go. That I wasn't meeting anybody and I felt lonely and I wished I had never come. No, because then they would tell me that I should have listened to them in the first place and stayed at home.

I just didn't know what to write.

I knew what I really wanted to write. I wanted to write: I

can't even speak English properly and I can't make friends because nobody thinks I'm worth knowing. Because of you, I have to lie and I don't know what I'm talking about half the time. I hate you for being poor. Do you know what I heard someone call me? A peasant. I hate you for giving me a bad start.

When I started writing the letter, the tears got the better of me and I told them everything they wanted me to tell them.

> *Dear Daddy, Momma, Joe, Urek, Krysia, August, Ignacy, Bernadette and Honey,*
> *How are you? I bet you are fine.*
> *Montreal is okay, but it isn't all that nice. I found a church to go to, a nice church and on Sunday I went to mass. I lit a candle for you. I'm going to light a candle for you every Sunday.*

I wanted to make the letter interesting, so I wrote that a man followed me home from the library one night and that I was really afraid but nothing happened. I told them that I couldn't sleep at nights because of all the ambulances and fire engines. Then I said how much I missed Jasno Gora.

> *And please Momma, please write to me and tell me what everybody is doing.*

Then I added something at the bottom.

> *I love you all and miss you all and God bless you.*

I was really crying now. This letter proved to me that, sometime in your life, you have to tell your parents and your family, that you love them. The easiest way is in a letter. I thought it was a bit daring, but I wanted them to know that really in my heart I did love them, and they shouldn't laugh at me for saying it to them.

After I mailed the letter, I was still worried. Had I made it clear enough that it was okay for Momma to write to me? Had

I made it clear enough that they were important to me and even though I was in Montreal they must write to me and talk to me as if I was there with them. That I wanted to hear the news from Jasno Gora.

But I knew I would never hear from them. It didn't matter how many times I underlined it, I wouldn't be able to make Momma understand. She would be afraid to send me a letter. She would be ashamed. She would say she didn't know how to write to someone who's in university.

Girls had come up to me to speak, but I had never gone up to anyone. Now, I could see the advantage in making the first move. If I went up to them, I could start asking all the questions first, so then I would know where I stood.

On the way to the very next meal, I saw a girl walking all alone. She would be the one.

"Hello, are you going to supper, I mean, dinner?"

"Yes."

"My name is Genia, what's yours?"

"Venitia."

"What?"

"Venitia."

I couldn't catch on to her name. I had never heard a name like that before.

"How do you spell it?"

"V – e – n – i – t – i – a."

"Oh, you mean Venitia."

She told me that I didn't pronounce it properly because I put the stress on the wrong syllable. "But it's okay if you want to say my name that way. I like it because it's different."

I couldn't figure out what she was talking about. I seemed to pronounce her name the same way she did. But I liked her. I liked her because she was all alone and she wasn't going out of her way to make friends and she never bothered to ask me any questions.

Now that I looked at her again, I could see she wasn't very good looking. She dressed richly but she didn't have a good figure and her face had a funny sort of nose and her skin was oily. Still, there was something nice about her. I decided there

112

and then that I was going to make her my best friend. I didn't really know how to have a friend but I'd learn.

"Where're you from Venitia?"

"Greenford."

I smiled. Well, she couldn't very well hold one over on me. From her rich window she must have seen some of the people from Jasno Gora come and go. She was so nice. She wasn't ready to cut me down and show me that she was better than me. I mean, when you think about it, she could have said Toronto. I wanted to be careful with Venitia. I would give it to her in small doses and maybe someday I would tell her the whole truth.

Now I was happy and started to see the good around me. It was always nice to meet Venitia, to talk and then come back to my room and not have to feel ashamed at what I had said, and kick myself for making a fool. Even my room was looking better.

The thing that pleased me the most was my closet. I could actually hang up my clothes, close the door, and not see them. It completely fascinated me and I couldn't stop opening and closing the door, admiring the way it worked. It was so nice to be able to shut your clothes out of sight. I wish Momma had this closet. I could remember how much she wanted closets on the farm. She said she'd get them some day. Now I was crying because my closet had come so easily and there she was in Polackville stuck with big four-inch nails in every wall.

I even started to see more things on the street. Like the nylon stockings. They were different, some sort that stuck to the women's legs like elastic. I wish Momma could see them. Old women with skinny legs had no trouble keeping them up. Young girls who moved fast had no trouble keeping them up. They weren't falling around the ankles, no one had runs, and everyone's legs looked nice in them. It looked like sheer nude velvet, you could hardly stop yourself from wanting to touch it. I wanted to ask one lady where you could buy stockings like that, but I didn't. I knew if I stayed in Montreal long enough, I would find out for myself.

I couldn't explain it, but every day I was happy. It was easy to be happy. There were so many wonderful things.

If I wouldn't have been suspicious, I would have started using the showers from day one. My hair always felt dirty and greasy and looked terrible but I decided the only thing I could do was wear a kerchief on my head to hide it, until it was time to wash it. I was used to washing it once every two to three weeks, otherwise I was sure it would dry up and fall out. But I couldn't help wondering why girls with shiny clean hair were going in to wash it every second day.

Then I started using the showers. God, I loved it. Fresh clean water. Unrusty water. Water that Daddy had spent his whole life looking for. Pouring down my body. Water that could get rid of anything – brown spots, black stains, things that were building up for years could be washed away. You didn't have to heat it in pots on the stove. You didn't have to wait until everyone got out of the kitchen so you could wash. You didn't have to worry that someone would walk in on you. Now I never thought twice about where the water was coming from. I started taking showers every week and then I took them twice a week. Then I realised I didn't even have to have a pattern. They were always there ready to be used, and I could use them whenever I wanted. I started to take a shower just whenever I felt like it.

That's the way I was leading my whole life now. Doing things just whenever I felt like it. Going to bed when I felt like, getting up when I felt like, taking a shower when I felt like. My God, it finally dawned on me, that I had no one to look after except myself. I didn't have to look after the children, or make meals for the family, or find Josef's shirts and Urek's socks, or worry about Daddy shouting and fighting all night.

But that made me feel sad too, because now I knew that poor Momma had to take it all without me. She only had Krysia now, and that wasn't any help because Krysia wasn't as strong or as hard a worker as me. And now she'd have to take all the blame and criticism alone. I wanted to share my luxuries with her. Maybe I should quit university and go back. She had been as good to me as she could possibly be. It wasn't her fault that she couldn't treat me like my brothers. They wouldn't have let her, and she was afraid of them. It wasn't fair that she had to handle the family all alone now.

I became really afraid that she was going to die of overwork. It was too much for one person – washing the clothes, baking the bread, making the meals, looking after the children, planting the potatoes, cleaning the house, running to M-J's cottage, sewing, knitting, quilting, mending. Everything you could think of. The horrible realisation came to me that nobody, not one person, had ever said thank you to her. For anything. No one even talked to her. She was always told to shut up, and if she didn't she would get beaten up. I ran as fast as I could for a pencil and paper and wrote her another letter.

Thank you Momma for all the stuff you did for me and please, please don't work so hard.

I couldn't control my crying.

Momma, please stay healthy. Please take it easy. And thank you again and God bless you.

I decided I would always write her letters with a Thank You at the end. She deserved it.

But I forgot things fast and the next time I went to dinner with Venitia I was laughing and happy again. At RVC there was no shortage of anything and Venitia was constantly amused at how much I ate. She only nibbled at a few vegetables because she was on a diet. She spent the rest of the meal watching me. Boy did I eat. I made up for every meal that I missed in my life. I had two or three glasses of fresh dairy milk, big helpings of meat, vegetables soaked in cheese sauce, and two desserts. I couldn't get enough of it inside me.

"It's a wonder you're not fat, Genia?"

She didn't know that I had been starving for seventeen years. I couldn't wait to get fat. That was the whole idea.

I didn't even realise that Venitia was jealous when she said she wished she looked like me. She couldn't stop complimenting me. She said I had healthy hair, nice teeth, wonderful eyes, beautiful clear skin and an attractive slim body. She said she'd never seen anyone so well proportioned, that everything matched – my hips, my breasts, my hands. She said she was going to like being with me because men would find me sexy and they would follow us. I didn't bother telling her that I never had any luck with men. I let her tell me all the nice things she wanted to, she was so kind. She even went so far as to say that she thought I was one of the most beautiful girls at McGill. I didn't really believe her but I knew something else. I knew now what it meant to have a friend.

12

Venitia was full of advice. She knew so much about university it seemed as if she had gone through it and was coming back for a second round. She told me that the only friends you have in college are the friends you make in the first few weeks there. I listened to her advice. I took this first few weeks business seriously. I decided to go all out. I could see that it was worth that extra work. Then as the years rolled on, I would have a lot of friends.

I wouldn't let a minute go by without making full use of it. I made myself smile at everyone and say hello. I walked around in my grey mini skirt with the frill, I sat everywhere I could think of to drink Pepsi Cola, I spiced up my stories so that anyone who spoke to me would want to come back and find out more. No one guessed that I was really the most unpopular girl in the world. Even when I told someone that I had been voted beauty queen in my last year of high school in Toronto, they believed me.

Lying became much easier. I found people were ready to believe anything. I told Sami that my father was a nuclear physicist, but I didn't know him because as soon as he invented the nuclear bomb the Russians made him move back to Poland. He believed me. But when he told me that he lived in a castle in India with twenty servants and hated it, I didn't believe him. I could spot a liar and I certainly didn't want to get stuck with one. I wanted the real thing. I wanted to find a real king, not a make believe one. Stupid Sami, I hated him for thinking he could get away with it with me. And his lies weren't even interesting. Nobody knew how to lie the way I could. Who cared about a stupid castle in India?

And then it came. The opportunity to get my husband. A residence entertainment council had organized a co-ed picnic for the first-year male students to meet the first-year female students. Everyone was hopping because they knew that this could be the most important day of their lives.

The men got to the picnic first. When our bus arrived they circled it completely and blocked the door, crowding each other out to get first choice. Some girls even got paired off from the windows. I didn't want to get off the bus. For the first time I was afraid that my mission wouldn't succeed, I wouldn't find a husband. What if those guys could see that once I had planned to be a nun? That I was the wallflower of the ball? That I almost ended up in an old maid's home?

My knees were shaking by the time I got to the first step. There should be a law that allows people to get off a bus and get their feet on the ground before you pass judgement on them. I had only one more miserable step to get down. Wasn't anybody looking me over? Then I heard a shout. I didn't want to look up too quickly. Then someone shouted again. It sounded like a hello. I stopped. It was me he was yelling for. There was no doubt in my mind. Right there on the steps of the bus, right there with God's light shining on me, I decided that what Venitia said must be true. I must be the most beautiful girl at McGill. I must have found a place in the world where small women with blue eyes are wanted. I looked up and smiled the biggest, happiest smile I have ever smiled in my life.

I could spot him weaving his way through all the other guys. I waited for him.

"Hi there."

"Hello."

"Do you want to go for a walk?"

"Why not?"

One of his friends from the back shouted, "Well done, Eimer."

In my head I congratulated myself. I had picked myself up a husband. A nice man. God, he was the nicest man I'd ever seen in my life. He gave me his hand to hold. It was as soft as a baby's.

"We'll just go over here. Into the woods a little."

He was wearing a sports jacket. Imagine a guy coming to a picnic in a sports jacket. He just didn't seem like a working man to me. There was nothing rough about him.

We stopped walking. "This is good enough." He touched my cheek with his other hand – the man I was going to be with for the rest of my life.

"What's your name?"

"David Eimer."

I hope he realised I wasn't doubting him when I asked him for some information. I knew he was wonderful, I just wanted to satisfy my fantasies.

"What's yours?"

"Genia."

I tried to act and speak as intelligently as I could. I owed him that much. I lay down on the ground beside him.

"Where are you from David?"

"Montreal."

"Mont . . . ?" I caught myself just in time. I was in Montreal. We were in Montreal. Then the whole situation hit me. I jumped straight out of his arms and into the air.

"You mean you're from here? I mean, you're really from the city, I mean, from this city, Montreal?!!"

Stupidly I had decided that everyone at the college, everyone in the park was playing a game like me. I don't know why, but as my confidence had grown I just assumed everyone was from some small town in northern Canada or from some deserted village in India. What else was I supposed to believe when they started talking about castles and big businesses and money pouring out of their ears – it sounded too much like my own stories. I figured that everyone was wearing their best clothes because everyone was looking for someone to love.

I didn't expect to run into the real thing so soon. I wasn't prepared for it. How did I know it even existed? But David Eimer was the real thing. There was no mistaking that. He wasn't lying. I only had to take another look at his hands to know that. They were clean and white and soft, they looked as if they'd never done a day's work in their life. Gentle hands. Hands that belonged to the sort of clothes he was wearing. Those weren't Sunday clothes he had on, he wore those every day of the week. It was clear in my mind that David came from the sort of family for which every day was Sunday. Those were the sort of things I would have to adjust to. Momma is going to faint when she hears this. A boyfriend from Montreal. A real genuine husband from the city. Without any lies. What would Josef and Urek think when they saw his hands?

I lay back down beside David. Closer.

I was trying not to get too excited. I could have kicked myself for having got a bit tongue-tied about Montreal. Now I was embarrassed because I didn't know what else to ask him. He was playing with the frill of my mini skirt. Here I was living in Montreal and I didn't know a goddamn thing about it. It's hard to pretend you're intelligent when you're lacking information. Even though I was nervous and confused, I couldn't stop talking.

"That means you're French?"

He was tickling me and trying to touch my breasts and kissing me on the neck. "Oui, je parle français un peu."

"Oh, that's good! I really want to learn French." He had more assets than I had even expected.

"Hey, wait just a minute. I'm not really French. Montreal has a lot of English people, too. I'm an anglophone."

He laughed. He had such a good sense of humour. I had forgotten what we were talking about. David was on top of me, rubbing himself against my leg. I knew he was trying to make love to me. But I expected this. And I knew I could handle him. I knew that guys from the city aren't as desperate as they were back home. Here, you could talk them into respecting you.

120

"David, I'm a virgin." I wasn't counting the years I spent in bed with my uncle or the night with Felix in the back seat of the car.

David was rubbing himself harder and faster. He tried to unzip his pants. He just felt it was his right, that's all.

"Did you hear me David. You're not allowed to do this."

He stopped and looked at me with unbelieving eyes. There was sweat on his brow. "Are you really a virgin?"

I was proud for my husband-to-be. "Cross my heart."

"Well, I tell you, you won't be for long."

So that was going to be our problem. My husband didn't trust me. Well I would show him. I sat up and looked him straight in the eye. "You wait and see – right up until my wedding night." I did up the buttons he had undone on my paisley blouse.

"You won't last."

I stood up. I had to make it quite clear to David that just because every other stupid girl let the city corrupt her didn't mean it would happen to me. I would make sure it didn't. It takes brains to remain a virgin.

"You'll find out one day David how well brought up I am, and with what fine morals and great ideals."

He decided to stand up too. We would take it slowly and carefully. He would learn to love me.

"Have you heard the RVC story yet? You know that huge grey monstrous statue in front of RVC? Well that's Queen Victoria. It's said that if any girl left the college still a virgin, the statue would get up and walk away."

"Well, David, you're going to live to see the day, because I came a virgin and I'm leaving a virgin."

Anyway I had to worry about getting pregnant. I certainly didn't want that to happen. But it would have been no use explaining that to David. Men just don't understand, they think they can do whatever they want and by some miracle you won't get pregnant. Well I had escaped it in Polackville, so I was damn well not going to fall into it in Montreal. No, if you wanted to be educated you had to act educated.

David walked me back to the bus. Three times we had to

change our direction because we ran into couples huddling together. But I knew I had played my cards right because when
David said goodnight to me he kissed me on the cheek. A re-
spectful kiss.

"So long."

"Good-bye David."

I squeezed his hand just a little to reassure him. He didn't
know what to say to me.

"Uh . . . I might see you at the McGill Disco if you're there
tomorrow night."

"Oh, I'll be there."

He walked away from me looking really confused. He'd forgotten to tell me that he'd pick me up and take me with him.
But I understood. There would be lots of time in our life to
make proper arrangements.

Anyway, it wasn't that difficult to find David the next night.
He was laughing and talking with everyone. He was everywhere.

"Hello David."

"Oh, hello there."

He was busy being popular. But I didn't mind waiting. At
least I got to speak to him as much as anyone else.

"David, I'm expecting you to walk me home tonight."

"Are you?"

I smiled. We were destined to be together forever.

And he did walk me home. We were on the steps of RVC saying goodnight.

"Genia . . . I'm not sure when I'll see you again because I'm
busy."

"I understand. I don't expect you to be able to see me every
single night of the week."

We both stood there and looked at the statue of Queen Victoria. Courageous Queen Victoria.

"Well, I'm going to a fraternity party on Saturday night. I
guess if you want to go, you can come too."

I wasn't going to let him make the same mistake he made
the night before. "Are you going to come and pick me up?"

"Do you think you can get there on your own?"

"No! I can't be walking on the streets alone at night."

"Okay, I'll come and get you."

I was a bit disappointed. It didn't seem as if he'd asked me properly for a date. But I forgave him quickly. How did poor David know it was my first real date? He'll feel so bad when I wake him up one night after we've been married a long time and tell him. My first real date. He'll want to cry for not having taken more care in the way he asked me.

I walked into the fraternity on David's arm. Like a bride. The party was swinging. We found a bench to sit down on. David stretched out his legs, put one arm around my neck and supported himself on my shoulders. It felt as if he was going to propose to me right then and there. How would I remember all this exactly? I was desperate. I'd forgotten today's date. And the time. I wanted to know what time it was.

"Genia, I have to tell you, I'm Jewish."

"Oh that's okay. I'm really religious myself."

I knew he was telling me because these are the sort of things a man and woman are supposed to clear up before they marry. But David looked positively unhappy. It should have dawned on me that he might be worrying I would try and convert him. I wasn't. I had already decided that whether I found a Protestant or Catholic, I'd marry them. I was even willing to marry an atheist.

"Look David, I really don't mind. There's nothing wrong with it. As a matter of fact, I'm sorta glad you're religious."

I could see it would be easier for me to explain my relationship with God to a husband who understood so much about believing.

"If I were you I'd cheer up David. At least you've got something that none of these other guys have."

"Oh no. They're all Jewish too. This is a Jewish fraternity."

He didn't say anything, and I didn't say anything. We sat in silence for a long, long time. I was trying to think if I'd ever seen a Jewish man before in my life. I remembered. Once, only once, did a Jewish man pass through Polackville. It was Friday night and Momma had just finished making supper and I was setting the table. I don't know how everybody knew, but somehow it got around that he was Jewish. He had just driven up to the farm in a rickety old grey dump truck looking to buy steel scraps. To me it seemed like a miracle. Only God could find someone who would have been interested in buying the junky old cars that cluttered up our farm. I was hoping he would take them all. I was sure this was going to be the last time in our lives that these abandoned cars and trucks would come in handy. But unfortunately the Jewish man only took a handful of scrap metal and put it in the back of his dump truck.

From the kitchen window we could see Daddy and the man coming up to the verandah. Who was this strange man that came out of nowhere and what did he want a few pieces of metal for? Beside him Daddy looked like a changed man. And he was sober. We heard him telling the Jewish man he could have the metal scraps for free and then he invited him to come in and have a bite to eat with us before he left. I think he asked Daddy what we were going to eat because we heard Daddy trying to explain to him about the white fish that he had netted the day before. Momma told us that she didn't expect him to come in because someone had told her that Jewish people don't like eating in someone else's house. We could see that he was having a hard time making up his mind, but he finally came in.

It didn't turn out to be a pleasure for us. He was a very dirty, untidy man. He was short and walked with his head and shoulders bent down. He had greyish-black hair and bushy eyebrows and an unshaven face. His clothes were all black and dirty and there were strings hanging out all over. He smelled. He had a hat on that he never took off. And he was very very rude. Unfriendly. All he did was mumble all the time. We couldn't understand if he was trying to talk to us or if he was just complaining to himself.

He rushed straight for the table and sat down. The rest of us all sat down after him, but nobody ate anything. We couldn't stop staring at him because he was so awful. He tackled the food with both his hands. White fish are the boniest fish in the lake and with both hands full of food he just spat the bones out. Bones were landing everywhere. He didn't notice because he never looked up, not once. They were all over and around his plate, on the floor, on his clothes, in his beard. Sometimes they ended up on Daddy's plate. I was sure Daddy was going to get up and hit him.

Finally the Jewish man finished eating and just like that stood up and walked out the door. He didn't say thank you or good-bye or anything. He had never looked up once so he didn't know how many of us there were in the room with him. I really felt like saying something to him. I would like to have told him he was the dirtiest man I knew. I would like to have shown him the mess he made and told him to clean it up. But he had gone and it was my job to clean up after him. At first I didn't want to go near where he had sat, I was afraid I would vomit. It took me three tries before I made it all the way. I had to hold my breath. There was half eaten food and fish bones and saliva everywhere. On the chair, under the chair, on the floor, on the walls, all over the table, in the margarine, on the salt shakers.

I looked back at my Montreal David with his sport's jacket and clean hands. Who would have guessed that I would have ended up with a Jew? I wouldn't mind cleaning salt shakers after David. Who would have guessed that a strange man from nowhere would walk straight into my life? Was that God up there letting these Jewish strangers cross back and forth over my life? Was that God up there sending me parables so I would recognize the chosen one when he came?

"You know Genia, I'll never be able to marry you."

I was out of that fraternity like a shot of lightning. He ran out after me, shouting, "It's only because you're not Jewish."

I ran away from the university buildings that were blocking my way, I ran across the roads letting the cars honk at me, I ran past all the strangers who might have wanted to rape me, I ran past big empty cement banks that were waiting to be robbed. I looked around to see if I had completely lost David. I was alone. He must have gone back to the party.

He might have said it as a joke. He had been sitting back with his feet stretched out and laughing.

My mind screamed at me. No, no he hasn't said it. David Eimer. The only decent man I'd ever met and now he tells me he doesn't have a mind of his own. Funny how one lousy sentence can change your future.

Even if he came back to me now or tomorrow or next year, I wouldn't be able to speak to him. I know he'd tell me he made a mistake. He'd tell me that he realised that he had lost the most beautiful relationship he could ever have been capable of having. We'd have been happy together. Wait until he finds out I know how to make home-made bread and change diapers with my eyes closed. He'll never find anyone who'll be able to tell him the sort of stories I was going to tell him in the middle of the night.

Still I would never speak to him again. My mind was made up. I would die keeping my word.

I sat down in my room, my unpeopled room, and I made myself understand the theory of short circuits. By the time something's said, it's already too late.

13

I'd say I was about one hundred years behind time. That hundred years that stood still in Polackville.

A college advisor had prepared a first year program for me of five courses. One of everything she told me, a political science, a sociology, a French, an English Literature, and an art. But I wasn't learning anything. I wasn't meant for university. I didn't have any of the things it takes to be able to get a proper education.

I was completely useless. I was failing in French because it seemed beyond me to pick up a new language. I mean, I still couldn't speak Polish properly and we used it every day at home. Sociology and political science were painfully difficult. I figured out a system that if I listened closely to the very first sentence of the lecture I could follow the professor's speech for a little while. But I never got past the first five minutes. On the first tangent he took I was lost and I never could figure out when he got back to the main topic. English Literature would have been okay but I had no background information to grasp onto. I was shocked when I found out that so much literature had been written. I cursed our school in Polackville for teaching us nothing but religion. If only the nuns would have taught us some of the things we had to know. Who would have guessed that you were supposed to have read all those books? Where would I have got them? And now where was I going to start? I had nothing to go by.

I was the stupidest person in every class. I knew that. That's why I never spoke up. I never once opened my mouth. I was afraid that I wouldn't be able to form a sentence, or use the right words in the right context, or my thick Polish intonation would come through and I'd be falling all over my *ths*. It was too great a risk. Besides, even if I could have found the courage to open my mouth, I had nothing to say. I started to spend all my time during classes trying hard to think of one thing I could say, but I could never come up with anything. I knew that my mind hadn't just gone blank, it had always been blank.

I thought Art class would be just the thing for me, because you didn't have to say anything, read anything, or write anything. You just had to use your hands. No one could say I never used my hands before.

One hundred and forty-four students showed up the first day so the professor had to pick his twenty students out of a hat. I was embarrassed when mine was the first name to be drawn out. He tried to make a joke about it. "Well, well, well."

Venitia leaned over to me. "See I was right, there is a horse-shoe up your ass."

But it didn't take the professor long to realise that he had pulled out the wrong one. I couldn't sketch, draw or paint. I couldn't judge the size of a still life and fit in into my canvas. I couldn't decide whether I should make circles or squares or triangles. Everything was flat, lop-sided and uninspired. I was hoping I could get the professor back on my good side by pretending I was a modern artist. But he never smiled at me again in his life.

I decided that maybe first-hand experience might make up for the background I didn't have. I gave myself an ambition to try everything at least once in my life. I even found a quote in the McGill orientation pamphlet that backed up this idea. *Montreal is a city to be lived. To enjoy it, one must smell everything, eat everything, see everything, hear everything, do everything.* That's what I planned to do. Everything.

I got the McGill college newspaper and examined all the notices. A political drama group announced that it was holding its first meeting of the year. It was the perfect thing for me because it was their first meeting so I would get in on it right from the beginning. There would be no catching up to do. I would know exactly what was going on. A fresh start.

Two members of the group came up to me as soon as I arrived. They explained that this was a very select, very small, very extreme left-wing political group and they had become a tight circle as they had come together quite a few years ago.

"From past experience we know that it's difficult for a new person to break into our group." His jeans were torn and faded and his printed t-shirt didn't hide his hairless chest. Something smelled, it must have been his feet. "We're not soliciting new members."

His long brown hair was tangled and I wouldn't like to say but it seemed dirty. The other guy was the same. And the others. They looked as if they were all related. "The advertisment was placed in the newspaper simply to inform our own members of our first meeting of the year."

They thought they were frightening me away, but they didn't. I was determined to stay and prove to them that no tight circle was too difficult for me to break into. I didn't tell them that, I just stood there and smiled my all-knowing smile.

Someone else who looked identical to him shouted out. "Oh fuck, let her stay tonight since she's already come out."

"Thank-you, I would like to."

God only knows what they were talking about. There were ten of them all hunched over, smoking their cigarettes one after another. They lowered their voices in such secrecy I could hardly hear them and there wasn't enough room for my chair in the circle. Their ashes hit the floor all at the same time. They all gasped at the mention of coffee. There was no distinguishing here at all. Even the girls said fuck. They used it so freely and in so many ways and with so much feeling. I told myself not to be shocked. The longer the meeting lasted the more I was convinced that it was definitely the best word to use to get the meaning of your message across to the next person. Everything was fucking good or fucking awful. There was fuck it, I don't care or fuck, it's getting hot.

I didn't mind hearing it, but I wouldn't dare to use it myself. I would be afraid it wouldn't sound natural and people would laugh at me. I would like to have been brought up using the word properly. In Jasno Gora it was considered a dirty word and I must admit somehow there it really sounded dirty. The only person in our family who used it was Daddy, but he only used it when he was drunk. Momma told us that we shouldn't listen when he said it because he had no control over himself at times like that and it was up to us to understand. If Momma could only see that here there were people, sober popular people, and girls who used the word about five times in one sentence. Sometimes they could make a whole sentence out of it. Fucking fucked fuckers.

I know that when Momma heard the word fuck, her whole body would shake. She would feel disgusted and it would mean that she'd have to say an extra few Hail Mary's that night. She worried so much about sin. Poor Momma, I couldn't wait to go home and tell her that really it wasn't a sinful word and that she shouldn't take it so much to heart. It made me feel sad that she had wasted twenty-five years of her life worrying about Daddy using a bad word when he was drunk. Someone should have told her sooner.

But I had my own worries. I had to spend the whole evening just sitting there, not saying a word, pretending. I pretended I was listening very hard. I pretended I understood everything everyone was saying. I laughed when everyone else laughed and shook my head in disagreement when they all did. I even pretended I had a lot to say but didn't really want to say it. I pretended I was saving it for the future. But underneath my pretending nods was a great fear. I was afraid they might pinpoint me directly and make me say something. I lived in fear that one day I would have to express an opinion. What would I say?

After the fifth hour, they made a decision that since they

lived in Montreal and Montreal was 80% French, they should conduct half their meeting in French. Everyone agreed. One of them half looked around to see if I nodded my agreement. How could I have said no? They might have asked me why not, and then what would I have said? God I hated when they spoke French. I spent the last three hours wondering if the meeting would ever end. I knew if we stayed any longer my mini skirt would fade.

Just before they all left, they made plans on where and when they would meet again. I felt that I really had to go to the next meeting because I had pretended I was so interested, it would have looked strange if I never turned up again. Anyway, I was hoping that the next meeting would be more interesting because they might get up and move around, do the drama. After all, it was supposed to be a political drama group. I figured that this week they did the politics and next week they would do the drama. They probably thought I wouldn't have the guts to come back.

I showed them. One of the head socialists rushed for me as soon as I stepped in the door. "Why have you come again?" He must have thought I was a spy.

"I'm very interested in what you're doing and if you don't mind, I would like to keep coming."

Because of his concern for society, he couldn't turn me away. But he did leer back at me. "We're a very committed group and we don't want people dropping in and out."

I just smiled. If only he knew what a loyal person I was.

Too bad it was so boring. I would like to have got something out of all those long miserable hours I sat there pretending. I would have been satisfied if someone there would have spoken to me for half a minute, just one English hello, that's all. But when they looked at me, they looked suspiciously. Sometimes they even had the nerve to whisper and laugh about me when I was sitting right there behind them. But I always smiled when they looked around to see if I was still there. God I was good at hiding my feelings.

The biggest problem I had was finding out where and when

our next meetings were. They were always meeting at the strangest hours, on different days of the week, in different parts of the city. Sometimes it would be in basements, sometimes in dirty restaurants, sometimes in a strange hall in the north of the city. Sometimes I was an hour late because I had trouble finding these places. But I always got there in the end. I often wondered if they changed their places of meeting because they wanted to be secretive or if they were only trying to run away from me.

Back at RVC, all my floor mates and Venitia were in awe of me. How brave and daring they thought I was to belong to an extreme guerrilla theatre group. They shivered when they saw me leave at all hours of the night and morning for my meetings. They marvelled at my hidden intelligence. They admired me for my dedication. If they only knew how I wished I could get out of it. But I had to keep going. Once you're in, you're in for life. If I could have thought of an unnoticeable way to get out, I would have. I hated them so much. We were spending half our life together and I still didn't know their names. I could see them ducking in and out of the corridors of McGill and up and down the streets of Montreal. The corners of their mouth would have turned green if they had to stop and acknowledge me. What if I just stopped coming. They could have stopped whispering then. They could have laughed right out loud – Ha, ha, I wondered when the fuck she'd stop coming. Well, the last laugh was not going to be on me.

What a relief it was when the first year of university was over. There was nothing I was looking forward to more than going back to Jasno Gora. To my sweet french fries, to Momma and to the children. Away from the guerrilla theatre group, unprincipled David, the agony of not understanding what the professors were talking about, and the endless catching up. How lovely Jasno Gora seemed. No worries, no frustrations. Just clean air and sunshine.

It wasn't until I got back there that I realised the sun doesn't shine on Polackville. Nothing at home had changed. Nothing. The farm still looked forsaken. The kids still cried and fought. Momma still killed herself with overwork. I went to the cupboards to get something to eat. They were empty. I was so used to eating, it didn't dawn on me until I was home two days that there was no food in Polackville. Only Daddy looked different, he seemed to be drunk more often. Momma told me that he was worse than ever now. It angered him that other people were out trying to make money and I was out there trying to spend it.

He never stopped bothering me all summer. He seemed to really have it in for me. He kept trying to find out from me what I'd learned at university. On Saturdays, he'd find something in the newspaper and he'd come running for me. "If you're so smart tell me what's happening in China?"

How could I tell him? I didn't know anything about China.

Then he'd wave the paper in front of me in his fist, "Come on tell me, what's the population of Australia?"

I just sat there and looked at him stupidly. "You don't learn things like that at university."

"Well what do you learn then?"

I just shrugged my shoulders. It would have hurt him too much if I would have said nothing. I wanted to cry. Then later he would come around to me with a pencil and paper.

"You're going to university, you figure out for me how much I could make if I'd sell two cords of pulp at two hundred dollars a ton."

I told him I didn't take mathematics.

"Well what can you do?"

"I don't know. I've read a few books and I can write a little."

"Well I can read and write and I've never gone to university."

Things that he always used to do for himself before, he would now ask me to do for him. I'd have to find a certain type of battery for his truck in the automotive catalogue and if I hadn't found it in two seconds flat, he would yell at me for being slow.

"Don't they teach you how to be quick in university."

He told me I was so sleepy that by the time I found the page in the catalogue the whole world would have passed me by and he would have lost a thousand dollars. Then when he wanted to send for the battery he asked me to address the envelope. "Can't you do anything right?"

He laughed at my address because I used all long forms and in this day and age he said everyone uses short forms and abbreviations for everything. "You can go to your universities, I'll still be smarter than the lot of you."

I knew he was right, but I couldn't admit it.

I decided it wasn't worth quitting university. My life in the city wasn't great, but at least it was better than this – anything was better than this. And maybe I hadn't tried hard enough in the city. In my second year, I would try harder. Just try harder, that's all.

14

There was curiosity, because Josef told Momma to tell me that he was going to drive me back to Montreal. For what? To see what it was like to go to university? To feel what it was like to live in a city? To try and copy it somewhere else if he could?

Once every hundred miles or so, Josef would ask me a question. It was always about engineering.

But I knew Josef would be lucky. He would never bother to lie. He would just never speak. Period. But for me, I could see that this year again I was walking straight back into a pack of lies.

Venitia had quit university and moved to a friendlier city. She had become an astrologer and 1970 was going to be a bad year for her. I had to end up sharing an apartment with Marilyn Hancock. I wanted to confide in Marilyn, start out with the basic truth, but that thought stayed with me for less than ten seconds. I just had to take one more look at Marilyn to know that was the wrong thing to do. She had an air of opportunism about her. Her ass jiggled the way Eileen Skuce's used to. By making up my mind to lie, I was doing both of us a favour. With her as a room-mate, I knew my chances to become sophisticated were good. If I wanted to get anywhere, if I expected to meet and be accepted by her friends, if I wanted to be asked to their parties, I would have to lie. I had no alternative.

Next year I would start telling the truth and stick to it.

In five hundred miles Josef and I never learned how to have a conversation. He couldn't change. This was still the Josef that only criticised and gave orders and grew silent. This was the Josef that kept everything to himself.

"Well here it is?"

"Doesn't look too great does it?"

I knocked. Tomorrow I would have my own key. I knocked again. Where was she? We waited for a few minutes.

"Marilyn, are you in?"

"Just a minute."

Josef started whistling. He looked around the archway and up at the ceiling. I'm glad Marilyn was in. What was keeping her? Maybe she was preparing a *Welcome to Montreal* surprise.

"Knock again."

"No."

Just then Marilyn opened the door. What a pretty girl she was. She had on a long yellow dressing gown. How cute she looked standing at the door buttoning it up.

"Hello."

"Hello."

Everyone was smiling. Josef and I walked in and put down our bags. Then we saw him.

"This is Rick."

He got up from bed, wrapped a towel around his waist, and went into the bathroom. I smiled to myself. This was going to be an interesting year.

"Would you like some coffee?" Marilyn acted as if nothing had happened.

Josef went out to get the rest of my things.

"No thank you."

I sat down. Where was I? I loved it. I loved the living room that was also Marilyn's bedroom. I loved the small kitchen where Marilyn made her coffees. I loved the cold back room that was going to be my bedroom, and I knew I would love the bathroom when I saw it. I had moved into a different world.

136

Josef came back. He looked out of place in my apartment. His shiny tight slacks and his thick black Luckoskie hair didn't fit in. On top of it all he starting speaking in Polish to me.

"Is that dirty skunk still here?"

"Shhh. He's in the bathroom."

"How long is he staying?"

"I don't know."

Josef couldn't see the beauty in anything. I could tell that he was going to go back home with stories about the sexy and dangerous life I was leading in Montreal. He would tell them that I was living in a house full of hippies. I tried to calm him down.

"Look Marilyn is a serious student. As soon as classes start on Monday, life will be back to normal."

What I hated most was, when he left, he didn't even say good-bye to Marilyn. He made such a bad impression.

When Marilyn left the apartment in the morning, I headed straight for her things. I had to find out what sort of girl she was. A quick look through her closet. Modern, expensive clothes. She had quite a few books. Lots of make-up. Her mother wrote her educated letters. In her bank account she had two hundred dollars. In her purse there was a note from her father saying that he would send her a cheque for one hundred and thirty-five dollars a month for expenses. In the bathroom, I found her birth control pills. I wish it would have been written somewhere on the package, just to be a hundred per cent sure. The Birth Control Pill. I felt nervous holding them in my hand. My cheeks were hot. My mouth got wet. It was like reading those dirty books. I was breathing faster than I was thinking. For a minute I pretended they were mine. How much fun it would be to punch out a pill every day. No wonder girls on the pill felt so important. I thought about stealing them. Or hiding them. What made her so special? I couldn't figure out what right she had to be on the pill anyway. I had heard the pill was bad for the body. I was glad they were ruining Marilyn's body and not mine.

I looked at Marilyn closely. She was still pretty but she

looked older and more tired out than me. We were the same age but I looked fresher. Marilyn was wearing herself out. She and Rick were at it practically every night. It was just a lot of whispering and breathing and bed movement, but I knew what was going on. Some nights I could hear Marilyn trying to cover it up.

"Rick, we'll wake her up."

"No, she's fast asleep."

Poor Marilyn couldn't see past the night. Now I knew what Josef meant by "going to the Dogs." Her breasts were sagging and on the telephone she talked about sex without love. She was so bored with Rick. Bored with everything that came with having a boyfriend. She never bothered discussing him with me. You could just see that she had enough.

It took her a week before she even brought up the subject of sex. I smiled. I knew she would sooner or later.

"Are you on the Pill?"

"Yes, of course."

God only knew what I'd find out now.

"Why don't you keep your Pill in the bathroom. I keep mine there."

"Oh well, I'm used to keeping mine under my pillow so I'll leave them there, if you don't mind."

She went to make herself a coffee. I should have followed her into the kitchen but I knew the discussion was over.

In a way I was glad Marilyn was so bored. I never had to answer another single question on the subject.

But you'd think she'd have more to say. If Rick wasn't at our apartment, she was at his. She'd pack a small bag and tell me straight to my face that she was going to be away for the whole week-end. I was sort of hoping that sex might be contagious.

I figured out a system for picking up men. I'd walk into a classroom, spot a guy sitting on his own, go and sit down beside him, and scribble boldly on the top cover of my exercise book. I'd underline the name of the manufacturer and underneath write, Mr. A.L.C. Luckoskie Sr., President. That's the way I got his attention. It never takes long.

"You're going to ruin your nice exercise book."

God I was good at this. I'd look at him slowly, almost sadly and smile.

"Oh this." Then a little laugh. "I've got hundreds. My father makes them."

"Oh! Where do you come from?"

I'd point to the printed address on the back cover. But that's as far as I go. I'd pretend I have no interest in him at all, and when the class was over I'd get up quickly, look at him coolly and most of the time not even bother saying good-bye. I've learned never to speak to the same guy more than once because I'm an ambitious liar and I have no control over my stories. The minute I hear something more exciting or more exotic than I'm already telling, I grab it and transcribe it into my own background. Even if I could remember all the variations, there was no telling if I could make myself repeat the same story twice. Even I had to wait to hear what I was going to say. And most of the time I surprised myself more than the guy I was trying to pick up. I knew I'd run out of people sooner or later, so from time to time I'd sit alone in the corner of the classroom. What did everyone think of me? That I was some very rich, snobby, spoiled little Daddy's girl, who just couldn't be bothered keeping friends? Hating everyone around me gave me my moments of glory.

But one of those bastards that I'd cornered didn't leave me alone. He kept coming back and asking for my phone number and my address and if he could take me to a movie some night. It confused me. Why was he asking me out? Did he really believe that my Daddy had paid a million dollars to have my baby picture hung in the National Gallery? Why wasn't he minding his own business? His persistence made me nervous. I had no time to think. I didn't know if he was getting me or I was getting him.

I wasn't at all impressed by Jesse Finkelstein. He was a short fat guy with a long full beard and thick curly bushy hair. He looked about fifty but he was only eighteen, a year younger than me. You could see the pimples under his beard. He was wearing baggy corduroy trousers that were too short, a black Mexican shirt that was too big, an Indian necklace, a green cowboy jacket, and yellow hunting boots. He looked silly behind the wheel of his mother's big purple car. I wasn't sure I wanted to be seen with him. If I didn't suspect he was from a very rich family, I wouldn't have gone out with him.

Jesse never opened his mouth without saying *fuck*. He hated everybody and everything. He didn't have any patience for other drivers and weaved in and out of traffic as if it was his right. He cursed at not being able to find a parking space close enough to the theatre. He cursed at the expensive prices for the movie. He ridiculed the ticket lady because she looked dumb. He cursed during the movie because it was too boring for him. He cursed at the people behind us because they were blowing their cigarette smoke in his direction. Everyone was getting in his way. It made me laugh. He was raging like a bull, but I knew he had a soft heart.

"Where are we going now?"

"To Miss Montreal to eat."

It seemed that everything was part of one big master plan and he knew how to follow every step.

In the Miss Montreal parking lot we met about fifteen other guys. You could tell they were all great friends, because as soon as they saw each other the cursing, the laughing, the shouting started. As they were standing there making noise, I had a good look at all fifteen of them to make sure that one of them wasn't really a girl. When I finished, I wanted to pull Jesse aside and ask him if he realised that I was the only girl there, but he was busy trying to be louder than everyone else. What a long way I'd come! This time it was me, only me, that fifteen guys had to turn to if they wanted to look at a girl. I had been chosen out of all the other girls in the world who were sitting at home painting their toenails and worrying. Me, hanging around with fifteen guys in a parking lot being popular.

What a carefree world it became. No one seemed to notice that we were carrying the noise straight into the restaurant with us. The other people who walked past us didn't seem to mind at all and acted as if nothing was happening. Nobody cared. Well, I didn't care either. I was having a good time. I laughed at everything they said and did. I couldn't stop laughing. I laughed so hard my belly ached.

We sat down at three different tables before we could find one that suited us. In the end, we settled for the biggest table in the centre of the restaurant. They kept the waitress waiting for hours as each one of them in turn described how they wanted their corned beef sandwich done. When she left they spilt all the salt and pepper into the ashtrays. They got rid of all the toothpicks. They complained because the water wasn't cold enough. I just kept laughing. I didn't know what they trying to prove.

They cursed like crazy when the food came. Nobody was satisfied with their sandwich except me. I thought it was delicious. It was the best meat sandwich I had ever tasted in my life. In the end, we ate everything in sight including the whole bowl of mustard and three dishes of pickles. When the bill came, it took all fifteen of them to figure it out. They kept arguing about who had what and what everyone had to pay for. They had to get the waitress over another three times to explain it to them. I knew they couldn't have been serious, they were all holding five- or ten-dollar bills in their hands. Jesse was holding a twenty. It would have been very easy to pay the bill whatever the amount was. They just loved making a fuss. It seemed to be in their natures to do that sort of thing. They were all so rich and so happy.

It was quiet in the car when Jesse drove me back to my apartment, but the noise of the restaurant was still booming in my ears and my belly still hurt from all that laughing.

"Who were those guys?"

"Guys I went to high school with."

"Did you know they would be at Miss Montreal tonight?"

"Ya, we used to hang around there almost every night."

"Who was that guy that never said a word all night?"

"Oh that was Saul."

He wasn't like the rest of them. He was quiet. In fact, he

was more than quiet. He was like a dummy. He made you wonder if he had a voice. You wanted to go over and carefully, gently, teach him how to speak. I thought he must have suffered from something and never gotten better.

"What's the matter with him?"

"Nothing. He just feels inferior because he isn't very rich. He's been like that all through high school because he's never had as much money as the rest of us."

"What does his father do?"

"His father's a music teacher."

Well what's wrong with that? To me it all sounded like nonsense. Saul didn't look poor. He had on a leather cowboy jacket like Jesse's and when it came time to pay up, he was holding a five-dollar bill. If Jesse thought Saul was poor, what would he think of me? I looked over at him. He didn't seem disturbed at all. Obviously he believed that I was a millionaire. Thank God for that.

Poor Saul. I felt sorry for him. He shouldn't have let his lack of money get to him like that. So what if he wasn't as rich as Jesse? They still liked him. They would have missed him if he wasn't there. And he was smart. And it was believed that he played the piano with imagination. If I would have known what was on Saul's mind I would have told him not to worry. Once he got out, he would go places. All he had to do was leave.

We were both looking straight out the window. Jesse was a good safe driver. "I guess you know I'm Jewish."

Well! That's luck for you. I can never tell until they tell me. But I didn't panic. I was going to learn to beat this problem once and for all.

"Well I don't believe in it or anything but I thought I'd just mention it."

I leaned over to Jesse. I lowered my voice. I was calm. "It doesn't matter what we are, does it?"

He looked back at me. Such soft kind eyes. I felt a pain go straight from the bottom of my stomach to my heart and back again.

"No. No it doesn't matter at all."

142

It hurt me to look at him, he was so beautiful. He was living proof that the rich can be generous. I looked back at the highway. At times like this I can thank God I'm short-sighted. It makes the streetlamps twinkle. I couldn't see anybody on the road in front of us. I wished that we were the only two people left in the world. In the distance, I couldn't see where the highway ended and the sky began. I wish we could have driven straight into heaven. I loved the darkness around us.

I looked back at Jesse. My first impressions of him were wrong. In between his beard and hair he had a beautiful strong nose and clear blue eyes. I should have known he had blue eyes. Good warm blue eyes. You could trust someone who had the same eyes as you.

I leaned my head back for a minute. I was so relaxed I could have melted into his car. But I wasn't going to make any mistakes this time. I had the situation all figured out sensibly. Jesse would never marry me and I shouldn't even expect it of him. But for the joy of it, for the pure pleasure of it, I let myself imagine what life would have been like with him. Living in a real home. I could see that it was people like Jesse who made homes. Homes that were safe. Homes where there was food in the cupboards. Homes that were peaceful. Homes where people cared. Homes where the woman was looked after. Homes that were homes.

I sat up and looked at him again. I wanted to squeeze in between him and the steering wheel. The closer I got to him the more comfortable I'd feel. Why wasn't there someone like Jesse for me?

He stopped the car and walked me to my apartment door. I didn't know what he was going to do and I couldn't have stopped him if he tried. He leaned over and kissed me. On the mouth.

"Goodnight."

Then he was gone and the night was over.

When I think about it, I didn't even expect him to kiss me. It was a good long wet kiss. You could never have guessed that he was capable of such a sexy kiss. I wish he would have kissed me just once more. I wish he would have gone further. But I didn't know what he was up to and I didn't want to push my luck. I was still feeling the kiss when he phoned me the next night.

"Are you alone?"

"Yes."

"Don't move. I'll be right over."

I was hoping he wouldn't sense how much I wanted him.

We hardly looked at each other when Jesse came in. We sat down on Marilyn's bed and started talking. I was in the middle of telling him that I was a world champion skier when he leaned over and kissed me again. On the mouth. I didn't care if I ever finished the sentence. It was a lie anyway. He kept kissing me as if we'd been doing it all our lives. I loved it but I was worried that he'd get tired. His hands went to my breasts. If only I knew what he was thinking. I opened one eye, half way. He smiled at me. We were both embarrassed but we didn't care. We weren't going to let that stop us. He took off my blouse and bra and looked. He sat back and looked again.

"Oh, my God!"

It sounded as if it was the most beautiful sight he had ever seen in his life. He swooped down on them. He couldn't stop kissing and fondling and admiring them. He was so wonderful.

Making love was easy. Jesse did everything. He undressed me one by one, until I was completely naked. He paused and looked and admired. He kissed and massaged and licked. It was as if I was a banquet table and he was having a feast.

And then, I think it was when my eyes were closed and I was thinking about how much I really did enjoy the very, very first night with my uncle when I was six years old, that my body started to shake. An electric current had taken over. I lost my mind completely so I don't know if I was shrieking or if I was just opening and closing my mouth because I had no control over my muscles. Jesse held me as tight as he could and I was grateful for that.

After he wiped away a little tear that reached my eye by mistake, he got up and started to take off his clothes. I jumped up and took his hands. I didn't really want to stop him but I had to let him know.

144

"I can't have intercourse with you, I'm not on the pill."

"That's okay, I brought a safe."

"But are you sure it's all right?"

"Yes, it's all right."

How strange Jesse looked. He had a wide hairy chest, a big protruding stomach, and short thin legs. His mouth and beard were dripping. He smiled at me. It felt stupid standing naked in front of each other, so I jumped back onto Marilyn's bed.

"Jesse, I've never had intercourse before. I'm not sure I know what to do."

He moved towards me with such intensity I knew he was going to look after everything.

But it happened too quickly. He didn't give me any warning. I didn't have time to tell him I was going to do it because I loved him. And when he was on top of me, I wanted to remind him it was me. Genia Luckoskie. I was trying to think of a way of stopping him, for half a second, to let him know that this was an important and special occasion for me. Then he halted.

"Jesse, you know I wouldn't let you do this if I didn't like you."

And rammed.

"I don't go sleeping with just anybody at all."

I don't think he said anything. He just fell down on top of me and sweated. But I convinced myself he wouldn't have done it if he didn't love me.

"Can I see?"

So that was semen. I didn't think about it until I heard the toilet flushing, but I should have asked him if I could keep it as a souvenir.

"Genia do you have anything to eat here?"

At least he was still talking to me. Thank God he wasn't ashamed. I told him where the bread and butter was. It looked as if he ate five slices.

"Well I think I better go home now."

It was four o'clock in the morning.

"Isn't your mother going to be mad that you're coming home so late?"

"Naw, she won't know. She'll be asleep."

I couldn't help wondering if she'd suspect what he had done.

That was really the start of something. Jesse came over every day now. We did it just before supper, at night, in the morning. Seven days a week. Day in. Day out. We did it more often than Marilyn and Rick. It worried me to do it so often. Even though I knew I would never get pregnant because Jesse had that all taken care of, I knew that somehow, somewhere along the line, I would end up paying for every ounce of moisture.

"Jesse do you think it's right to make love like this all the time?"

"Yes of course, you have to enjoy yourself while you're young."

Maybe I worried because he ate so much afterwards. Every week he went through three loaves of bread and two pounds of butter. Before the year would be over, he'll have gone through a hundred and fifty-six loaves of bread and a hundred and four pounds of butter. It'll cost me a hundred and twelve dollars and eighty-four cents. I won't be able to afford it. It would have been much better if he stayed in bed. And I would have liked it. It would have given him inspiration to say nice things to me. Why didn't he say nice things to me?

Why was he coming over so much if he didn't love me? He must love me. Maybe he needed a hint. Maybe he thought that I wouldn't understand if he said it. But I would. Maybe he didn't know how to say it. I didn't either. But I knew it had to be said. It was important. I decided to break the ice. Oh, I know it wasn't right that I should, but someone had to do it.

"Jesse can I whisper something in your ear?"

I should have stopped myself right then and there.

"I love you."

Where did I get the guts to say it? I dropped my head in the pillow beside him. I had collapsed from nerves. But at least it was done. Now all I had to do was wait.

I idolised Jesse. To me, he was God. He didn't like it when I told him so, but it was plain to me that he had what the nun's

146

used to call God's arrogance. As soon as he walked into a classroom he could command a presence, people knew he was the
one who was going to speak out, they waited for him to argue
every point, they listened with respect. When he left the room,
you could feel the power going out with him.

I couldn't figure out where all the information he had came
from. There wasn't anything he didn't know about, there
wasn't anything he couldn't talk about. It seemed as if there
was a secret to it. That there was one input place that not
everybody knew about. Something that kept you up-dated
from minute to minute. And I knew it must have been something that was kept at his home, but I never asked him because I wanted to show him that I wasn't the sort of person to
pry into his private life like that, and I didn't want him to find
out about my stupidity.

Even though it was my second year at university, I was still
as stupid as the day I was born. I knew nothing. But I don't
think he suspected it. Even though I was always asking him for
an answer, he didn't notice. Mind you, he didn't seem to notice anything about me – that I didn't have the million dollars
I was always talking about, that my grey mini skirt with the
frill was three years out of date, that I loved him so much I
used to follow him to the bathroom.

I knew it was a good thing that I was attached to Jesse. I
didn't mind that we never went to dances or parties or mixed
with anybody else. I started taking all the same courses he was
taking and every night I went with him to the library to study.
Somehow the car radio was always on when we were driving
home from the library. I couldn't help hearing the sadness in
the love songs.

> *I've seen lonely days*
> *when I could not find a friend*

It seemed as if the singers were crying instead of singing because they knew that everything they said couldn't be heard
by the person they loved.

147

"Oh, Jesse, listen! Isn't it beautiful?"

"Ya, it's my favourite."

"What's the name of it?"

"'Fire and Rain' by James Taylor."

But I always thought, baby

I'd see you one more time again.

I wouldn't tell Jesse why they made me cry and why I wanted him to hold me as much as he could and why I wanted him to squeeze me tighter and tighter. He was so close and it wasn't close enough. If only he'd tell me once – just so I could hear it. Even if he didn't mean it, I wanted to hear what it would sound like. I wanted to hear it. But I didn't ask him. Maybe I hinted but I didn't ask. I'd whisper his name over and over. Jesse. Jesse, my Jesse. And then he said it. I love you. Just like that. I love you.

"Oh Jesse, say it with my name. Use my name."

"I love you Genia."

"And are you going to say it always? Always?"

"Yes always."

I kissed him, but what I really wanted to do was say thank you.

15

Slowly, Jesse let me into his life. I knew he would sooner or later. He just needed a little pushing because for a man he was still young and he didn't trust his own feelings.

"You know Jesse, I don't know where you live?"

"You can come over this Saturday and listen to records."

"Oh no, I better not."

"Why not?"

"Oh you know, your parents might . . . ."

"They're not going to be at home."

"Are you sure?"

"Yes."

His father was playing golf and his mother was having her hair done.

I pretended not to be too impressed by their house. I didn't want Jesse to notice me eyeing everything.

"Take your shoes off."

"Why?"

"My mother would kill anybody if they walked on the carpets with their shoes."

What a strange way to live, never being able to wear shoes in the house. He was right. There were carpets everywhere.

Blue carpets throughout the entire house. They were soft, about two inches thick. No, I'd say more like five inches. Easily.

"No! You can't go in there!"

"Why not?"

"That's the living room. My mother doesn't allow us to go in there. I've only been in there twice in my whole life."

From the archway, I could see the silk couches, the shiny grand piano, the fragile china, the mother-of-pearl coffee tables, the oil paintings. We ended up in the kitchen. It was the only safe place.

I wondered if they really lived in this house. It smelled of too much wax, protected by too many closed curtains, humidified by too much clamminess. To me, it felt like a church without a God. If I could have just seen one thing breathing, like a plant or something, I think I wouldn't have been so nervous.

"Please Jesse could we go?"

"We only got here, sit down and relax."

Relax! I wasn't perfect enough to relax. I had pains in my stomach. "Please, I feel sick. Let's go for a walk or something."

"Oh Christ! I don't know what's got into you."

No, I could see I was right the first day I met him. He would never marry me. I wanted to break up as soon as possible. Now before it's too late. There was no point in going on and if we left now at least we could still be friends.

"Jesse, I think it would be best if we broke up."

"Why? Why should be break up? We love each other don't we? Are you getting tired of me?"

I did love him. But it would have been dangerous to waste my time when there was no hope.

"Well we've been alone together for so long you haven't had a chance to see if you might want someone else instead. I mean, we could break up for even a week so you could see if you really want me."

I knew if I could just get away from him for one day I'd be able to think straight again. I wanted to remember that if you

150

plan to have a wedding day, you have to find yourself a husband that will marry you.

"But it's impossible not to see each other, we're in all the same classes.

"I know, but please can we give it a try?"

"It won't work."

He was right. The separation didn't last. Jesse got three of his friends to sit with him in his mother's car. They worked out a way to get special permission to park on campus. Every once in a while, one of his friends would come out and follow me on foot and then report back to Jesse. Later on in the afternoon, another friend came out of the car and asked me to reconsider. Towards the end of the day, the third friend said that Jesse was crying and that I should come to the car if I could.

* * *

When Jesse asked me to go with him to Eaton's to help him pick up a few things, I got so carried away with the notion of shopping that I forgot he said it was for things he needed. I was sure that it was a modern unsex-related way of saying the trip was for me, that he was going to make it a sort of present to me for having stayed with him. We would just be walking along and with his far-sighted good eyes he would spot a dress in some window. He would say that it would look beautiful on me. He would insist that I try it on. Then he would nod and smile and when I wasn't looking he would buy it for me. He could see that I needed clothes. By now he should have noticed. Anyway, what did he need? He wore a fresh new shirt to classes every single day of his life. God who knows, he might buy me a whole wardrobe. I'd like to have had a dress or a pair of jeans or a nightie or maybe a long yellow housecoat. I needed gloves and a scarf and a sweater and I could use a new pair of shoes. But I only put down the most urgent things on my list – two spools of thread, a pair of socks and brown shoe laces. I decided to leave the rest up to Jesse. It would be some proof at least that we had a serious relationship.

I wanted to walk slowly around the entire store, see everything inch by inch, think about this and that, this and that, and then finally make our purchase. I was ready to start anywhere. Every counter interested me. My head was swimming.

"Christ I hate shopping. Let's find the men's section, get what we want and get the hell out of here."

Before I had a chance to say or do anything, Jesse was walking fast ahead of me, ploughing through the people, trying to get to the men's section. I had to run to catch up with him and I didn't see anything at all on the first floor. Going up on the escalator, we passed everything else. One floor after another full of women's shoes and women's dresses. Women's coats, handbags, nighties, jewellery. It was all so quick I couldn't have a proper look. If I looked to the right, I missed the left. If I looked to the left, I missed the right. If I looked ahead, I missed what was behind. What was it that was sparkling so much?

Nobody had to tell me that by the time we got up to the seventh floor, I was experiencing depression for the first time in my life. I knew that the size of the lump in my throat wasn't normal. I knew that your heart doesn't get so heavy if it's not sinking in your chest. We started searching for the things Jesse needed. Twice I had to hide behind a rack of dull men's clothes so I could stop myself from throwing up. Jesse loaded his arms with four or five pairs of trousers and went to try them on.

"That's too many pairs. Why don't you just decide on one thing and get it?"

"Naw, I'm right out of everything. Go find me a few shirts."

"I don't know what sort of shirts you like. Maybe you should find them yourself."

Jesse went to a shelf and pulled out four shirts. He didn't even look to see what colour they were.

"Did you like the cords on me Genia? Do you think they're okay?"

It was hard for me to smile because I felt like spitting at him, but I told myself not to be so stupid and to make an effort. After all he really hasn't done anything wrong has he? He hasn't yelled at me or hit me.

"Yes Jesse they're beautiful. They look very nice on you."

152

He was still as ugly looking as the first day he came running for me. No one, anywhere in the world has invented a new pair of corduroy trousers that would help him look any better.

We took the four pairs of trousers and the four shirts to the counter. As the saleslady was tallying up the cost, Jesse reached over and took a leather belt.

"What the hell, throw it in with the rest of the stuff."

"That'll be eighty-nine dollars please."

I couldn't believe my ears. Jesse had just bought himself eighty-nine dollars worth of clothes without blinking an eyelash. I simply could not believe it. Jesse looked at me and smiled. Then he pulled out his mother's charge card and paid the bill. I tried not to look shocked but I was.

"Is your mother not going to be angry that you bought eighty-nine dollars worth of clothes?"

"Ya, she'll probably raise the roof about the belt and I'll have to bring it back." He picked up the shopping bag. "Let's get the hell out of here." Back down the escalator. Past all those bright colourful women's clothes, past the beautiful dreams, past the sparkling hopes. But there was no activity in my heart now.

"Was there anything you were going to buy, Genia?"

If I hadn't been so overburdened by low spirits, I would have screamed at him, *I don't even have five cents in my pocket. Do you hear? Not even five cents. I couldn't afford to buy a bubble gum.* The clothes I was wearing were tiring me out, they felt heavy the way old clothes do. I felt too poor to answer his question. I looked at him. I looked at his perfume soaked face for as long as I could. Then I took his hand and tried to smile. I felt sad for him too. Today would pass but God would remember that he didn't buy me the pair of brown shoelaces I needed.

When we stepped out of Eaton's into the street, I swore to myself I would never go shopping again in my life. Jesse stopped to switch his parcels from one hand to another.

"Christ, I'm glad we got that over with. I fucking hate shopping."

"So do I."

*   *   *

If I had to be stuck with Jesse, I thought I better try and wake him up. Tell him the truth about myself.

It isn't easy to stop lying once you've started to depend on it to get you through the day. But I made an effort. I started by giving him little hints here and there, so that he would get a truer clearer picture of who I was without feeling that I had down-right cheated him. I told him that I had become sick with depression because my Daddy had stopped sending me my one hundred and eighty-five dollars allowance every month, because he'd gone and adopted seven other children because he'd moved from our block of privately owned highrises in New York because he wanted to settle in a small place in northern Canada because his favourite pastime was driving a half-ton truck.

It didn't make me feel any better, I was still depressed. Jesse never asked me anything, never wanted to discuss my problems. And it wasn't any fun at all getting up depressed, following him around from one class to another depressed, coming home and having sex depressed.

I thought maybe if I got him out into the air, that would help. Alone in the country, on a little hill somewhere, I could finish telling him the true story. There would be no book for him to read, there would be no bread to butter, there would be no paper to play with.

"Here, Jesse. Let's sit down here and have a talk."

But I'd forgotten about the horizon. What was he looking at out there? What was in the distance that held his attention so well? What was there that I couldn't see?

"Jesse, I told you we were upper class, but you know in the country, you see, now, we're really no class. I mean, we're classless."

I knew he found it difficult to concentrate on things close at hand, but this time I was going to make him listen to me.

"You see, I mean, really I should explain this so you'd understand, because, well I've been thinking, that the same things that make one class here are not the same things that make the same class there. So you see if you've always been a city

154

person you wouldn't understand and just assume we were all lower class."

He wanted to get up and walk around. "Is that all you wanted to tell me?"

I wish he'd look at me. If he only looked at me once he might see how important it was for me. If he was telling me something important about himself, I'd sit and listen. I'd be interested. It was that goddamn computer brain.

"I really hate sitting around and talking about nothing. I just like to know the facts."

But I had to describe it. If I just told him the facts he would pick up and leave. I had to explain to him that it was just fate that I was born in Polackville to a poor family. At times like this facts aren't any good because they only tell what happened, not what should have happened. Facts don't give you a chance. Facts show you're stupid, when you know that you're smarter than most people you've met in the city. Facts say you're not worth bothering about, when you know you've got potential if you only knew how to make use of it. Facts say you're a liar, when you know you're the most honest person alive.

"Please Jesse sit down and listen to me." I was almost crying. "Don't you want to know me better?"

"Okay, but don't take all day, I want to walk."

If I could just zero in on my father. That was the key to it all, because if it wasn't for Daddy I'd be much better off today. Everything always depends on the father.

"Well, like I was saying you couldn't really categorize us."

He was impatient again.

"Well if you want to know the facts, we think we're rich but we haven't got any money. And my father ... my father ... "

For a long time I sat, quiet. I don't know why you could hear me crying?

"For Christ's sake what's wrong? Look are you going to tell me or not?"

"I just don't know how. I don't want to hurt you Jesse."

He softened up a little bit. "What is it?" He came up close to me.

"No please don't hug me, because you won't like me anymore."

"Yes I will, tell me."

Who was this stranger that needed to have everything?

"No, I'll never tell you."

Jesse took his arms away and got up. "Well suit yourself."

For the first time in my life, I said it out loud. "My father's an alcoholic."

It sounded worse than I thought it would. I was crying hard now. I had to get away. I started running. I ran as fast as I could. Anything so long as I could get away from Jesse.

I stopped and cried and cried. I hoped he wouldn't come after me. I hoped he'd get straight into his car and go home. It would be easier to end the relationship this way. I would never have to look into his successful face again. I could either stay in the woods until I died or maybe eventually I could find my own way back to the highway and hitch-hike home. I wasn't worried about my alternatives. It didn't matter anymore.

But Jesse found me.

"What are you trying to do, running away like that? Come on, let's go home."

He thought I was the same person.

"You go home. I'm not coming. I'm going to stay here."

"Oh stop acting like a baby. Come on."

I kicked him in the shins. But he just held on tighter and kept shoving me. I wasn't going to let myself get trapped by another Mauldoon. This time I wasn't going to stop at anything to save myself from being pushed into a car with someone who had planned how he was going to destroy me. Why did they want me so badly? Why was it always me? They'd already travelled more times than I could ever count from my little breasts to my vagina and back again. I couldn't think of anything else I had left but I wanted to keep something for myself. I made myself fall down. I wanted to hang on to some shrubs or the trunk of a tree. He dragged me along the ground at a faster speed. Then I started praying out loud.

"Holy Mary, mother of God, pray for us sinners."

He let go. Looked at me. Thought for a minute. Turned and

started walking away. He almost got out of sight. But then he came back. He was even angrier now. He banged his fist with all his might into one of the trees. I screamed hysterically.

"Look you bastard, leave me alone. Can't you understand English."

His whole body softened, he walked up to me gently, bent over and kissed me. On the forehead.

"Look, it's okay, now please come home with me."

I got up and walked back to the car with him. A few times I wanted to break away and run again, but something stopped me. Maybe Jesse understood, even if he didn't tell me he did. Otherwise, why wouldn't he have let me stay in the woods? But he never said anything. All the way home no one spoke. We sat like two lumps of stone. I looked over at him. There wasn't so much as a flicker in his eyes. Maybe he hadn't heard me. Well, I wasn't going to tell him again. And if he heard me, it didn't seem to bother him because we went home and had sex as if we were celebrating a great occasion. It seemed as if the whole incident on the hill had never happened. Nothing was important. Nothing meant anything.

*　　*　　*

Jesse's parents told him to invite me to their place for dinner so they could meet me. I spent hours finding myself a pattern, getting material, and cutting out the dress. I wanted to look as pretty as possible. And I was going to try and sound as intelligent as I could. I went to the library to find out the date of the Second World War. September 3rd 1939 to May 8th 1945. 5,-820,960 Jews were killed. I used every minute I was sewing to memorise the facts, and practise what else I was going to say. September 3rd 1939 to May 8th 1945. 5,820,960. I wanted to write it somewhere on the sleeve so I wouldn't forget, my mind still hadn't improved. September 3rd 1939 to May 8th 1945. 5,820,960. I knew they didn't like the Germans so I'd make sure to point out that I was Polish. I had found a book in the library once that said the Polish have a reputation for being ingenuous, creative, intelligent, hard-working, good people.

There was no reason why I shouldn't be proud. I would have to show them I wasn't afraid of their rich house and that I was good enough for Jesse. Maybe I'd even show them that I was better than Jesse, so they'd think he got himself a winner. But I was fighting time.

At seven o'clock the dress wasn't finished and I had forgotten the dates of the Second World War. I decided it would be better if I didn't go. The phone rang.

"Where the hell are you? We're waiting."

"Jesse I can't come, I have nothing to wear."

"Don't be so stupid, put something on and get over here, they're waiting."

I ran to my dresser. There was nothing there. The grey mini skirt with the frill had seen its day. I couldn't bring myself to put it on three years after everyone was wearing midis. I ran back to the machine and started sewing my dress more frantically. The phone rang again.

"For fuck's sake, are you coming over or not?"

"I think it's too late now, anyway I don't think I'll be able to find your place by bus."

"For fuck's sake, take a taxi and get over here right away. I swear if you don't show up I'll never speak to you again in my life."

He sounded in more trouble than me, so I helped myself to one of Marilyn's dresses and left. Two hours late.

Even the taxi driver was confused that night. He lost his way and we circled Goldstone Avenue three times before we found number two thousand. I gave him everything I had in my purse and he let me off with the extra dollar I owed him because he said that if he would have found it straight away it wouldn't have cost so much.

I was afraid to ring the doorbell in case it would sound too loud so I knocked. The door was bigger and blacker than I remembered. You couldn't hear my knocking. I knew in the end I would have to ring the doorbell. I wish there had been another way of doing it. It seemed as if the door opened instantaneously. There they were. Mr. and Mrs. Finkelstein together. It shocked me. I had never dreamt that a man and woman

158

could answer a door together. They looked as solid as a cement building. They almost completely blocked the entrance. I wondered how I'd manage to get in the door. It didn't occur to me that they would back up and let me in. They were smiling. Who would have ever thought that such perfect people existed? Here they were in real life standing in front of me, looking as if they had just stepped out of my card-board box. The brown-eyed wonders of the world. There wasn't a crease anywhere. Mr. Finkelstein had on a white shirt, stiff collar, and tie. Mrs. Finkelstein had on a tailored dress, tight hair and neat make-up. Perfect. They looked lovely. But they scared me. I still couldn't believe they were real. But before I had a chance to turn around and go back home, they spoke.

"You must be Genia?"

I couldn't find enough voice to say yes. I just nodded and giggled a bit and tried to squeeze inside. I was in a great hurry. Mr. Finkelstein held out his right hand to shake. I didn't know quite what to do, so I ignored it, smiled embarrassedly and started to take off my things. I had to unbutton my coat and take it off, and my kerchief, and my shoes.

"You don't have to take your shoes off, Genia."

But I remembered what Jesse had said about the carpets.

"Oh no, I don't mind at all."

They kept insisting. They were so polite.

"But please, you don't have to."

I took great effort to line them up neatly in the vestibule. That was one thing I felt I had done right. I looked back proudly to see my shoes standing perfectly at the door. They were the only pair there.

Mr. and Mrs. Finkelstein kept trying to talk to me, ask me questions. But I was in a great hurry.

"How are you?"

"Did you find your way easily?"

I was trying to get past them to find Jesse.

"Did you have far to come?"

I managed to get in front of them and walk away. They followed me.

"Did Jesse not tell you to come for seven o'clock?"

159

Finally, I got away from them. From far behind, I think they were still asking me questions.

"Would you like to sit down?"

But I had no time to answer.

When I found Jesse, I told him I didn't know what to do.

"Jesse what should I tell them, if they ask me questions about my family?"

"They won't ask you any questions."

"Yes they will. They were asking me questions the minute I got in the door."

"Well, tell them the truth. But don't go into detail. Just answer briefly. But don't mention anything about your father or my mother will drop dead of a heart attack."

"Do you think I should go down there and offer your mother help to get the dinner on the table?"

I walked very quietly to the kitchen. I wish I wasn't so nervous. And I couldn't trust my voice. I knew it would let me down. Right in the middle of a sentence it would crack and I would have to take a big gulp.

"Mrs. Finkelstein?" I cleared my throat. I was trying to get a big enough breath to see me through the sentence. "Would you like me to help you?"

"Oh no, thank you. Everything's more than ready."

I giggled a bit and went as quickly back to Jesse's room as I could. Why did I come? I wish I was anywhere else in the world but here. And why was she going through all that trouble to make a special dinner for me? Everytime I heard a pot rattling in the kitchen, I felt more guilty and more ashamed. I wanted to tell her to stop. I knew I wasn't worth it.

Dinner was called.

"Genia you can sit here."

I sat next to Mr. Finkelstein and Mrs. Finkelstein sat across from me and Jesse was way over there across the table, in the far corner. Everyone was watching me. I was too afraid to start eating because I knew I wouldn't be able to swallow the food. I was too afraid to even pick up my fork because my hands were shaking so much I knew I'd touch all the other cutlery, and

160

there would be such a noise everyone would wonder and look, and how would I be able to explain? But still everyone waited for me. I couldn't see how I'd manage to get through the meal. I decided the best thing to do was not to eat at all. That way, I'd make less of a fool of myself. I'll just pretend I'm not hungry. Anyway, I didn't even have an appetite. There was so much food on the table and it was all probably very good, but for the first time in my life I couldn't even smell it. My senses were completely shot.

"Pitch in Genia. Don't wait for us. Just go ahead."

I looked up at her. She was smiling.

"Well you see, I'm not very hungry."

"Oh I know. I always make the portions of chopped liver too big, but eat as much as you can and leave the rest."

She handed me the plate of sesame biscuits and told me to take one for the chopped liver. I reached for the sesame biscuits and just barely got one in my hand. I knew she saw it shaking.

"You will have a little won't you?"

I looked down at my plate. I didn't care if I turned to stone. I was so embarrassed. But when I looked up, they were all eating so for a moment they had stopped looking at me. I ate a bit of the chopped liver on my sesame biscuit. I couldn't taste it. It just sort of went down. All I was hoping was that I wouldn't choke on it. Now they were looking at me again. I knew I had to continue eating or they would think there was something the matter with me. I knew they saw the fork shaking as I lifted it to my mouth and once I missed my mouth altogether and the chopped liver fell off my fork. I wish they'd stop watching me. I never realised before how difficult it was to eat. To actually get the food on the fork, lift the fork without spilling the food, find the mouth without missing, and then trying to swallow the food without choking.

Now the questions came again.

"What does your father do, Genia?"

I tried to get Jesse's eye for the right answer but she caught me, so I had to think fast.

"He's a doctor."

"Do you have any brothers or sisters?"

"Yes, there's eight of us altogether. Four older ones and four young kids."

The smile dropped off her face and the eyes popped out of her make-up.

"Eight!"

She got up and busily started taking the chopped liver plates off the table. She was in the cupboards taking things out and putting things in. She wasn't looking at me at all now. I knew she didn't like the idea that there were eight children in my family. I looked over at Jesse. I wanted to catch his eye for a smile or a nod of affection or something. He didn't look up. He was busy eating everything in sight. How had he ever learned to fit in? When Mrs. Finkelstein came back to the table with the salad she tried hard to put the smile back on her face.

"My goodness, how did your mother ever manage?"

I looked up at her. Now I knew what the secret was. If I mimicked the way she spoke, I was sure to be all right. When she spoke, it was so sweet and smiley the words dropped like sugar from her mouth. I tried it.

"Oh you know she has help. We all give her a hand."

It's quite hard to speak with a smile on your face.

Now Mrs. Finkelstein was into the roast beef.

"What cut do you prefer Genia?"

"I don't care really."

"Well would you like the outside cut? I know some people prefer it to the lean meat inside."

I wish she wouldn't ask me any questions at all. If she'd only just give me the food and not ask. Of course I didn't want the outside piece, but I didn't know how to explain which piece I did want so I just nodded and she gave it to me. I hated it as much as I knew I would. It was too hard to cut and too difficult to chew. I put the whole piece in my mouth and hoped it would melt away. I chewed and chewed and it wouldn't get smaller.

"Does your mother mind living in a small town?"

How was I going to answer her question with my mouth full of this unchewable piece of outside beef? She was waiting for an answer. I pushed the whole wad of beef with my tongue to one side of my mouth.

"No, she doesn't mind."

I knew you weren't supposed to talk with your mouth full but there was nothing else I could do. Then I noticed that they had all just about finished eating and I still had this piece of beef in my mouth. I wanted to take it out and put it on the side of my plate, but I knew that would look awful. Somehow I must try to swallow it without choking. I did. But tears came to my eyes. God Almighty, that was a hard meal to eat.

Jesse was full and happy. He kept saying over and over what an excellent cook his mother was.

"Didn't you think that was one of the best meals you've ever had?"

"Yes Jesse it was very good."

I felt sick and I had Marilyn's dress on, and I wanted to get home and take it off before she found out I was wearing it.

"Jesse I'm going to go home now."

"We can't go right away."

"Well if you don't take me home, I'm going to walk."

On the way back to my apartment, Jesse didn't speak to me. I don't think he was thinking about too much though. I had a feeling he was just waiting for us to get into bed so he could have his second good meal of the night. But I was angry. I didn't have a chance to say any of the things I wanted to say. And now I could think of a hundred other things I should have said. I should have told her that I'm even more Canadian than her. That my family were the first ones to settle in Canada and we didn't even know that 5,820,960 Jews were being killed. Nobody in Polackville knew about the war. We were busy trying to stay alive ourselves. I should have told her that I wasn't used to people getting their faces all twisted up in a smile when they spoke. If you smile you're happy, and if you want to speak you say something. And my mother. I should have told her exactly how hard my mother works. And that no no one lifts a finger to help her except me. How she has to wash clothes in rusty water, how she has to work at other people's cottages to make money to buy the flour for bread, how she has to get out and shovel snow in the winter and dig potatoes in the summer. How she'd run around helping anyone, anytime. She quilted and cooked, knitted and sewed, baked and brought up children until her bones crumbled away from wear and her skin dropped from tiredness. And on top of it all she's given blood seventeen times. And Mrs. Finkelstein. How many times has she given blood?

I looked over at Jesse. He had been given blue eyes. I knew, in my heart, that God intended him to be more than just her son.

16

All I could remember on the bus going back to Polackville were the orgasms, and how tight he held me and how many times a week he asked me if I still loved him. I knew it was going to be another hard lonely summer, but summers don't last forever thank God. And then Jesse would be back from his trip to Italy and we'd get an apartment together and sooner or later we'd get married. I could see the advantages of having your own man. It would be harder for Josef and Urek to kick me around now that there was someone standing behind me. Once my hand came up to my face and slipped down my shoulder and touched my breasts by accident. It made me smile. Maybe I was a woman.

This time everyone noticed me when I walked in the door. "Genia's home."

I was still smiling about being a woman, and when I sat down I couldn't help noticing that my legs reached the floor. I crossed them three times in three different ways to make sure. Did Momma notice that there was something different about me? I tried to stop smiling because I didn't want to make anyone jealous that I was happy. And I had to watch the way I walked. Could anyone see that I made love every night of every week of the past year? I tried not to say too much because every time I opened my mouth it seemed as if I sounded educated. I dropped my head into my hands and thought about it for a minute. It must have happened in the middle of all that loving for Jesse. I could have told them right then and there that they were looking at Genia Finkelstein.

I waited until after supper. I wanted all the control I could get. I went to sit down with them on the verandah. There were wild geese in the sky. I didn't know if they were coming or going. I'd already forgotten how many times they crossed over Polackville in a year.

"Well I have a boyfriend." I started speaking faster. "I mean a real boyfriend. It's serious. We've been going out together for a whole year. I mean we'll probably get married."

I stopped smiling now, so Momma wouldn't catch on to what we had been doing. "He's very rich and he's really nice." I didn't bother telling them he was Jewish.

"Well, where is he?"

"Oh, he's gone with his parents to Europe."

"Tell him to come down sometime."

"Oh no, he wouldn't be able to come. He's too busy."

"I guess we're not good enough for him eh?"

"That's not true. I'm not ashamed to bring Jesse here and if you want me to, I will."

Not one of them believed me. They thought that education had made me too good for my own pants.

Once I had started, I couldn't stop talking about Jesse.

"And you should see their house. Carpets five inches thick."

I cornered Momma every chance I could get – in the kitchen, in the fields, near the washing machine.

"And they have a lady that comes in every day and does their cleaning for them. And Mrs. Finkelstein goes to the hairdresser every Friday and she wears make-up even in the house."

I wanted her to ask me questions about him. But she didn't.

"And they eat in a restaurant one night every single week."

It seemed as if no one in the world was interested in Jesse except me. "They have so much money, when Jesse goes shopping he buys eighty-nine dollars worth of clothes."

Even when Momma was trying to get away, I walked after her.

"I think they're richer than the Montgomery-Joneses."

I know as a fact she didn't hear me half the time.

And I knew another fact. These were not the sort of suppers I wanted to invite Jesse to. What would he think when he saw Daddy sitting at one corner of the table with his stack of potato peelings on one side of his plate and his half pound of baloney still in the brown paper wrapping on the other? Everything was in pots, and people fought to get to them first, and there was never anything left for the last three people.

Momma was always last. When it was too late she came to the table with a piece of bread and margarine and a cup of tea. How crouched over she sat. Her head seemed to be hanging closer to the table every year. She never looked up. She was so sad. On her upper arm there was a black mark that had almost faded away and on her lower arm there was a new one ready to take its place. Poor Momma, now she had low blood pressure and kidney stones, and her teeth were falling out. There was no calcium or iron or protein in bread and margarine, and that's all I've ever seen her have for supper. I knew she was dying. I could have killed Daddy. He'd never share his baloney with her. One night at the table, Momma told him what a real sin it was not to buy food for the family, but he told her it was his money and that he had done plenty and worked hard enough and that some of us should do something for a change. He looked straight at me.

"She's so smart going to university, why doesn't she help out a little."

I gave him the dirtiest look I could find, but before I could get away from the table he flung his stack of potato peelings into my face.

I decided that I was going to try and talk Jesse into helping me take Bernadette and Honey to come and live with us in the city. Even though I still had another year left at university, I knew I could give them a better life than they were having on the farm. It would be no trouble for Jesse and I to look after them, because they'd go to school in the day and we could certainly find enough food somewhere to feed two little kids, and I wouldn't mind staying home every night babysitting them. That was the least I could do to help. The more I thought about it, the easier the plan seemed to be. I couldn't wait to ask my capable Jesse.

Someone must have spread it around in Hopefield that I was educated, because I couldn't get one person to say hello to me on the Post Office steps. Everyone disappeared like mice at a light. Once I went right up to Mary Poderskie sitting in her half-ton truck waiting for her husband to come out of the liquor store, but she turned her head the other way and froze. She was pretending she couldn't hear me knocking on the window. Agata stopped when I said how are you, but I couldn't hear her answering me. Her voice seemed far away. She had a glazed look in her eyes. I know she couldn't see me properly. Her lips were moist and half open. She put me in a trance just looking at her. They shouldn't have been running away. I wasn't looking for their bruises. I wasn't going to use a word they wouldn't understand. I wouldn't tell anybody they had stopped looking good. I just wanted to talk to them, see their babies, look at their kitchens, smell their bedrooms. I wanted to tell them I knew what it was like having a husband.

As I saw it, Jesse and I were already married. We had given ourselves to each other like a man and wife. All we really had to do is get to the wedding.

But I could see that my wedding was going to be one big headache. If no one actually picked a fight with Jesse I figured I could get him through the day without too much trouble. He'd be asleep through most of it anyway, and I could steer him toward the food any other time he started getting upset by what was going on. But I could see that for Mrs. Finkelstein it would be a long hard haul. Her painted eager eyes would notice everything. She'd shake Daddy's black hands and notice his pink-stained tie and faint. Someone would give her a tight hard pinch on her ass by mistake and she'd faint. Somebody's grandfather would get corked up enough to sing "My Little Brown Jug and Me" and she'd faint. All day long she'd be fainting. I'd have to spend my time running back and forth trying to stop a crowd from gathering around her and cheering. And I didn't think she knew how to square dance, so what fun would she have at the wedding? I could see that I had to discuss it with Jesse.

In the day it was the worries, and in the night it was the sadness that ate me up. At first I pretended I didn't hear the weeping. But I couldn't sleep. The tears were too close. It was Krysia in my bed right next to me. Doesn't matter how many times I turned sides I couldn't shut it out. Once, I almost touched her and asked her why she was crying. But I turned around and went back under my pillow. I knew why. She was hungry and lonely and sad. She hated Daddy and felt sorry for Momma. She wanted a boyfriend and love and happiness. I knew how much her stomach ached and how swollen her heart was. How could I give her any comfort when I knew that once the pain starts it never stops? I had to stay awake and watch the ceiling and listen to her crying. And later on in the night, I heard someone else had started to cry. And then someone else. It sounded as if there was someone crying in every bed. So long into the night. How was it possible that a whole house could suffer?

I turned back to Krysia. She was so close to me I could see the black circles under her eyes. Maybe she didn't even know she was crying. I wanted to wake her up and tell her she could have Jesse. No wonder everyone hated me. They needed so much help and there was nothing I could do for them. Things really had changed, now it was me who had someone and they had no one. I was the only one in this house who could get up in the morning and remember a better life somewhere else.

So I put an end to Sunday mornings.

"Hurry up and get ready for church, Genia, or we'll be late."

"I'm not going."

"What do you mean you're not going to church?"

"I don't believe in God any more."

Momma shrieked, the children were shocked, no one could figure out what had happened to me.

"As old as I am, I've never heard anyone say that before."

I didn't care. I was sick of praying. "I've been going for almost twenty years and I've still not got anywhere. You're not going to catch me going another twenty years."

Momma told the kids not to listen to me. She told them to cross themselves and say one Hail Mary and get quickly onto the back of the half-ton before I said anything else.

The farm turned spooky when everyone left for church, but I made myself sit on the bench on the verandah underneath the straw cross. I wouldn't let it haunt me. And I was still sitting there when they got back. I could tell from all their red eyes that everyone of them had offered their Mass up for me so that through the grace of God I would be put back on the right track. It was such a waste of time. How many favours had God done us in the last twenty years? Or in the last fifty years? Or in the last hundred years? Where did all our kneeling get us? It would be worth going to hell just to show God that he couldn't push me around any longer.

*   *   *

Jesse had found a one-room apartment on the twelfth floor of a highrise. He wasn't going to move in himself, but he would be there three quarters of the day, every day, and he'd pay half the rent. Just me and Jesse in our own place. One minute after I stepped in the door I had a perfect idea of what a lovely home I could turn it into. I was going to make sure it would be warm and comfortable. And spanking clean. And once a week as a special treat I was going to bake Jesse a pie. Cherry pies and lemon pies and apple pies. I wanted to buy a little glass statue and put it at the very edge of the coffee table to show that anything could survive in our place. I felt like a bride coming home. And as a matter of fact, that was the only thing left that we had to solve.

"You know Jesse, I've been thinking all summer about us getting married. . . . "

"Don't worry about that now."

"But I have to start worrying about it because I can't figure out what sort of wedding we'll be able to have with my father and your mother and . . . . "

170

"We can get married on a ship."

He always had an answer for everything. But it wasn't as simple as all that. I didn't want to be a sea bride. I wanted to stand in the middle of my hill and stones and let the rest of Polackville see that Genia Luckoskie had her day.

"But are you sure you can get married on a ship?"

"Ya, people do it every day."

I wonder if he realised what had happened. It was the first time he'd admitted in his own Jesse way that he would marry me. And that's what was important. More important than anything else. I would marry him anywhere he wanted. And who knows, it might even be fun on a ship.

There was so much hope for the future and yet I knew that Jesse wasn't happy. The very next day after we moved in, he brought over magazines and books on dogs.

"What do you think of bloodhounds, Genia?"

I didn't have a chance to bring up the subject of Bernadette and Honey coming to live with us.

"I guess they're all right."

"Would you split half in buying one?"

I could see what he was getting at. He wanted to get his share of splitting for the rent and not living here twenty-four hours a day.

"Do you think we really need one?"

"Look, I've never had a dog in my life and now that I have a place to keep it I'd like to get one."

I could see that it would have been the end of our relationship if I said I didn't want a fucking dog.

"You have lots of room at your house, why didn't you have a dog?"

"My father is allergic to animal hair."

If my heart wasn't aching so much I might have felt sorry for him. But at least I could see it would give me a chance to do something for him that no one else could, not even his parents.

"Come on, Genia. You wouldn't be human if you didn't like a dog."

"Okay, but only because you want it, Jesse."

I went over and kissed him but I don't think he noticed.

It was like buying a child. It was so cute and cuddly. We called her Paladin because Jesse had just finished writing a major paper comparing cowboy and western television shows which he was going to use for four of his classes, and Paladin from "Have Gun Will Travel" was his favourite hero.

But Paladin didn't stay small. In two months she was bigger than me. And she had become a queen. She had collars and chains and brushes. We took her to a vet twice a month. She had dog food and dog candies and dog toys. She came to all our classes and at nights we never went anywhere unless we could take her with us. Jesse never got tired of catering to her. Paladin was happy. She knew everything was hers. And she never stopped growing. In four months, there was no room for me in our one-room apartment and I had lost everything I had ever owned. She got into the closet and ripped up my clothes. She tore up all my books. She destroyed the mattress, the blankets, the pillow cases. She gnawed away every leg of furniture. And I still had to continue paying half her upkeep. There was no money left in my bank account and there were no pretty glass fixtures on my broken-down coffee table.

I hated her. Paladin sensed it. She spent all her time waiting for Jesse to come over and take her out, and Jesse played up to her all the time.

"I think Paladin likes me more than you, Genia."

"It doesn't matter, Jesse, she's only a dog."

But it did matter. I tried to get Paladin to like me again but I couldn't get her attention away from Jesse. Nothing I did interested her. One Friday, when Jesse wasn't coming over because he was going to dinner with his parents, I decided I would kill Paladin. Do away with her. All night I tried to get her to come out onto the balcony. In the end, I had to bribe her with the cherry pie. When she finished it, and I finally got her into my arms, I didn't have the strength to lift her over the rails, she was too heavy. I think at last she started to catch on, because she kept running away from me. But I kept trying, nothing was going to stop me. Finally she went into the bathroom and laid down and wouldn't come out. If I even walked past the door she'd growl at me and once I touched the door and she made a lunge for me. I wasn't able to use the bathroom until Jesse came over the next day.

The first telephone call came late at night. We were in bed, just getting started. I got the shock of my life. I didn't expect it to be her.

"I want to speak to Jesse."

Mrs. Finkelstein. But I couldn't believe it was her voice. It sounded so clear and mean and hard. I held the receiver for a moment and stared at it. I didn't say anything. I was still in shock. I handed over the receiver to Jesse. When he got off the phone, he looked as if he was in shock too.

"What did she say?"

"She told me to teach you how to answer a telephone." He seemed angry at me. "Why didn't you say one moment please?"

"I don't know. But if you want me to Jesse, I'll always say that from now on."

A lot of people have hated me, but no one has hated me with such a passion as Mrs. Finkelstein. She hated me so much that she started to get migraine headaches and had to see her doctor twice a week. She lost control of her crying organs and was howling uncontrollably all over the city. She got her husband in on it, and got him so upset that he started losing business. Jesse kept me up-to-date on everything that was happening. Poor Jesse. There was no peace for him. They screamed at him before every time he came to see me and after every time he got back. They promised that if it was the last thing in the world they'd do, they were going to break us apart. I felt sad.

"Why don't they like me Jesse? Is it because I'm not Jewish."

"It has nothing to do with that. It's just that they don't think you're nice."

He repeated it about three times. He imitated how his mother had said it, out of the side of her mouth. It was hard to see where she left off and he began. "I don't know Jesse, she's just not nice. Not a nice girl."

I didn't know what he meant. He didn't either. He just knew what he was told, that you can't learn to be nice, you're either nice or you're not nice. And I wasn't nice.

"Do you think they'll break us up Jesse?"

"Naw. My mother is always arranging dates for me with her friends' daughters. You've heard of Stitberg, haven't you? Well they want me to meet their daughter. I'm not going."

"Why not?"

"Ah, I find them all too boring. They all have too glorified a picture of themselves."

That made me feel good. When it comes to love, it doesn't matter who's daughter you are. In my own little way I felt I was as good as Miss Stitberg. We both wanted Jesse and I got him. And who knows, maybe one day his parents will change their opinion of me. First impressions don't last forever. And anyway, I only met his parents once, how did they know I wasn't nice? Where could they get enough reasons?

But they did. She was getting new facts every day. They brought Jesse's friends into their house, one by one, and made them testify that they suspected I was using Jesse. Some said I was doing him in or taking him for a ride or going to ruin his career when he became a lawyer. She even dragged in Saul, who never spoke, and made him nod his head that I was trying to trap Jesse into marriage. She had more stories about me than a whole village full of ladies working full time. They told her they didn't know anybody at McGill who liked me, that a political activist movement had taught me how to make molotov cocktails, and that I might be on heavy drugs because I always walked around campus looking dazed.

The next time she rang, I practically ran to the telephone. I would have done anything to look good in her eyes.

"Oh yes he's . . . Can you hold the line . . . Can you wait . . . uh, just one minute, I mean moment, please. Thank you."

This time she asked Jesse what I was spouting off about. Poor Jesse. She never stopped criticizing me for five minutes. And when she was too ill to phone, she got Mr. Finkelstein to do it.

"Is that Genia?"

"Yes."

"I'd like to speak to Jesse, but before I do, can I have a word with you?"

"Okay."

"I don't know if you know what's going on, but Mrs. Finkelstein hasn't been able to sleep at nights. Jesse has become very rude and disobedient to his mother and he's never been like this before. Now it doesn't matter what religion you are, you must know about the holy fourth commandment, that children must honour their father and mother."

When he finished, he thought he'd solved her problem. But he could quote all the commandments to me he wanted and it wouldn't work. Poor Mr. Finkelstein. He didn't know that I didn't like God.

And they never stopped plotting either. Some of their plans were really good. They knew that Jesse wanted his own car. He was an independent person. His own man. He couldn't be without one. They helped him pick one out, they ordered it for him, they paid for it, they even had an extra mirror on the right hand side installed for him. All he had to do was break up with me. Jesse had to tell me the condition or I might have unknowingly spoilt it for him and they would have taken the red car back. I was getting used to the idea of not expecting anything but I was still shocked when he told me.

"Look I had to promise them I would or they'd think I was using them. It has nothing to do with you. It's something I have to fight out with them"

I didn't care if he said it was only his battle. I was still hurt.

"Look, all you have to do is not answer the telephone, and in the next few weeks I won't see you as often because I'll have to stay at home a few nights with them. But in a few weeks it'll all blow over."

I couldn't see why he wouldn't tell his parents that he loved me.

I just didn't know what love was anymore. I thought love was something you wanted to tell the world about. I thought love was something that was celebrated not destroyed. It never dawned on me that love would be something you could trade in for a car.

"Well, you'll have to let me go now, Jesse."

"No, Genia, not now! Please don't leave me now."

"But I have to."

"We've gone through too much together to give up now. Don't you see, I can't let you just walk out on me now. It would show that I didn't care for you."

I had lost complete control over my life. I had to be with him for better or worse. He made me get in the new red car and like it. When he said duck under the dash board in certain sections of Montreal so his parents or their friends wouldn't see me, I'd duck.

"The thing is, Genia, that I'm quite an eligible man."

I pretended I hadn't heard what he said. I already knew the key to Jesse was his eligibility.

17

I would have been able to forget about my background completely if it wasn't for the letters. Momma's letters. Letters she'd learned how to write. Letters that read as if someone was speaking to you. Sad little letters that followed you everywhere you ran.

Dear Daughter,

Just a short line because I haven't got much time. There's so much to do. I never seem to be able to catch up with my work. You mighta heard, Franek Poderskie passed away. Everyone said he was looking kinda sick but it still came as a shock. Everything is okay with us. Daddy's getting pretty bad. He drinks more than ever now. He's kicked Urek out of the house so I guess Urek won't be able to finish school. It's just as well I guess because he could never study at nights with all the shouting and fighting going on.

There are certain people, right from the beginning of civilization, who are cut out for only one thing – to kill someone. It comes to them in a dream, or someone pays them or they read it in between two sentences in a letter. You're not supposed to do anything about it until you get your message, and it was crystal clear to me that I was getting mine now. It came so strongly to my mind, I know it would have been a sin not to follow it. And it didn't frighten me at all that I had to kill my father. It made sense that I should have been the one picked to do the job.

I couldn't let him get away with anymore. I had enough of him. Just enough. He had ruined everybody's life - Momma's, Josef's, mine, Urek's, Krysia's, the four little kids'. In my mind, it didn't seem fair that none of us ever had a chance.

I sat down and really thought about it. I was prepared to sit in jail for the rest of my life, but I knew that if I was careful I could pull it off without any more hurt at all. I would have to do it right. The way God would have done it, if he was a murderer. I took a deep breath and consciously calmed myself. I knew the planning stages were the most important. My heart fluttered a little bit for two minutes and my hands felt a little bit sweaty, but that's as far as my nerves got with me this time. There was such an important reason to go through with this, I wouldn't let another little twitter spoil it. I started to plan.

I'm going to go to a big department store here in Montreal and buy some rat poison. That way I won't have to go into Stedman's store in Hopefield and have Mrs. Yakaruskie make me buy a trap instead. I'll do everything very carefully, so no one will be able to trace anything. I'll take the rat poison to the bus station with me, go into a cubicle in the ladies washroom, open the box, pour it into a clear plastic bag, without any writing on it. I'll tear the box into tiny pieces and flush it down the toilet. Then I'll put the bag of rat poison into my suitcase, get on the bus, and head for Jasno Gora. I'll just pretend I'm coming home for the week-end to announce my marriage engagement. When I get home, I'll get Daddy's bottle of wine out of his hiding place in the dirty clothes basket and mix all the poison into it. There'll be enough dirty clothes in the basket to wipe my finger prints off the bottle. Then I'll put the bottle back in the hiding place. He never goes for the wine until he's so drunk on beer he won't even notice he's drinking rat poison until it's too late and his guts seize up and he's dying. It was fool proof.

At the funeral, everyone would look at everyone else to see who was smiling the most. And once they'd decided who they thought had done it, they'd nod their head ever so slightly for the brave favour. We all wanted him dead.

The police would come around asking questions but no one would talk. No one would say one word. The police would have to give up sooner or later, they would never be able to pin-point exactly who did it and they couldn't very well hang the whole family.

Life would be so happy without him. Momma could find a new husband and Urek could go back to school, and the small kids could learn how to laugh. Later on, if we felt like it, later on, when we'd forgotten what suffering meant, we might talk about him. It would be easy to talk about him once we knew he was in the ground, once he was a dead duck. Dead. Nothing would bring him back. He could curse all he wanted now about who that little bitch was that spiced up his wine. But it doesn't matter how much he yelled - he wasn't coming back. No more.

I got up, found a clear plastic bag, took the small suitcase, wrote a note for Jesse – *Please don't worry, I'll be back in a few days* – and left.

As soon as I stepped onto the goddamn street, Jesse rolled up in his red mini. I couldn't believe it was just coincidence. It was as if the detectives were already at work. I would have to play it very cool with Jesse, because when they start searching, these are the sort of things that come out.

"Where're you going with your suitcase?"

"Oh Hi Jesse, I left you a note. I'm just going away for the week-end."

"Where?"

He could get vicious sometimes. Maybe he'll be the next one I'll do away with.

"I'm not sure yet."

"Look, for Christ sake, where're you going?"

"Home."

"Why?"

I tried to smile and keep control. "For a visit."

"Well get in, I'll take you to the bus station."

"No, I can't. I have to do something else first."

"What?"

I couldn't figure out why I was being cross-examined even before I got started. It made me angry.

"I can't tell you right now. I'll tell you when I get back."

He stared at me. I tried to stare right back.

"It's something very, very important."

He kept staring at me. I couldn't tell if he was the lawyer, the judge, the jury, the jail keeper and Mrs. Finkelstein all in one. Or if he had been, or if he would be. I couldn't tell when I'd been condemned. My mind snapped and I started crying.

"Oh, for God's sake, what's wrong with you now?"

"Leave me alone. This doesn't involve you at all."

He gripped the top of my arm and wouldn't let go. It hurt.

"I'm going home to kill my father."

"Stop acting so stupid."

"It's not stupid. You don't have to live with him so you don't know the hardship he's caused everyone."

He dragged me straight up to the apartment, straight into the door and pinned me on the bed.

"It isn't up to you to judge whether he has the right to live or not."

"But I have a right."

"No you don't. Forget the whole idea."

I couldn't think straight any longer. I was so fed up with everything. I just wanted to close my eyes and cry for the rest of my life.

"Genia. . . ."

He was so relaxed. His white shirt sparkled and in between the buttons I could see that his belly was tanned.

"I think that there's probably something wrong with you."

"What do you know?"

"It's not normal to desire and plot to kill your own father."

I knew there wasn't much logic left in me, because the only thing that I was thinking about was how shiny and red Jesse's mini must look parked outside in the sun. He kept talking.

"Lately you've been going to pieces. I've seen you become a nervous wreck right under my eyes."

I wanted to ask him what sort of pleasure he got when he sat behind the wheel and drove up and down the freeways of Montreal.

"I don't think it would be a bad idea if you saw a psychiatrist."

I cried hysterically all the way up to the Allen Memorial Hospital. I was so tired and I wanted to eat a decent meal so badly and I felt so unimportant. Some nurse at the hospital gave me a valium to calm me down. Then she showed me into another room, and let me rest for half an hour. A valium rest. I could feel the valium taking the build-up off my bones and letting me melt into a dream. I didn't even bother to see what the room looked like, I was resting. I didn't worry about what time or day of the week it was, or wonder where Jesse disappeared to, anticipate what was going to happen next. I have never rested so blissfully in my life. The nurse came back, took a few details, and gave me an appointment to come to see a doctor on the staff for free counselling once a week. I sailed back down the hill with Jesse. Everything was all better again.

The first Friday I skipped all the way up the hill to the Allen Memorial Hospital. I was alone. Jesse was going out to dinner with his parents. He always missed the important occasions. But I was too happy to let that bother me. What would the other people on the street have thought if they knew that I was seeing a psychiatrist once a week? What an impression I would make if I told them. I knew that in real life psychiatrists cost about seventy-five dollars an hour and only rich spoiled people who have nothing better to do go to them. Now it was me. Now, for the first time, I had a status symbol.

I was taken into a room and told to wait for the doctor. It was a small wooden room without any coloured stuff like curtains or rugs. There was a desk without anything on it and two wooden chairs placed haphazardly. I wish I could have figured out which one was for me and which one was for the doctor. The couch was there too. It had a sort of grey vinyl covering on it. I didn't know if they expected me to lie on it but I decided not to because I didn't want it to look as if I knew all about psychiatrists and that you are supposed to end up there. I finally decided on the chair closest to the couch, because I didn't want it to look as if I knew nothing at all either. I hated the chair. It had a straight wooden back and high legs so I could hardly touch the floor with my feet. I felt stupid sitting there with my little legs. I tried to get it off my mind so that I could concentrate on the major problems of my life. I wanted to think as clearly as I could so that I would get everything solved once and for all. I was a little bit nervous because I wondered what the doctor would think of me.

Then she came in. I jumped off my chair in case she wanted it.

"Uh . . . I didn't know where you wanted me to sit so I sat there."

"That's fine."

She took the other wooden chair, brought it up close, and sat directly in front of me. She crossed her legs. Nice thin long legs that touched the floor. She wore make-up and she had on a red skirt and a white medical jacket. And blonde hair. I had a feeling we were going to have fun. I always wanted to find out what blonde-haired women really thought about.

"Don't worry about this pencil and paper. I'm just going to jot down a few things as we go along so I won't forget. That's all."

"Oh, I don't mind at all."

I wanted her to write things about me. In the end, I knew it would be easier to figure out a solution for me that way. Daddy used to always scribble things on a piece of paper. He told us that it was easier to think if he had a pencil in his hand. I think that's why he used to be so angry when he could never find a pencil in the house. Pencils just seemed to disappear on the farm. You could never find one. Poor Daddy. If only we could have worked out a system so there would always be a pencil when he wanted one. I knew that even if I went back today or tomorrow or fifty years from now, there still wouldn't be a pencil to be found. Now that I think of it, it was little things like that that made our life so miserable. Little things, and big things.

"We want to find out what's bothering you. Tell me about yourself."

182

I told her my name, that I was a student at McGill University and what I was studying. I was using the most sophisticated tone of voice I could think of.

"Where were you born?"

Goddamn tricky question! I didn't want her to know I was from a small farming community that no one's ever heard of. I wanted her to respect me and know that I was an important person. That it was important that she should help me. And now this has to come up. I decided not to answer the question. It would be better not to. So we just sat there looking at each other.

"Where were you born?"

"Jasno Gora." It hurt me to have to ruin my image so early in the game. "You might not have heard of it, but it's quite a large prosperous centre in northern Ontario."

I moved around in the chair but I still couldn't get my goddamn feet to touch the floor.

"Now tell me when you came to Montreal, how you've got on since you've been here, if you have made any friends and how you like the city."

"I came three years ago. I love Montreal. It's a very beautiful city. And I'd say I have, oh about one hundred friends."

I didn't like the way she was looking at me. She had sat back in her chair, closed her pad and held it sideways to rest her arms on it. Her legs seemed to tighten their grip on each other. Even though she had blonde hair, she wasn't all that pretty. Her skin looked cold. The make-up looked as if it had been applied by someone as an afterthought, to try and make her look more life-like. It didn't suit her. The coldness was making the lipstick get redder by the minute.

"Do you think you might be suffering from culture shock?"

"No, I really don't think so. I mean even though I said I was born in Jasno Gora doesn't mean I lived my whole life there. I went to visit my uncle every summer from the time I was five until the time I was twelve, and when I was thirteen, I went away to work for a week and now I've already been in Montreal for three years. If I wasn't used to city life, I would have had problems the first year and I didn't. I fitted in right away."

She wasn't listening. She looked at her watch.

"I won't keep you any longer today. You can go now and I'll see you the same time next week."

Just like that it was over. Not one word of advice, nothing. If I had been really mentally sick, how could I have got through the week? Just like that she let me go.

It was having to admit that I was from Jasno Gora that had turned her off. I knew that. She's not interested in spending her time trying to help someone from a small community nobody's heard of. What interest would I be to her? Lazy, ignorant bitch, anything for a easy way out. How dare she think I didn't belong in Montreal. I probably knew more about the city than she did. I hated her guts. All she had to do was sum it up as culture shock and sit back and be really proud of herself that I was such an easy case. She probably wouldn't even bother showing up next week. She was too stupid to realize that maybe I wasn't meant to be born in Polackville.

I told Jesse that it was wonderful and that I couldn't wait to go back. In a way, I was looking forward to Friday again. Maybe I hadn't given her a fair chance, maybe I would win her over yet. Somehow I would make her see that I was meant to be an important person.

Things were moving along just fine. This Friday we sat in her office. It was the same as the other room, except there were a few things on her desk including a telephone. She sat behind the desk and I sat in a chair in front of her.

"Why don't you tell me something about your family? How many brothers and sisters, their ages, how you got on together, your mother and father?"

She was at it again. She couldn't get it into her head that I was a rich spoiled girl needing to whine a little bit.

"Oh let me think now. I had a very happy childhood. We've got quite a large family – two brothers and one sister. I like my father but I hate my mother."

I knew I was sounding more interesting this week.

"You know, I never really think about my past. I think really most of my problems come from the fact that I find that I'm too good for people and that I don't bother keeping my hundred friends because I find them beneath me. I don't think I have patience."

"Why do you hate your mother?"

"Because I think she's stupid. She never takes control of the situation and she let's everyone do what they want. I don't think she's very strong. I think she's a weak woman and I hate weak people."

I wanted to keep away from the subject of my family as much as possible. The time was too precious to spend talking about them. I wanted to push on to more important things. I wanted to talk about Jesse.

"I have to tell you that I'm in love. And my boyfriend loves me so much and the two of us are trying to figure out how we can get Jesse's mother to like me because she wants to break up our relationship."

But again it was time to go and nothing was solved. She wasn't so bad this time. We were getting closer and closer to the real thing. By this time next week, we would have got to the heart of it.

I was ready to start rolling right where we left off. But the next Friday, she had forgotten that it was Jesse we were going to talk about. I knew she wasn't interested in talking about him, but I wanted to get these interviews into the right perspective.

"I think you'd understand me much better if you met Jesse because Jesse is a really big part of my life, a bigger part than my parents."

"It's such a shame that Jesse can't hear what's going on because he would understand me better too."

"You know, I think our problem is a mutual problem and even if you and I hit upon a solution it wouldn't help because Jesse will be left out of it."

"Can Jesse come to these sessions with me?"

And then the phone rang. How differently she acted. It helped me see exactly where I stood. She smiled and her eyes lit up and for that five minutes even her hair looked blonder. She was making an arrangement to meet someone. I knew it was her husband. On the hand that stroked the telephone cord I could see the big sparkling diamond ring and wedding band. Who would have guessed that there was so much playfulness in her? How she had him fooled. He probably never saw the side of her that I saw. I had the feeling that he was such a wonderful, exciting, handsome man. She didn't deserve him. She had a mean one-sided heart. If only worthiness could count for something. It sounded as if they were going to a really good restaurant for dinner. I wondered what they would have. They would probably kiss when they saw each other.

When that telephone call was over she changed back so quickly to her normal self I had to pretend it never happened. But it had, because now she had lost interest in me completely. She couldn't even remember what I had been talking about. I tried to tell her all over again about Jesse but she couldn't concentrate. Her mind was a million miles away. She was thinking about the telephone conversation, about meeting her husband, about his warm kisses, about the dinner they were going to have. I bet she was trying to make up her mind about whether to have a glass of wine or not. She touched her lips a few times and looked at her nails. I could tell she was itching to go and put more make-up on. The third time she looked at her watch, I was convinced that seeing her was a total waste of my time. I knew that she would only be interested in me if I was her husband, or the wine taster or the *maître d'*, or another psychiatrist. She didn't even bother looking up when I said good-bye from the door. There had been too many good times in her life.

I decided I would have to approach her from an entirely new angle. I was determined to get something out of all that walking up the hill to the Allen Memorial every Friday night. I was going to ask her for advice. Real advice. Something concrete. After all she had a husband and a successful career. She obviously knew what to do and what not to do. On the very next Friday, I came prepared.

"I know there's nothing really wrong with me. Okay so I hate a few people, but I can learn to live with that. What I really need is someone to sort of advise me about what I should do. I don't know how to go about getting a job, and how can I best use my education? How do I know when I choose something if I've taken the right step? You see, I don't want to be a failure in life, but I might be because I don't know what I should do and how I should go about doing it."

"Those are the sort of questions you should put to the McGill Career's Advisory Service."

God, she was useless. Couldn't she see I was really asking how a woman goes about getting that diamond ring on her finger.

"I might add that I don't think at this stage I can be much help to you, so I'm recommending that you join the group therapy sessions. I'll make the arrangements for you."

"But why should I go to group therapy?"

"Well it's a way of learning to cope with anti-social behaviour. You will meet other people your age with similar problems and through discussions you'll come up with useful ideas."

Nothing was going to fool me. I knew I wouldn't get any answers there either. Nobody is ready to give you answers. I didn't know how I'd ever find out about things but I certainly knew it wouldn't be here. I had enough of the Allen Memorial Hospital and psychiatrists for the rest of my life. I wasn't going to waste another day of my life climbing up that stupid hill.

Anti-social behaviour. That wasn't it at all. I could have told her fast enough what my problem was. I could have told Jesse. I could have told the whole world. My problem was that I had a dog who ate better than I did, I lived in a one-room apartment that felt like a barn, I wore out-of-date clothes that were chewed up, dried in animal saliva and hairy.

My problem was that I had boyfriend who cried if he couldn't be the ringmaster, who spent hours calculating everything to the nearest penny, splitting bills straight down the middle, collecting receipts I'd never heard of to make sure I'd always pay my half, who forgot that I was still little and gave me more sex than I needed.

My problem was that I never grew up into the woman I wanted to be, that I was never seen at a hairdressers, that I was never given jewellery, that I was never taken on a vacation.

My problem was that in one month I would be finished university and I had no idea where I would be going or what I would be doing. I had spent all my time waiting for the promise, expecting the engagement. It had never dawned on me to plant a garden, water the trees. Now there was no opportunity, no contacts, nothing to look forward to.

Anti-social behaviour. She should count herself lucky that she had worked out a system of getting rid of her patients before they got rid of her.

I just hoped with all my heart that there would be moments, quiet moments, like the valium induced moments, moments taken away from God, in which I could not remember my own terrors. I just hope with all my heart, that I wouldn't discover that you can relive your past, but not redeem it.

I had the same worries when Momma first started teaching me how to make bread. She told me she couldn't tell me exactly how to do it and she couldn't write it down. All I could do is stand beside her and watch. She said I'd catch on. That for bread you just know when it's right. You just know. I didn't know how I'd ever know. I didn't know if you felt it, or there was a sign, or if you just had to put all your faith in it. So all day long I kept running back and forth, punching it down and it would rise, punching it down and it would rise. But Momma told me that if you punch it down too many times it won't rise properly, and then when you bake it it'll come out tough and leathery and be hard to eat. But she wouldn't tell me how many times you were supposed to punch it down and how many times it was supposed to rise before you could put it in the oven. She told me it depends. That I'd know. But when would I know?

I had to find her letters. Where did I put her letters? I searched the whole room until I found every one of them. Some were hidden under the bed, some were stored inside my winter boots, some were scotch-taped under the seat of the chairs. I read them all, and re-read them. Followed every word with my finger and underlined things and memorized things and re-read them again. Over and over.

I pray for you every day. Look after yourself because you can never tell what people will try and do to you. Things will work out for the best, maybe not the way you want it, but the best for you. It's time for me to get on with the washing and get some bread into the oven, so I hope this letter will cheer you up.

God bless you,
Momma

18

For Jesse there was no shortage of opportunities. How could he miss?

"My father's taking me to China with him this summer."

I could see it was another plot to get him as far away from me as possible so the bond would weaken and break.

"That's pretty good, I guess."

He had started to jump around on his toes, deluding himself that he was dancing, with the natural rhythm of fat people.

"Good?! It's the best thing that's happened to me in my life."

He did a clumsy sort of leap with a side-kick, used his hands for an awkward gesture in the air, and tried to do two spins and swivel his hips.

"I hate to say this, but it's even better than an orgasm." Dancing all by himself.

"But what are we going to do about Paladin?"

"Well you'll just have to take care of her."

Nothing in the world was going to stop him from going.

"How can I take care of Paladin? She's stronger than me and she doesn't listen to me. I know she'll break away from me when I take her for a walk and she'll get run over and then you'll blame me."

"Look go home for the summer. You live in the country, don't you? It's the ideal place for a dog."

"I can't."

"What do you mean you can't?"

It was a pity I had never told Jesse any of the facts. He had no idea that Daddy would kick Paladin around morning, noon, and night, that there wouldn't be anything for her to eat and she'd get skinny, that one of the neighbours would try and shoot her, that one of the mongrel dogs would mate with her and before we knew it we would have more dogs than we'd know what to do with.

"I mean, I think it's unfair to make my family look after something that's our responsibility."

Every one of them would look at me with their unhappy eyes and wonder why I was bringing more misery to the farm.

"Well you'll be there."

"But I don't even want to go back to Jasno Gora. I want to stay here and find a job."

"What'll you do?"

"I don't know. I'll find something."

"Naw. I think it's better for you to go back. It'll give you time to think about what you want to do."

Jesse went to China. At least no one could say I stood in his way. I didn't even bother him with the fact that it was the summer of my graduation.

Only Momma got excited about my having finished university. She wrote me a letter saying she was going to come to Montreal for the graduation ceremony and then would help me get my things back to the farm. I didn't think too much about it because I figured it was another big dream of hers—like those closets she still doesn't have.

The kids must have cried their eyes out when they saw her packing a suitcase. Daddy probably tried to stop her and told her if she stepped out of the house not to come back, and followed her in the half-ton, yelling, as she walked every inch of the twelve miles to Hopefield to get the bus. I should have known that nothing would stop her. I almost didn't have the heart to tell her.

"Momma, I wasn't really thinking of going to the graduation, maybe we should pack everything up and head back for Jasno Góra as soon as we can."

She looked so sad. Then I noticed her fingernails. She had borrowed some red nailpolish from someone and painted them.

"Okay, look if you think maybe we should go, I'll go."

"Well, I don't want to push you if you don't want to go."

"No you're not pushing me. You know maybe I should go. I mean, I passed university and I am getting a BA."

She started smiling and she looked straight into my eyes. They were so blue and they sparkled so much. They embarrassed me with their bravery so I looked away.

"Yes Genia, I think you should go. You're getting a BA. It's something to remember for the rest of your life."

I looked back at her. Why wasn't it her? I wanted her to have it.

"Momma, I don't think I've really achieved anything."

"Yes you have. No one else from Jasno Gora has gone to university. You should be feeling proud."

I wasn't feeling anything. I looked at our chewed up apartment and our unhappy dog. I thought about my boyfriend floating around in the middle of China. I remembered the hard summers that had gone and the ones that were still to come. What did I have to proud of?

But graduation was nice. There were thousands of people in the big hall. All of them were milling around, heads up, hair pasted into shape, chests puffed out. It gave me a good feeling to know that Momma was going to be able to enjoy it just as much as every other parent there. She deserved a great occasion like this.

As I walked down the aisle in procession with all the other McGill graduates, I saw Momma pushing her way ahead of the crowd trying to snap a picture of me. We were moving away, and she got so nervous she could hardly take it. I saw her smiling and there were tears in her eyes and her hands were shaking. But just in time I stopped the procession, and I stood still for her, and she snapped my picture. I wasn't ashamed now. I would have stood there for her until the master of ceremonies threw his hammer at me. She snapped my picture again. I was proud. This is what I was proud of, that my mother had the courage to push between all those big strong fathers who were snapping pictures with their electric powered Nikons and their zoom lens, and there was Momma with her borrowed Brownie taking my picture. I smiled back at her. I was so proud of her. I knew the pictures wouldn't turn out, because her hand was shaking too much and I don't think the flash cube was screwed on tight enough because it didn't flash, and as it turned out the batteries in the camera were dead because it was Aunt Zosia's and she hadn't used it for five years. But that didn't matter. I was happy. I knew I didn't need prints to prove to me that my mother had taken my graduation picture.

It was hard to hide the fact that Paladin was a nuisance. A minute after we got back to the farm she was slobbering all over everybody. The kids started screaming. Daddy came out of the shed, half-cocked and roaring mad.

"What's that?"

"That's my dog."

"Get it out of here. I don't want to see it around here."

"Well, I'm only staying for a few days."

Paladin didn't learn to stay out of Daddy's way until he gave her such a good kick that she limped for a week and I thought he'd broken her hip. After that Paladin was afraid of Daddy and would run away every time she saw him coming. I was so worried that Paladin would get skinny that I fed her my french fries all summer. Everyday when I went to close the chip stand, I would bring her back a pail full of soggy cold greasy french fries. Thank God she liked them because there was nothing else I could find for her to eat.

I made August work in the chip stand for most of the summer because I had other plans. I wanted to spend all my time fixing up the farm so it would look decent enough when Jesse came to Jasno Gora to pick up Paladin, after he got back from China. Momma and Ignacy loved the plan. They had always dreamed about fixing the farm up someday. I used all the money we made at the chip stand to pay for everything we needed. Momma painted the whole outside of the house and I painted the window sills and verandah and doors. Ignacy cleaned all the nails and bottles and rusty cans from the yard. Every day we took loads and loads of garbage to the municipal dump. We brought good gravel and patched some of the worst holes in the road leading to the house. We cleaned the inside of the house from top to bottom. There wasn't anything we didn't wash. We were exhausted every night but we never gave up and every morning we looked forward to another hard day of work.

In the back of our minds we remembered it was Jesse. That it was worth it.

I think Daddy had a hint of what was going on, but nobody told him for sure. We didn't want him to spoil our plans.

Aunt Zosia came to pick up her Brownie camera and joked with Momma about how hard we were working to fix the place up.

"What're you getting ready for – a wedding or something?"

Momma didn't say anything. She just smiled some more. I had never seen her so happy in my life.

I thought I'd go crazy when the day arrived for Jesse to come. There was still so much that could have been done. Unless you remembered that the house used to be black, and that you stepped on rusty nails everytime you turned around, you could hardly tell we had done anything. I wish we could have got rid of the old cars and trucks in the open fields or could have planted some flowers. I wish that flowers would have been able to grow.

I was worried that Jesse wouldn't find his way to our farm. Since the day I wrote down the instructions for him on a piece of paper, the barn just outside of Hopefield where he was supposed to make a right turn had burned down. Everything was making me nervous.

Then I saw his mini tackling the gravel road, collecting dust. Small stones were banging on it, little shrubs scratching it, marshy patches splashing it – by the time it reached the house you could hardly tell it was red. I knew that everyone was at different windows watching, and I was glad. I was proud of Jesse. I wanted them to see what a wonderful boyfriend I had. How perfect he was. Jesse stopped his car and it rumbled, I knew the shock absorbers were done for.

Paladin was jumping all over him, so he had to kiss and hug her first. But then he came to me and took me in his strong arms and hugged and kissed me. Right out in the open. In Polackville. I looked around to see if they were still at their windows. I didn't want them to miss a thing. I wanted them to see how much Jesse loved me. But then the kissing and hugging stopped, Jesse stood up straight, and with his twenty/twenty eyes took one look around. I knew he saw everything. I smiled and got nervous and started gesturing profusely.

"Well, here's where I live."

I was trying to be proud and courageous. Right here in the open there was nothing I could pretend about, nothing I could hide.

"Come in and meet some of my family."

I knew that Momma would make him a cup of tea and offer him a piece of apple pie. It was all planned. And I knew that Daddy was sleeping and I was only hoping that he wouldn't wake up for the next few hours. We went into the kitchen. Momma was at the sink. She turned around and I introduced her to Jesse. Momma was really nervous. She didn't know what to say or do. She got her sentences all mixed up and mispronounced all her words, and her accent got thicker and she got all red in the face and started smiling and laughing. Everyone was so nervous. Even Jesse looked nervous.

Jesse started eating the pie, but before he could finish I thought I heard Daddy cursing in the back. I rushed Jesse out of the house immediately. I told him we should take Paladin for a walk and see a bit of the country. I had to try and keep him out of the house as much as I could. I was too afraid Daddy would slap Momma across the face in front of Jesse or call me a whore because I wasn't married yet. My plan was to keep Jesse walking until it was time for supper. It was going to be a special wonderful supper. Momma was going to use a large piece of beef and cut it up into small pieces and serve every one of us a piece like a steak with potatoes and carrots. There was going to be enough for everybody this time. Even the kids were going to get one piece each. I didn't want her to go through so much trouble and expense, but she told me she didn't care what Daddy would say about using the meat. She said that we deserved a good meal once in our lives and if we didn't have it now, when would we have it? This time we were going to have the meat all in one meal. And for dessert we were going to have the rest of that apple pie.

One of the kids came running after us and wanted to whisper something in my ear. She told me that Daddy had got up and was really mad about Momma making steaks and was cursing and kicking things and drinking out in the open. She said we shouldn't come back for a long time. I told her to tell Momma to try and feed everyone and put two plates in the oven for Jesse and me and I'd try and get back as late as I could.

I walked Jesse around the whole farm and down the country roads two more times. I could see that he was tired and hungry and he was trying so hard not to lose his temper. I might have risked doing the complete walk for the third time but I had run out of fancy excuses to stay away. I had no choice but to take him back.

Just as we got close to the house, one of the kids ran to me and told me that Daddy wanted to see me in the shed. Jesse looked at me with concern.
"Do you think it's important?"
"Yes."
Important? Do you know what would be important? If you took me in your arms. And held me tight. And told me I'd never have to worry again. If you told me you didn't notice that we were poor and that we had a hard time living and that you wouldn't hold all this that you see against me. If you looked into my eyes and told me that now that you'd come to this farm you realized that I was the right girl for you, and

196

that you would never find anyone better and that since God wasn't good to me, you would be.

"Please excuse me Jesse. I promise I'll only be one minute."

In the shed, I could hardly find Daddy. He was sitting in the corner, in the dark, on a pile of boards. He was dirty and unshaven and he had his bottle of wine on one side of him and his soup tin for his snuff spit on the other. He was drunk, and his eyes were red and unable to quite focus on me. He looked so dejected I tried to control my voice for his sake.

"What do you want?"

He was incoherent as usual and started muttering. He said he had heard that my boyfriend had come and that he was a nice boy. Then he lowered his head.

"I don't know what's wrong with Momma."

"Ya, ya."

I didn't have any patience for him anymore. I went back to Jesse.

"Jesse can you wait outside for just one minute. I have to see my mother."

I went into the kitchen but I couldn't see her. I asked everone of the kids where Momma was, but they said they didn't know. I looked upstairs, in the bedroom, all over. I couldn't find her anywhere and I started calling and shouting for her. Then I opened the basement door and there she was. In a bundle at the bottom of the steps. I ran down to her. Her left eye was purple and swollen and her leg was bleeding.

"Are you okay?"

"Yes, just help me up the steps."

I sat her on a chair in the kitchen. Her face was white and I knew she was going to die. I was praying, in my head, that her heart wouldn't give out.

"Why did he do it?"

She wouldn't tell me. She was trying to act normal. She was pretending she wasn't dying.

"Your two plates are in the oven."

"Why did he do it?"

"He was mad at me for using the piece of beef and cutting it up into steaks instead of saving it for stews."

He couldn't stand seeing her make a fancy meal. He said he wasn't a millionaire and that piece of meat could have last us half the winter. He said he didn't want her catering to anybody. He wasn't running a hotel. And when she tried to stand up to him and answer back that it was her children she was doing it for, he shut her up by pushing her down the basement steps. Even though I was crying, I was furious.

"That bastard can keep it. I wouldn't eat here if you paid me."

I ran out of the house. I told Jesse that he and I and Paladin and as many young kids as we could take were getting in the car and going into town.

"Why? What's going on?"

I know I made his life difficult for him, but I couldn't help it.

"Please Jesse don't ask questions, let's just go."

When we got into Hopefield I asked Jesse to stop at the grocery store. How was I going to ask him for some money? I knew he expected a free meal. I didn't have a penny on me. We had to eat, we were all hungry. I looked at the kids all crowded in the back seat – if only we could have scraped together a dollar between us. But I knew Jesse was the only one with money. I was afraid to ask him. I got out of the car.

"I'll be back in a minute."

I went into the store and looked around. I'll keep it as cheap as possible – a quart of dairy milk, a loaf of bread, a half pound of cheese, and a bag of marshmallows, as a treat for the children. I took the groceries to the counter.

"Oh, I'm sorry, Mrs. Konarskie, I forgot my purse in the car, can you hold these for me a minute?"

I went back to Jesse's car.

"Guess what Jesse, I completely forgot to bring money – can you give me three dollars to pay for the groceries."

I could see he was really angry at me. He didn't trust me that I would pay him back the money.

"I promise I'll pay you back as soon as we get to the house. God, I'm sorry about this, but I can't very well leave them there on the counter."

He couldn't make up his mind what to do.

"Look, I promise I'll pay you back, I just forgot that's all."

He only gave two dollars and thirty cents because he didn't want to break a five-dollar bill. It wasn't enough so I had to put the marshmallows back.

When I got back into the car with the groceries, I said that we were going to eat in the country, a picnic. The air was so nice, it would be a shame to stay indoors. Jesse said I was crazy because it was dark, but then he stopped the car and we got out and started to eat. By now everyone was in a bad mood and it was hard to eat. Especially for me. I've never had such a big lump in my throat in my life. And poor Jesse, usually he can eat anything anywhere anytime. Now he took one bite of cheese and was full. Even the children had a hard time eating. But Paladin ate everything that was left. I was glad someone was happy.

On the way back to the farm, in the dark, Jesse ran straight over a stone jutting out somewhere and ripped the muffler right off his car.

I took Jesse upstairs and gave him him my bed to sleep in. I don't think he liked the idea of everyone sleeping in the same room but there was nowhere else for him to sleep. I told him that I was sleeping downstairs. I pretended that there was another bedroom down there that he hadn't seen. I was going to stay up all night and guard the door. Daddy was still in the shed and I knew he was sleeping but I didn't want to take any chances. I knew if he woke up he would roam all over the house, shouting and cursing and keeping everyone awake. I wanted Jesse to have some peace. I kept myself awake by thinking about all the tricks I could use to keep Daddy out of the house until the morning. Once I almost fell asleep so I went to sit down at the door so if he wanted to get in the house he would have to trip over me and that would wake me up. But I never fell asleep again, and the morning came.

Jesse wanted to leave as early as he could but the clutch had worn down on his car, and he had to wait until August and Ignacy got a few things from the abandoned cars in the field to fix up his mini, so it would do until he got back to Montreal.

"I think a year's separation will do us good. Give us time to think. Every relationship needs to have time apart to prove whether it's good or not."

I stood there and watched as he helped Paladin into the back seat and tried to make her comfortable.

"And anyway even if they would give me money if you were in the same city, I won't have any time to fool around this year. It's going to be fucking tough getting into law school."

Then he came to say good-bye. He hugged me and I didn't want to let go. And he kissed me and I wanted to kiss him one more time. I could tell he still loved me. I could tell.

Jesse got into the car. I wanted to kiss Paladin good-bye but she was busy playing with a toy bone Jesse had bought her in China so she just growled at me. Maybe the next time we get together both of them will have forgotten all the bad things that happened.

Jesse rolled down his window.

"Let me know, when you decide what you're going to do."

"Maybe I'll go to Toronto."

When he started his car, it made so much noise I didn't quite hear what he said, but it sounded like something about Genia always going from place to place looking for a mecca. I wanted to tell him if he was going to get poetical, he should have said manger.

There was so much I forgot to tell him. I wanted to tell him that I would prove to him yet that I was as good as everyone else. I ran to the high pasture and stood on the biggest rock I could find. I wanted to shout it out to him so that he'd have something to wait for. But I only caught the last glimpse of the red in the distance.

Nobody bothered saying good-bye to me when I left for Toronto. I couldn't really blame them. I knew they were as sick of seeing me leave as I was of leaving. I found Momma. She was starting the washing.

"I don't want the chip stand anymore. It's yours. You can do whatever you want with it. If you happen to sell it, you can send me half the money or something. Okay?"

She started the washing machine. I couldn't even see her head between the baskets of dirty clothes.

"Good-bye."
 Then I said it again louder.
"Good-bye."
 She looked up for a minute.
"Eh?"
"Oh, nothing."

19

It was in all the papers. A city on the make. Growing. Moving up. Expanding. Thousands of jobs for everybody. People were coming from all corners of the world. To Toronto.

I didn't exactly believe every word but I expected to have some luck in Toronto. I figured if Toronto could be everybody else's city, it could be my city too.

I hit the streets with a passion. Eight o'clock every morning I was buying a newspaper and chasing after the jobs advertised in it. My head was spinning I was so ambitious. I applied for everything. I was ready to tell the employers that I would do anything, that I was a quick learner, that I was better for the job than anybody else I could think of.

I walked up and down the streets, from one end of the city to the other, from this block to that block, from one office building to another. I had to walk. I calculated that if you did it the easy way, by taking a bus or a subway or a street car, it could end up costing you over three dollars a day. I needed to save my money to buy the newspaper to find the jobs, to make the telephone calls, to arrange the appointments, to buy the stamps to send them more information on me. I asked people for directions, and if I was going to be late because they told me it was far, I ran. Maybe I wasn't going about it the right way, but how are you supposed to find a job if you don't go out looking for it?

At the end of the third week, I had applied for a hundred and twenty-nine jobs. Nobody could use me. Nobody really needed me. Nobody would put their faith in me. I had never done anything before so they had no proof that my eagerness would make up for my lack of experience. My clothes looked a bit shabby so they didn't believe that I could make myself look nice. They seemed like a different set of people in Toronto. I don't think any of them realised that I was a fellow Canadian.

And the money was slipping through my fingers faster than I could make up new budgets. Even though I had cut down eating to once every two days, and even though I was postponing paying my rent for my room in the rooming-house and letting it add up, and even though I started borrowing newspapers instead of buying them, I couldn't make my money last. And there was the money that I had to pay back on the student loan. I had a debt of four thousand dollars and the interest was adding up every day. When would I ever start paying it back? And where would I find the extra money if my shoes gave out on me?

And then I got the pain in the back of my neck. I tried to smile and pretend it wasn't there. But every day it got worse. I cursed at it and tried to ignore it. But it wouldn't go away. The more the pain hurt, the more I walked. It drove me to try twice as hard, apply for twice as many jobs. Not even the rain stopped me. I like the rainy days better than the sunny ones. It hurt a little bit less then.

At the end of the fifth week, I watched my last ten cents slip down a pay phone:

"Listen Miss. . . ."

"Luckoskie."

"Yes my dear. It's four o'clock Friday afternoon. I don't see any point in you dragging yourself out to see me, so I suggest you leave it and get in touch with me on Monday."

"But I could be there in fifteen minutes."

"No, I'm going off early for the week-end. Why don't you just enjoy the rest of this nice sunny day."

She had hung up the receiver, and locked her office, and left for her week-end, but I was still talking to her on the phone. I told her that the pain had paralysed my neck and I could only turn five degrees to the left and I couldn't turn to the right at all. I told her that I had already applied for two hundred and fifty-seven jobs and I was hoping that she'd be the last one I'd have to call. I asked her what I could do, who I could speak to, where I could go now? "You know what it's like," I told her. "You're a woman. I'm sure you understand, don't you? If I menstruate to-morrow, it'll fall on the street."

I thought I'd better get to a doctor before the paralysis spread to my spine and I'd have to go running around looking for a job in a wheel chair.

"I don't know why I have a pain in the back of my neck. I haven't done anything unusual. No heavy lifting, nothing."

I tried to stop myself from breaking down into tears but I couldn't. I had become so weak and stupid, I'd start crying every time I'd move. No one would ever have guessed that I came from good hardy strong Polish-Canadian stuff. The doctor put his hands on the back of my neck. Skin to skin. He kept them there. Touching me. How wonderful it was. Did he know I could feel him touching me? Did he know what it felt like to be touched? So good. Even after he took his hands away, I could still feel exactly where he had touched me on my skin. You have to touch, always touch. Even if you do it for one minute, you can give enough to help somebody. I just hoped with all my heart that I would remember that you have to touch. Someone.

"You've got a charlie horse."

"What's that?"

"A charlie horse is a cramp that seizes the back of the neck muscles and causes pain. It's caused by tension."

"I'll give you a prescription for some valium to take every day and have a hot pounding shower beat down on it as often as you can."

Valium?! Second time round you begin to realize that there is something funny going on. It seemed that every goddamn time I was stepping into a doctor's office, they were prescribing valium for me. I guess they'd like me to be lying on some bed somewhere slipping into a state of rest. I guess they think that's all they can do with a Canadian Pole is put them to sleep. They keep forgetting that sometime in your life you wake up. Walk around the earth. See the world. Realize that everyone else is working. And then who can you yell at, who can you kick, when a hundred years have past and all you were doing was sleeping. Thank God I didn't have the money to have the prescription filled out. The charlie horse would have to go away on its own. And what the hell was it doing in my neck anyway?

At the beginning of the sixth week, I saw a little sign sitting on a window of an old building. You'd almost miss it unless you were walking slowly and carefully because you were tired and poor.

Earn up to $200 a week.

No experience required, only enthusiasm and hard work.

Apply within.

All the offices on all the floors seemed to be shut down. By the time I climbed up to the third floor and still couldn't find an office that was being used, I decided I'd give up. That sign was probably put there years ago, before the building fell into dilapidation. I had no energy to climb any more steps. But what if there was a job up there at the top? What if I'd come this far and just missed it? I sat down and got up some more strength and started climbing again. On the fifth floor I found it. There was a small paper hand-written sign by the side of the door, *Chaime Sneltzer*. There wasn't a handle on the door so I pushed it open and walked in. There was a middle-aged man sitting behind a worn-out desk. No one else was around so I figured he was Chaime Sneltzer. He pointed to a chair. It rocked underneath me when I sat. The building didn't look professional, and the office didn't look professional, but I took the interview seriously and I was a bit nervous. I thought I probably wouldn't get the job because I felt too tired to have any enthusiasm and looked too weak to make him believe that I could work hard.

Chaime sounded smart and businesslike. You could tell he tried his best to run the place like an office.

"I'm not going to be bothered interviewing a lot of people. When I find the right person I'll hire him on the spot and I'll forget about the others. You know, I want to get straight down to work."

He took a minute to look at me. I wanted to look back at him, into his eyes, but immediately he lowered his eyelids and I never saw them.

"I'd be interested in employing you and if you want to work with me and trust me, I'll explain the job and you can have it."

"Oh, that's very kind."

He was straightening up his body more now, but his eyes were still hidden.

"This is a telephone campaign job. Basically what it is is that I give you a list of people in the city to phone and you ask them if they would like to buy an advertisement space in a magazine I'm going to publish on football and which I'm going to distribute free at the final football match of the season."

The cheapest advertisement was twenty dollars and they gradually scaled upwards to a full page for two hundred. It really depended on how much the people wanted to donate and how much they wanted to advertise.

"There'll be no problem selling the advertisements because the whole world loves football."

I smiled to myself. He sounded like me with my french fries.

The money arangement worked like this: on the completion of the sale of the advertisment, that is, after the money was promised and then actually delivered I would get 5% of the advertisements I had sold.

It sounded a bit risky, but since we were going to be working in the same office I could keep my eye on him and the money that was coming in, so I decided to take my chances. As

Chaime explained to me, I had nothing to lose and I had the possibility of earning two hundred dollars a week. At least I didn't have to go door to door to make my sales. I think it was the thought of never having to walk again that made my decision instant and final.

He got up to show me the office. There was no need. From my unsteady chair, I could see the streaky little window with no curtains, the forty-watt light bulb, the four copies of the Yellow Pages.

"I've had an extra telephone installed here you see."

He looked back at me for approval. I nodded my head. He came back to sit at his desk.

"When would you be free to start?"

"I could start right this minute."

He was right. The advertisements sold like hotcakes. Chaime told me that I wasn't to be afraid to stretch the truth, swing the lead, try a bit of bluff, to sell the advertisements.

"The name of the game is to get them, and the more of them you get, the more money you make."

He was overjoyed when he found out that I was a great liar. We cooked up stories and made up names and trumped up business like two old sinners who hadn't seen each other for a long time.

Every time I was promised an ad, I could see the dollar signs flashing through my mind. Five percent of twenty dollars, five percent of a hundred dollars. I was making on the average forty dollars a day. When the week was over I had earned one hundred and fifty dollars, but Chaime reminded me that I'd have to wait for at least another week before I would see any money, because it would take that long at least for it to come through in the mail. But he promised me that it would pay off in the end. The first day I walked in, he gave me two dollars for food and every week he gave me ten dollars as an advance, just to keep me standing up.

I know some people that passed thought it was strange seeing me walk with an old man into a building that looked as if it was condemned. But I loved my job. It certainly wasn't hard work and we could sit in the hide-away office all day and nobody in the world bothered us. Chaime taught me how to smoke a cigar, so I'd have one cigar with him every day. Whenever we'd get tired phoning we would stop, sit back, put our feet up, smoke our cigars and talk to each other. He asked me all about myself.

"Do you have a boyfriend?"

"Oh yes. We've been going out three years now. We're really in love. We'll probably get engaged this year. He's what you'd call nice. He's Jewish. He's going to study Law at McGill University."

"Are you sure he's going to marry you?"

"Of course, I'm sure. We're in love. His parents are trying to break up our relationship but Jesse won't let them. He's different, you know. He doesn't think like other Jewish boys. We know the problems, but we're going to face them together and get over them."

"He won't marry you, Genia."

"How can you say that? You don't know him. You don't know what he's like."

"Look, I'm Jewish. I know."

Wouldn't you know it! It seems as if I'm bumping into a Jew every time I turn around and I still can't recognize one when I see one!

"I didn't know you were Jewish. I used to go out with another Jewish boy, David, so I know what you mean. But Jesse's different. You don't know him, but I'm telling you he's different. Doesn't matter what you say, I know he's different."

Chaime wouldn't give up trying to make his point. He took my hand, squeezed it in both his hands, and let me see his eyes.

"Look they all say they're different, but mark my words little Genia, he'll never marry you. Do you hear me – he'll never marry you."

Even though I could see his eyes were real, I didn't believe Chaime. He was a failed Jew. If he couldn't get ahead, he wasn't going to let any other Jew get ahead. I wasn't going to let him think bad things about Jesse. The Finkelsteins were successful Jews.

"If you're Jewish, what are you doing having a job like this?"

208

"I was a lawyer too, but I had trouble with a case and was accused of embezzlement and was disbarred. But I'm trying to get it all staightened out and in a few months I shall be a practising lawyer again. This job is to bring in the bread and butter in the meantime. You have to do these sort of things to be able to support the family when things go wrong. And you've got to be prepared to do anything. Anything. I've even had to buy girls' panties and have girls wear them for a day and then sell them to men, to make money."

After the third week had come and gone I was getting a bit suspicious about when I would be getting my money. I knew there was money coming into the office but Chaime told me they weren't from my clients. They were his. I sat on the telephone for one more week. At the end of the fourth week, I definitely decided that Chaime was trying to pull one over on me. I told him that first thing Monday morning of the fifth week, I wanted my money. Real money. No more advances. No more promises. I wanted my true commission or a salary. I had two month's rent to catch up with, and I had a four-thousand-dollar loan plus interest to pay back, and I wanted to start eating meals.

But Chaime was one step ahead of me. At first, I thought I was on the wrong floor but it didn't take me all that long to realize that Chaime had moved out. His run-down desk and my shaky chair were there and there were a few bits of paper on the floor, but the telephones had been removed and my pen was gone. I slammed the door that wouldn't bang. He had even remembered to take his paper sign. Funny, but I didn't cry. It was all over and I didn't cry. All I kept thinking was that there was a real difference between us. He was a dirty liar and I was an honest liar. But I didn't hate him. If I bumped into him on the street I would pretend he didn't owe me anything. I'd probably just ask him why he didn't leave me a cigar.

Up there in the dingy office, I could smile about our misfortunes and love him because he was Jewish and we both had ended up in the same boat, but now that I was out in the street again I wasn't laughing. Maybe I should have laughed. I should have sat down and laughed my head off. Everyone could come to Toronto, from every corner of the world and make their fortune. Except me. I had been here two and a half months and I didn't have one penny to my name. Not one penny. I couldn't go into the cheapest café in the city and order myself a half of a used tea leaf.

One night I got a cramp that completely seized up my abdomen. In the morning, I couldn't get up. In the afternoon, I couldn't get up. At night, I couldn't get back to sleep. The next morning, I still couldn't get up, and I was starting to get more worried. I must try. Don't be stupid Genia, get up! Sickness is a state of mind. I got up and started for the door, to go to the bathroom. I couldn't do it. I fell back on the bed. How did I get so weak? God my life had slipped from me so fast. Dying at twenty-one. I should go to the bathroom. I don't need to go, but I should go. It's not right not to move from bed for two whole days. Then the night came again. The cramps were getting worse. I couldn't sleep. The morning came. Maybe it was the fourth day. I don't know. Somebody must help me. I heard a noise outside. Where I got the energy this time, I don't know. I think the pain must have driven me from the bed. It was a garbage collector.
"Please can you take me to a hospital."
I couldn't get back into my room, so I just fell on the step.

How I got to the hospital, I'll never know, but I was there. I loved the big strong white bed under me. I loved the three dying old women in my ward. I loved the intravenous needle in my arm. I loved the bedpan that was brought to my bed because I was too weak to be taken to the ward bathroom. The nurse said they had diagnosed me as anaemic and dehydrated. By vitamin injections and intravenous feeding they were going to build up my system again. But they were puzzled about the cramps and were going to run a series of tests once I was strong enough.

I didn't want to get better. I loved being in the hospital. They took such care of me. Life was so easy. And now I really didn't care about dying. It would have been easy for me to pass away in the night. I wouldn't have felt it. So much easier in a hospital than in a rooming-house. It was even easy to commit suicide in a hospital. All I had to do was let a little air into the intravenous tube that ran directly into my blood and I'd be dead in an hour. Why couldn't I bring myself to do it? I had nothing to live for. If only I had something to die for. Or someone. Who would I write my suicide letter to? And what would I say? Jesse wouldn't care, he'd still become a lawyer and doesn't matter how you cut the cake, he'd still have a happy life. And Momma. Well Momma prays for me whether I'm dead or alive. I don't really have a life anywhere, not in Jasno Gora, not in Montreal, not in Toronto. Suicide would be futile for me. How can you take away something you haven't got? No, the hospital suited me. I better stay as long as I can. I just lived from day to day, and my greastest joy was when they took the intravenous tubes away and I could have solid food. Every day I had a choice of what I wanted to eat. It was like living in a free restaurant.

The tests for the cause of my cramps continued. The doctors were running around like crazy trying to figure it out. I could have told them why I had pains in my stomach. That's where I was kicked and punched, when I lived on the farm, more times than I could count. That's what seized up every time I got depressed with Jesse. That's where more suffering took place than anywhere else in the world. But I didn't tell them. I wanted them to figure it out on their own.

One of the doctors, the youngest one, always kept hanging around my bed. He was looking for clues. I could tell he wanted to solve it on his own, to prove himself, to move up faster than everyone else.

"You're not Jewish by any chance, are you? You know that that would really answer a lot of questions, if you were?"

I wanted to give him a break. I smiled and I nodded. I've never seen a happier doctor in my life. He ran out to find his colleagues. Four doctors came back, circled my bed and drew the curtains. They were ready to make a diagnosis.

"We believe that what you have is Crohn's disease. It's a disease that attacks the intestines and eats them up. A person is then unable to pass food. We understand you're Jewish."

I wanted to wink at that young doctor.

"Yes, that's right."

"You see, we were originally puzzled but this explains it. This is a rare disease and it only occurs in Jewish girls between the ages of fifteen and thirty. But there isn't too much cause for worry. You will have to watch what you eat, but you should be all right. If the intestine deteriorates to an uncomfortable level it will have to be replaced by a plastic one. Once you are strong you will leave the hospital and see an outside clinic once a week for check-ups. The only prescription we will give you at the moment is valium."

They walked away proudly in their stiff white jackets. They were pleased with themselves. Well I was pleased too. I was pleased because the doctors had really believed my lie. They believed that I was a Jew and they confidently explained to me that I had a Jewish disease. I couldn't wait to tell Jesse, so he could tell his mother. Now she would have to accept me into their family. I had another status symbol. I was so damn proud to have Crohn's disease.

It shocked me when the nurse came and said that they needed my bed.

"You can go home now."

At first I didn't think she was serious. But nurses have a way of turning off when they know you're no longer officially sick.

"Can I please just stay the night and I promise I'll leave in the morning?"

I cried all night. I didn't want to go. What would I do? Where would I go? It was stupid sending me home. On my own, I couldn't keep my strength and I would become devitamized and anaemic again, and before they knew it I would be back in the hospital. I knew if I told the doctors I really wasn't Jewish they would let me stay another week so they could figure out once and for all what was wrong with me. But I couldn't put the poor doctors through all that trouble again. I would have to go.

The nurse was there kicking me out of bed bright and early.

"Is there someone I can telephone to come and pick you up and take you home?"

212

"Oh no, everyone at home will have gone to work so they can't very well pick me up."

"Well you better get a taxi right out the door."

"Oh yes, that's no problem."

"Now you're sure you have someone at home to take care of you for a while. You're still weak and it wouldn't be very good for you to be on your own immediately."

"Of course. I'm well looked after. I live with my fiancé and he takes very good care of me."

"Now here's your prescription for two bottles of valium and a bottle of codeine for pain. Don't forget, take it very easy for the next two weeks."

It was easy for her to talk. She probably ate three square meals a day. If I didn't go out and find a job, I'd be back in this hospital before her duty for the day would be over. I was hoping she felt sorry for me as I walked towards the door. But she didn't call me back. I even stopped at the door for a minute to give her a chance. But I didn't turn around because I knew she wasn't there.

I walked back to the rooming house. My steps were weak and I had to stop after every block to sit down and rest. It made sense that my body should have gone weak. My mind was weak. I was a weak person. I never had the strength to do anything. All those years ago when Josef and Urek called me a *maly biedok* – the stupid little weakling, how right they were. Why hadn't I closed the switch on the intravenous needle in the hospital that night? The nurse had explained it to me carefully. Why didn't I realize that maybe God had sent her to show me how easy it is to slip away if you have to. I think God expected me to commit suicide.

But really the street was the perfect place for it. It wouldn't look like suicide. I would take one weak step out onto the road and some fast strong car would come by and mow me down. You'd really just disappear. And that's what I wanted to do, just disappear.

The only thing that they could trace on me was the prescription. I walked to a garbage can and threw it away. I wouldn't have had any money to buy the medicine anyway. Now there was nothing on me. No proof. How would anyone know who I was, where I had come from or where I was going? I stepped out onto the road. And a car whizzed past me. God, I almost had it then. It didn't give me enough time. Those mean bastards wouldn't give you a minute to say something nice to yourself, like, "Thank-you God for everything." I hated that car that almost got me.

I needed something slower, more satisfying, but just as deadly, like a red mini. I wanted to step in front of a red mini. I saw one in the distance and I chased it but I couldn't catch up. It got ahead of me, made a corner, and was gone. I thought that the roads would be full of red minis, that there'd be one lurking around some corner waiting for me, but I never saw another one.

At the rooming house there was a letter from Momma. She had sold the chip stand and had sent me a money order for three hundred dollars. She sold it to a man from Greenford for four hundred dollars but was keeping one hundred for a few things that she needed. Good, clever Momma. How many many times she has helped me. You could always count on Momma. That was one thing I could always say for her. What a good strong woman she was. And still alive.

20

I was getting really fed up with being a failure. Somehow I would have to take complete control of my own life. I didn't want very much. Simple things. To be able to tell the truth and to get a job.

I'd start small. I'd get a job as a cleaning woman. In the university. It was the best place I could think of, where I would be sure of getting a job. I would have a vital edge. They would have to favour me over the regular cleaning ladies since I was a university graduate.

But when I got to the English Department and had a second look at the secretary who said hello to me, I decided to go one step higher.

"Oh yes, hello miss."

I would love to have been a secretary. Such good honest work. Work that other people depended on. Work that made other people happy. You could type, telephone, write in, erase out, file, post, water plants, dust your desk, and if you got all caught up you could sit back and read a magazine. Your boss would come out of his office and smile at you for having done something well. There was obvious love and security. And if you were one of the lucky ones you might get a hard tight pinch on your ass. It was perfect.

"Is it possible to get a job as a secretary at the University here? I have a BA."

"I'm sorry, there are no vacancies at all."

She could smile all she wanted, I wasn't leaving.

"Well if you don't mind, I'm going to sit down here and wait."

She didn't know whether to laugh or cry. Every once in a while she looked up from her work to see me sitting there. I was hoping she'd get ill so that I would be right there on hand to replace her. For once in my life, I wanted to be in the right place at the right time.

I sat there and wouldn't move. All morning people kept coming in and going out. The different professors, the students, the Chairman of the Department. What I couldn't understand was that the whole world looked relaxed. The professors stopped to joke about the weather, the students meandered into every corner of the room to touch every brochure they could find, the Chairman of the Department made himself a cup of coffee. It dawned on me while I was sitting there that I could probably stand on my own two feet like everyone else around, if I only had learned a few things in my life. If only somewhere I could have learned the basic facts. And I could still do it, if I picked up some sound knowledge, a proper education. All afternoon people kept coming in and going out. Everyone that passed had a look at me. Well, they could look at me all they wanted. I was busy planning my life.

After the third cup of coffee, the Chairman of the Department came over to speak to me. He bent right over me, he was so worried.

"Is there anything I can do for you?"

"No thank you."

I gave him a waxy smile. I didn't mean to. It's just that I couldn't help it. My face was starting to harden like wax and when I smiled I could feel it creasing my skin. The secretary got really nervous and got up and followed him into his office. I didn't care. He came back out.

"Perhaps you'd like to come in and talk to me for a minute."

Now I could see that I was getting someplace. I nodded a

thank you to the secretary as I walked past her into the Chairman's room. I sat down in a nice green plush armchair. So soft and comfortable. There were plants in his office and a brick fireplace and on his desk were all sorts of paper neatly piled. The organization in the room gave me strength. I felt I was a very important, very intelligent person. Maybe I was a diplomat? All of a sudden, I felt I was going to get anything I wanted. It got me all excited. What should I ask for? I felt charming and nice and pretty. I was wearing my black coat that I had bought for first year at McGill. All the silver buttons had fallen off so I had it pulled tight across my chest with a safety pin. I had lost the belt with the silver buckle but it felt like the coat of a queen. Nothing would have made me take it off. What made me think that I was worth a million dollars?

The Chairman was busy putting the tobacco into his pipe so I got a head start.

"I'll tell you why I'm here." I crossed my legs. "I'm looking for a job. I'd like to work as a secretary at the university but I'll take anything, you know, like cleaning or something until the vacancies come up."

"But why come to the University of Toronto if you just want a job?"

"Well I've got a BA so I thought this would be the best place to come because I'd be right on hand anytime there was an opportunity for something better."

I knew I better start spicing it up.

"And I thought that I'd like to continue my education so if I worked here I could sort of continue studying you know during my lunch breaks."

He raised his eyebrows and started taking longer and harder puffs on his pipe.

"I mean that's what I really wanted to do in the first place. Get an MA."

The last thing in the world I wanted to do is go back to university, waste some more time and get further and further into debt. But it was the only way I could keep him interested. He took his pipe out of his mouth and started banging out all the spent tobacco.

"If you were thinking of doing graduate studies, why didn't

you get an application in to us in plenty of time for us to consider you?"

"Well I wanted to but I couldn't because I was in China."

He was going to put some more tobacco in his pipe but instead he decided he better sit up and listen to me.

"Of course you know that I couldn't let anything stop me from going to China. It was the opportunity of a lifetime so I had to take it. But I'm a hard worker and I know that I could catch up."

It was the end of November and I'd already missed two months of classes but he was still listening so I continued talking.

"It should be possible in a graduate course to do that sort of thing. I know you don't make it a rule but please can you make an exception in my case. You see, I had no way of contacting you from China."

He was still listening to me.

"And another thing, I took some courses when I was out there so if you'd like I could write the university in China and ask them to send you the results of the tests and you could count that towards the courses I've missed here."

He just sat there and looked at me. It was one long uninterrupted gaze. Eyes that had been warmed by too much tobacco smoke. I just sat there too. I had finished. Anyway all I wanted was a job.

Then he moved. He picked up his pipe, held it in both his hands for a few minutes, then put it in his top pocket. I could see that he was going to make a bargain with me.

"Generally people take the MA course in one year, but I suggest you do it in two. That way you can do both the things you want to do – work and do your MA over an extended period of time."

It made sense, because if I enrolled in a university course, the four-thousand-dollar debt would remain frozen and interest free and through the course of the year I could handle a few subjects while I held down a job.

"Next year you can file your application in plenty of time and I see no reason why you shouldn't be eligible for a bursary."

In fact, by going back to university and working at the same time I could get my finances completely under control. And especially next year, if I got a bursary and still kept my job, I could leave university with an MA and all my debts paid. It sounded like a good enough deal, so I accepted. He got on his phone to everyone to make all the necessary arrangements – enrolment, financing, transcripts, appointments, courses I should take. Here was a man who knew how to do business. I didn't have to lift one finger or walk one inch. I wanted to remind him that I didn't have a job. But I didn't. I knew when you're doing a deal you have to meet your partner half way. I decided I wouldn't bring it up again. That half was up to me.

I found out that there was a trick to getting a job too. I cursed all the way down to the Manpower Centre. Why had I never heard of it before? Why had no one told me that something like this existed for people who just wanted a job, work, money? I always find out everything at the last minute. I was down there like a flash. I didn't even wait to make out an application form, and I wasn't going to wait to be interviewed and I couldn't wait for someone to hand me a job. The room was full of people and I didn't want to run the risk of there being no jobs left by the time it was my turn. I read every single advertisement on the wall, I wrote down the names and addresses of all the plants and factories looking for extra workers, and then I headed straight for them. Within five hours, I was all set up with a job at a bakery. Three evening shifts a week and all day Saturday and Sunday. I had to punch a clock so I knew I'd get paid, and there were about five hundred other people working there so I knew they wouldn't close down on me. I wish Chaime Sneltzer could have been here to see me get paid every single Friday at one o'clock on the dot. Oh, I know they only took me on because they needed the extra help to get all the mince pies out for Christmas, but I had a feeling I would never get laid off. All the old men that worked beside me told me that the foreman liked pretty girls, and if you were pretty you would get to stay on. And when I walked into that factory, I knew that every single man there thought I was the prettiest thing in the world.

The only thing I didn't like was getting up when it was dark and coming home when it was dark. That was the only sinful thing about it. At four o'clock in the morning, even before the alarm would ring, I could feel someone coming into my room and stealing my life from me. It was always too early to see the sun rise. And it was always damp and cold. The streets were big and empty. I felt like a baby, so small and scared, walking up one way and down another to get to the factory. Once I tried to make contact with God, but he wouldn't speak to me. I wasn't going to ask for anything. I just wanted to tell him that I knew that behind everyone of those dark windows there was a man and woman making love. He was angry that I had given him up. I had really lost him now, I knew I would have to walk these streets for at least a hundred years before he would even consider forgiving me. I was a criminal among criminals. It was right that there should be nothing in those mornings and nights except the cold and the dark.

I had my job in the factory and I had my classes for my MA at the university. I worked like a bastard, but I was proud because it felt like success.

Until the tired little mind of Professor Fairclough tried to get me. He thought it was one big joke to hand me back my first English Literature paper with a red F. I would have spoken to him right there and then but he told me he only speaks to people by appointment. I didn't have enough goddamn time to cater to him but I had to because I could see he was going to use his power to fail me. Sister St. Jerome had caught up with me.

I opened the door of his office with a big smile. For effect. How ugly and small he looked in his big grey swivel chair. He was wearing grey trousers and he looked pallid. I wondered how he had the strength to keep his legs crossed. He was the weakest-looking man I had ever seen. His chest was caved in and his chin was sinking. Men shouldn't look like that.

"Please Professor Fairclough, I wanted to discuss my term paper with you. You see, I think you failed me."

"Well you don't expect to walk into a class two and a half months after everyone else and pass do you?"

I could see that the first round was only going to last five minutes because he knew what he was going to say and I knew what I was going to say.

"But I can't fail. It's too important. I can't afford to go to university for a year and fail."

"Well we can't pass people just because they want to. We have our standards to maintain. There would be no point to a university if people didn't meet the approved standard."

He got up and moved from his grey swivel chair to his brown straight armchair. I think that was the only fun he ever got out of life, because he did it with so much attention and with such a big stupid grin on his face. I had to follow him around in his goddamn little room like a tiger.

"Well can you give me another chance? Can I please rewrite this paper for you? If I don't write a better paper on my second try then I will understand that you have to fail me."

I don't know why he was sitting by his window anyway. It was a useless window. I knew that there never was a day when any sunshine came into his office. Even if you stood in front of it and looked straight out you couldn't tell if it was a rainy or a sunny day.

"Well can you at least please show me what I've done wrong and how I can write a better paper in case I ever have to do another one?"

"Let's have a look at it then." He sighed.

I handed it to him. His hand had liver spots all over it. Anybody could see they were weak hands. But they were still vicious hands and as he quickly turned the pages of my paper all I could see were the huge red lines and circles and words that he had smeared my work with. But then he stopped, and page by page, he described why he commented and why he criticised and why he failed me. The paragraphs were too short, many were only one sentence long. One long rambling sentence that didn't make any sense. Words used incorrectly. Paragraphs with no consistent theme. There was no structure, no purpose, no meaning, and no logic. The only thing he liked were the quotes I found, but he couldn't understand why I used them.

"It seems as if you didn't really care when you were writing this paper. It really does look like a child's you know."

He was right, I didn't care. But I did care about failing so I had to learn to beat this problem once and for all.

"Professor Fairclough, I'm sorry but I just don't know how to express my thoughts. They're in my mind but I just don't know how to write them down."

He looked up from the paper and into my face. I didn't realise he wore glasses. And he had thin lips. How awful it would have been to kiss him.

"Can I ask you something? Do you really have a BA?"

I could see that that was a very good question to ask me. I had to sit and think about it for a minute. Of course I had a BA, but I never once put it into use. Then the whole secret about education dawned on me. You have to use it. Make it work for you. That's what everybody must have meant when they said your education would come in handy someday. Days like today when you have to stand up and prove you're educated. To take the first step for yourself.

"Well you see, our generation was brought up on television. Very few of us read any books."

You have to catch an idea.

"We just saw and heard things and that's how we learned."

And develop it.

"We never got used to writing. I mean, we don't even write letters. When we want to speak to someone we just telephone. Doesn't matter where any of your friends live, if you have something to say you phone them."

And pass it on.

"And we never really thought too much about what we said or how we said it, we just said it. So you see, we never learned how to put our thoughts on paper."

Like all those lectures I had sat through, he was listening.

"And then I went to McGill and you know what McGill's like. It's a progressive university and they take pride in the fact that instead of writing papers and theses, you can pass by doing practical projects like conducting an oral seminar where four or five people will discuss an idea and then only one person will act as a secretary and write down the collaborative ideas and submit that paper on behalf of the five people."

As long as you kept talking, no one could doubt you.

"We never ever really had to write a paper. And in some classes if it was required you would be allowed to put down the information in point form or make up a bibliography."

And if you talked with enough energy you could even prove what you were saying.

"At McGill they were interested in interrelationships between subjects and new and different ideas and thoughts. The more innovative and unconventional your idea, the greater the chance you had of passing. They weren't concerned with what they gave us, they wanted to know everything we could give them."

And when you're finished, your head starts spinning because you didn't realize you knew so much.

Professor Fairclough cleared his throat. His voice had weakened so much I had to really strain to hear what he had to say to me.

"Well one of the most important things about an education is that you must be able to write well."

He got up and pulled out a book by Bernard Shaw.

"You see, Shaw was a marvelous writer. You should read a lot of Shaw. It would teach you how to write well. Then you should also have a look at this very elementary but very helpful language and grammar book which teaches you how to make correct sentences and paragraphs, how to structure a paper, and how to present your ideas."

"Oh, thank you so much."

"Then when you know what to do, it's up to you to do it."

"So you think that if I read all Shaw's work and followed the outline of writing as they suggest in this grammar book that I should be able to write a decent paper?"

"I don't see why not. Of course you won't be another Bernard Shaw. . . . "

And he laughed. What a weak miserable laugh it was. What would he have thought if he had seen the way I used to belly laugh with Jesse?

"I mean, do you think I might be able to come up to the standard of your class and pass?"

"Well, we'll just have to see."

I felt proud and full of energy. Even though there wasn't much I could do with his advice I felt good that he had offered it to me. I stood up and gave him my hand to shake. After thinking about it for a minute, he shook it. Poor Professor Fairclough. I must have upset his day, because he wasn't very happy about shaking my hand. It was a trick I learned from Mr. Finkelstein. A handshake can put anyone off guard.

"I'm very grateful to you for talking to me about my paper."

By the time I got to the door and turned around to say good-bye, he still hadn't got out of his chair. I knew he was suffering from the handshake.

I smiled.

Everything went click, click, click.

The legs on the chair in my room were unchewed, I knew where every penny that I made went, and I calculated that in ten years I could save enough to pay back all my debts.

Fourteen people lived in the rooming house and we all shared the same kitchen and the same fridge. It was a poor man's paradise. Fanny was a vegetarian and health food fanatic and every night she made a fresh container of orange juice, so I helped myself to a glass of it every morning. I even started drinking a glass every night until she started complaining. She could never find out exactly who it was that was taking her juice because there were so many of us in the house. I was safe. Anyway I figured if she can afford to have orange juice every day of her life, she can afford to spare me a glass. On my budget, I couldn't plan for anything except supper – three carrots, two potatoes and a pork sausage. Fanny hated watching me prepare my supper every night but as soon as she heard the sausage frying she couldn't stop herself from rushing in. She watched every move I made.

"Aren't you bored eating the same stuff every night?"

"Oh no, you see I'm on a selective foods diet."

That enraged her. She thought it was a new diet that she

hadn't heard of. She drew charts comparing and combining the food value of a carrot to a potato to a sausage. She searched the libraries for ancient and new books. She questioned me every night about what I meant by selective foods. I didn't tell her that my food budget was two dollars a week, that was just about all the store near the factory sold, that sometimes those damn carrots would get stuck in my throat and almost choke me. But I made myself eat them every night because I didn't want to get sick again.

I had the occasional supplement. Whenever someone bought milk or cookies, I would always help myself to a little bit. I was a genius at putting everything back exactly the way I found it and I was so quick at getting things, I never got caught. Even if all thirteen of them were in the kitchen with me I never worried. I could take things when they bent down, or rubbed their eyes, or turned their backs for half a minute. In my time I had a taste of honey and peanut butter and a golden delicious apple and raisins.

But I wasn't trying to fool the world with my success. Every once in a while I got severe hunger pains in my stomach and I knew I was still the little girl standing around the corner watching the onion eater and wondering when I'd ever get my piece of bread and margarine. I could see my fancy cut-outs in real life going into and coming out of restaurants. Sometimes I'd follow them up the steps to the door and stare inside. All I could ever see was the double decked trolley full of chocolate puffs and strawberry mountains and golden cake. And there was cream on top of everything. Once when I was coming down I bumped into a man going up to take my place.

"Hey do you think you can give me a dime for a cup of tea?"

And I started crying.

"Holy jumpins, I'm sorry. No, listen you keep your dime. You keep it. Hey listen, do you want a cigarette?"

I was sad for him because he was older than me.

It was slimy, rooming-house rat, professor-imitating Charlie that told me that my father had come over in the afternoon.

It couldn't be Daddy. He never left Polackville. Why would

he want to come to Toronto and ruin my life? Now everybody'd know all about me, my lies would have gone to waste, and next year I'd have to find another city to move to.

"No, it couldn't have been my father. My father's on a business trip in the Orient."

"Well he said he was your father and he sat in the kitchen and waited for an hour and I talked to him."

I could tell he was going to turn the knife for all it was worth.

"I didn't know you came from the country?"

I pretended to laugh.

"Don't we all?"

I wanted to know what Daddy looked like and if he was drunk but I didn't dare ask long-nose, pain-in-the-neck Charlie. I had no idea how much he already knew and I certainly didn't want him to know more.

"Well, anyway, I told him you go out every night until eleven o'clock so he said he'd come back then."

That gave him pleasure. He couldn't wait until eleven o'clock so he could rally the whole house together to see me fall flat on my face.

"Did anyone else speak to him, or were you the only one?"

"No one else was in."

Thank Christ for that. Fanny's IUD would have popped out if she would have seen my father. I had her convinced that I was a millionairess. Oh, I knew it was him all right. It didn't matter how hard I tried, it seemed that I would never be able to have my own reputation. God hadn't even scratched the surface of his vengeance for me.

I ran all the way home from the factory so that Daddy wouldn't get there before me. And anyway what was he doing all night? Sitting in a hotel getting drunk? And what the hell was he doing in Toronto? Where did he get the money to come all this way? Imagine what Fanny would think when she got up in the morning and saw his old half-ton on the street outside the house. What if he couldn't get it started and sat there all day cursing. It would take me the rest of my life to get over this blow. I sat in my room and waited. At one minute to mid-

226

night, I became so afraid he would fall all over the steps and wake everybody up and frighten Fanny that I went to sit outside on the doorstep. It was a good idea because this way I could sneak him into my room before snaky Charlie got together his contingent of supporters.

Then Daddy drove up. He parked the truck and walked to the door, straight as a judge. Ignacy was with him. Good Ignacy, I knew he'd kept him sober for me.

"Hi Daddy."

"Genia."

And I kissed him on the cheek. God we've come a long way since those miserable days when he couldn't stand the sight of me.

"Come in."

Now that we were safe in my room I was glad he was here. It was nice to see him. And Ignacy. They seemed happy. It seemed to me that Daddy really like travelling. I sat him in the armchair by the lamp. You could see his intelligent face. I stopped breathing for a minute. I never realised he was such a good-looking man. Now I could see his high aristocratic cheekbones and his distinguished blue eyes. I could tell from the way he sat in the armchair that he had sophistication. Sophistication that's born in the bones and that no amount of alcohol can dissolve. No one, anywhere in the world, will ever be able to see an old armchair so beautified.

"You must be tired from travelling all day and hanging around all night waiting for me to come home?"

"Oh no, we're not that tired."

Good strong Daddy. I wish I would have had enough money to give him back the money he had to spend on gas to come to Toronto. He deserved someone to give him money. Such a gifted man deserved to be successful. And he crossed his legs and sat back in the armchair and I wanted to bow for him.

"I'll make you a cup of tea. Wait here, I'll be back."

I made some tea and then I searched the whole damn place for something special for Ignacy to eat. I found two chocolate covered digestive biscuits hidden behind three tins of soup in the top cupboard. There would be hell the next morning if I took them but that didn't stop me. Nothing would have stopped me from stealing those cookies for Ignacy. Daddy smiled when he saw me walk into the room with a plate and two cookies on it. I smiled back. And Ignacy ate them. I don't think I've ever been happier in my life.

"Me and Ignacy will have to start heading back home soon, but could I lie down and have a snooze for five minutes first."

I jumped to attention.

"Of course you can lie down. And you'll sleep all night."

I opened up my bed for Daddy and put a blanket on the floor for Ignacy and me.

"I'm not going to let you leave in the middle of the night. And in the morning you'll have breakfast and then you can go."

I watched as Daddy laid down his kingly head.

I showed Ignacy the way to the bathroom. I waited for him in the kitchen. That's when I spotted the grapefruit in the fridge.

"This isn't a very nice place you live in, is it?"

"Ignacy, what did you and Daddy come to Toronto for?"

"Oh Daddy wanted to see about buying parts for the tractor because he's ordered some and they haven't come. And he needs to get the tractor going because he can't do any work in the bush."

"How come he's not drunk?"

"Oh no, you don't know Daddy. He's been really good now for two weeks."

Ignacy and I tiptoed back into the room to sleep.

In the dark and light of the room I could see the shadows of the King. His head didn't sink into the pillow. It lay on top like a carved piece of priceless crystal. I was so afraid it was going to shatter from disappointment. They couldn't find any parts for the tractor in Toronto so they would be going home empty-handed. I couldn't stand thinking about him spending money to come to Toronto and not get anything for it. No wonder he needed alcohol. It was something to cool the pain. I got up and took the two dollars that was next week's food budget and put it into Daddy's coat pocket. And there was that grapefruit. If it would be still there in the morning, I would be able to send them off with a good breakfast. I had refused to pray for such a long time, but now I decided to try ten Hail Marys. I knelt by the window and negotiated every single difficult word in my mouth. I got up and went to the fridge, took the grapefruit and held it in my hand under the blanket for the rest of the night in case God hadn't heard me.

The grapefruit was the turning point of my relationship with Daddy. He was the first one to greet me the very next time I went back to Polackville.

"Oh here's Genia."

He was almost jumping he was so excited. And he tried to stay sober for the whole week-end.

"Momma, did you know that Daddy came to visit me in Toronto?"

Momma said that he was moping around all winter, complaining and not doing anything that she suggested to him that he should go and see me.

"He always complained that the kids never did anything for him, but I told him that I had nothing to complain about. When I went to your graduation in Montreal you treated me like a queen. So I guess he decided to go. And he doesn't regret it. He talks about it every day."

She was right. Daddy never stopped talking about his visit to Toronto. He even brought back men he bumped into at the liquor store to show me off.

"This is my daughter, Genia. You know she treated us well in Toronto. She even gave us a grapefruit for breakfast."

Then he looked straight into my eyes.

"You know I'll never forget how good you took care of Ignacy and me. No man could do better."

At last.

I could now live in two worlds comfortably.

I wanted to write Jesse immediately to tell him how ready I was for him. There was still three months to go before our trial separation would be over but I couldn't wait. I wanted him to know that he was going to get more than he expected. I could feel that I had become all right.

> *My Darling Jesse,*
>
> *I can't tell you how much I've missed you in the past year. I hope yours has been a good year. It certainly has been for me.*
>
> *I've done so many important things, special things but I'm going to save telling you until I see you in person. They'll make you so happy. You are going to be really* proud *of me.*

Being proud can keep anyone together.

> *How's Paladin? I bet she kept you good company all year because I know how lonely it can get one night after another. But you and I will never have to be lonely again because we'll have each other. When we're alone together my darling nothing will stop us from being happy for the rest of our lives.*

I knew that once we were married everything would be okay. I knew I could make Jesse happy. If only he would have faith in his decision. All he needed was faith.

> *I love you, my sweet Jesse.*
>
> > *All of me,*
> > *Genia*
>
> PS: *I don't mind waiting for four more years until you're finished law school.*

Really, when I think about it, Jesse and I had put behind us four of the hardest years. There would only be good times for us now. I used to always overhear Jesse tell his friends that as the years roll on life gets easier. That's what I felt, too. Maybe the people that suffer end up having a better life after all. I decided you have to live a long time before you get comfortable.

21

But if I got anywhere it was a shaky step and there was spasmodic pain.

Now that I'd learned how to speak up for myself, I'd stop the professors short every time I didn't know what they were talking about. Redrup would get blood blisters on her neck, Fairclough shut up like a clam, Pepet twitched. After about the fourth time I'd interrupt, they'd say they didn't want to spend class time answering my questions, and if I wanted to discuss any point, I could speak to them afterwards. I would have obliged them but I knew it was a trick, because whenever someone else asked a question the professors would get all excited and smile and spend class time answering it. Hours and hours of class time. For them. And when these interesting people spoke they didn't even want answers. They just wanted to hear themselves talk. Or to hear each other talk. But I wanted an answer. I always wanted answers. I only asked because I wanted to know something. And I'd keep on asking.

But they had it all tied up. Them and the professors. The professors and them. I needed three letters of reference to apply for a bursary and I couldn't get one professor on my side. Every one I asked said they couldn't give me a letter because they'd already written letters for at least two other students.

231

When I wasn't looking, those lovely talking bastards had edged me out. The professors said it wouldn't be fair to those people to give out another letter because then the ones they'd already written wouldn't mean anything. Every day the deadline got closer until there was only one day left. I wasn't going to give up. I wanted to apply, I wanted to try my luck at winning a bit of the free money, like everyone else.

I went back to Professor Pepet.

"I'm sorry, Miss Luckoskie, but I just don't know you or your work well enough to be able to write a letter on your behalf."

"Yes, I understand Professor Pepet, but I don't have anyone else at the University of Toronto to ask for a letter. Nobody at all."

I kept looking at him. He thought for a long long time.

"Would you please be kind and write me a letter even if you have nothing to say about me?"

I was still looking at him. Finally he said okay. As soon as I left him I wrote to a couple professors at McGill and asked them to forward the two other letters I needed. I figured it was better to have letters from professors who didn't know me, than no letters at all.

From the point of view of letters of reference, I sort of suspected I was running the risk of not getting a bursary, but I was counting on the fact that there just might be one poor soul on the selection committee who knew what it was like to eat boiled carrots every night. I knew a person like that senses everything.

I lived in hope. Just the expection of having free money to go to university on made me feel dizzy. What would it be like? I'd have enough money to see me through the year. I could buy one or two of the books I really needed. I could have a full cafeteria dinner once a week. And I could plan. Really plan for a fresh start in life. When I got the bursary I would use that money to finish university but I would still continue working full time so that I could pay off my student loan. It would make Jesse so happy. I knew he didn't like the idea of marrying someone with four years of debts hanging over their head. But would I feel guilty that maybe there was somebody else who needed it more than me?

I wish there had been someone around to help me open the little brown envelope that arrived so soon. But it was only a notice to inform me that the committee was unable to process my application because they had not received any letters of reference. What had gone wrong? I went straight to Professor Pepet's office.

"I sent it, Miss Luckoskie."

I showed him the notice I received as proof of what I was saying.

"Well could you please write me another one because they won't consider me if they don't have the reference letters in their hands."

It sounded as if he was snorting. "I'll type up another copy of the letter I sent and I'll give it to you personally to mail so that you'll be satisfied I'm not trying to be difficult. But I'll tell you, if I hadn't kept a carbon copy, I wouldn't be doing this."

Why do people turn nasty when you ask them for a favour? I couldn't understand why he didn't want to help me. I would have helped anyone in the world if they would have asked me. I watched his cold bald head as he typed up the letter, put it in an envelope, sealed it, and gave it to me to mail. I didn't have a stamp or money on me so I had to take it home with me for a night.

I stood it on my dresser and tried to stop looking at it. I was tempted to open it but I told myself not to because it wouldn't be an honourable thing to do. In the end, people respect you far more if you're honourable. I tried to go to sleep but I couldn't forget that it was there in the room with me. And my room felt so small, the committee felt so far away. And what if he knew things about me that I didn't even know? I got up and opened it.

Dear sirs,

I have known Miss Luckoskie for only six months and have therefore really nothing to say about her. She does however strike me as being a fairly energetic young lady.

> *Yours sincerely,*
> *Prof. Pepet, Ph D*

How was I going to get a bursary based on a letter like this? Why hadn't Professor Pepet made more of an effort? He could have lied for me. He had nothing to lose. What a miserable useless creature he was. I could have killed myself for having thought he was unique when he told our class one day that he took a twelve-hour train journey so he could read *War and Peace* in the right atmosphere.

What could I do? I got out another envelope, put the letter in, sealed it, and mailed it off. It obviously wouldn't be fair to dismiss me for a letter like that. The committee is sure to recognize what a mean selfish man he is. It obviously says more about him than it does about me. They'll invite me to come before them. They'll ask me why someone would write a letter like that? They'll allow me to state my own case.

But I didn't get that far. The professors at McGill hadn't bothered to write letters of reference for an unknown ex-student, and on the basis of incomplete documentation the committee abandoned my application for a bursary. I received another little brown envelope that asked me to try again next year. They must be crazy. Do they think I can afford to wait from year to year to get money? What am I supposed to live on from one hungry day to the next?

I think I could have handled it, if I wouldn't have found out who got the bursaries in the end. Can you imagine how fat Jack and ugly Julie must have been dancing that night? In every class, the Professors Redrup, Fairclough, and Pepet stood up and asked us to extend our congratulations to Jack and Julie and the million other students who had been successful in getting scholarships and stipends and bursaries. I wasn't going to congratulate them. What for? For being tricky enough to get to the professors before me? For being able to get the professors to lie for them? And what really angered me beyond words was that they weren't even Canadians. Jack, Julie, the whole stinking bunch of them were Americans. I could see them winking back and forth, patting each other on the back, shaking hands. I tried to sit as far away from them as I could. I had started to talk out loud to myself.

234

"Don't turn around and look at me for congratulations because I'll kill you."

How unfair and stupid the government is. To give these American students our money when they or their families haven't worked a day in Canada. Here they were sitting in our universities, living off our taxes, burning our cheap electricity, and thinking they were the greatest intellectuals in the world because they had fooled everyone around them. Well they might have fooled the government and they might have fooled the university and they might have fooled the professors, but they hadn't fooled me.

What a deceitful girl Julie Glossop was. She was going to use the money to carry on her sneaky love affair with Jack. What else did she need the money for? She was married and her husband paid for her three-room apartment and everything else she needed. And Jack was going to use the money to buy himself a car. I guess he was getting too fat to walk around anymore.

How unjust the Canadian government is to its own people. We were the first people to settle in Canada. We are absolutely the oldest Canadians. There's a goddamn blue historical plaque sitting on a post outside Jasno Gora to prove it. Since we came to Canada one hundred years ago, we have never left yet, not even for a day. None of us. And we haven't complained either. They have never had a word from us. We took that handful of stones they gave us and kept our mouths shut. We've just worked. We didn't spend our time planning ways to cheat the government – we didn't know you could.

In Polackville unemployment insurance was unheard of because everyone was self-employed on their own farms and bush lands, and where would they get enough stamps to be able to claim unemployment? And we didn't even have a public school. We only had the small schoolhouse that the church built and kept up from donations we gave them every Sunday. Sometimes the nuns would ask us to bring them things for teaching us. We took them wood or apples or our mothers would bake them bread or knit them woolen socks. In the winter no snow plow cleared the roads for us. We had to tramp by foot with snow up to our ears to get anywhere. And we didn't have a hospital. The church was saving up money to build one but we'll all be dead before they save enough. And now after one hundred years of never getting anything, I ask them for one lousy small bursary and they turn around and give it to an American.

Scrupulous.

Yes, Father Anotskie was right. I was too scrupulous. That was my biggest problem in life. Why was I born of such conscientious, gut-working, reverent stock? We had to learn everything the hard way. The rich American cottagers took advantage of us, the people that passed on the roads laughed at us, the educated repatriates denigrated us. Just for one drop of pity, one word of advice, a few simple answers, a half a pocketful of help. We'd been kicked in the teeth so often we'd forgotten it hurt.

If only Julie had been more modest, a bit grateful, it would have been easier to take. But she strutted around the university without any shame at all. And every day she had new things. She threw away her glasses and bought contact lenses, she bought a really expensive long purple Indian dress from a boutique on Avenue Road, she was always sitting in the student cafeteria eating pizzas and drinking coffee and smoking cigarettes. The money was just pouring out of her ears. But for me there was no chance. Canada is no place for a hard-working, scrupulous Canadian Pole.

Try again? Like hell. They were never going to catch me applying for another bursary. What did they want from me anyway? Did they want me to stay in university for the rest of my life and get more and more in debt until they woke up one day and realized I needed help? It would have to be a day when there were no more hypocrites around, and I couldn't wait that long.

I was learning fast now. I knew it didn't matter how long I stayed no one would help me. Look how long we'd waited in Polackville. In those hundred years, Canada had grown into a great nation, but it belonged to someone else. Our people cried and prayed and then gave up. Now they're all sitting in their unpainted leaky farmhouses, looking at their two hundred acres of hard stone and drowning their lost hopes in alcohol.

It took the full one hundred years before Canada remembered it had one rough little corner up there. Then one day we were made note of in the government files. We were registered as a depressed area. If you broke your back in the bush, they'd give you a little bit of free money. But who wants it now? I was ready to leave university for good. I hated everybody I could think of. I would have quit right then and there, but I figured it was worth starving another six months so that I could leave with a lousy useless MA. I couldn't let Julie have everything.

* * *

My brother Josef has stopped talking altogether. He lives in his silent world of rage. He hates students too. He says they are nothing but a bunch of parasites. Nobody knew, but Josef slaved through university and got himself an engineering degree. But you would never have caught him eating pizzas or applying for bursaries. The day he finished he got a job in a big electrical company and within a year he had paid back all his loans. He never got a free cent from the government in his life. He wouldn't even think of trying to get one. He had a word for it, a Polackville word – suckholing. He goes to work, comes back to his room, sits down and goes to work again the next day. And every week-end and every vacation, he travels the two hundred miles back to the farm. He buys as little as he can in the city. He would never shop in a big supermarket. Even though he had to pay more, he always went to his local corner store.

And when he comes home, he buys as much as he can in Hopefield to take back, just to bring them a little business. As soon as he's saved enough money, his first investment will be a piece of property in Jasno Gora. Everyone thinks he's crazy, but I know he's right. You don't have to travel the world to know that the best people live in Polackville.

But sometimes I feel sorry for him. I'm afraid he'll turn into an alcoholic. In his room there's a display of all the bottles of booze he's drunk. There are bottles from over the past two years. In total they must number about one hundred. Which is only a bottle a week. I hope he doesn't drink any more than I can see. As long as he keeps it in the open so we can keep track. It's once you start to hide it it gets dangerous. I don't want him to give up so soon. I could see that he was slipping on the line between bitterness and culture. I wanted him to remember how he tried to use big words, how he used to find things to discuss in those newspapers he delivered every week, how he heard things on his transistor radio long into the night when everyone else was asleep. I tried to explain to him that that's how culture started. When the first man stood up and said what? why? where? You have to break the chain, fight your way out, pull yourself up, tear yourself apart, search. It takes courage and pain to stand up and become cultured. But I wanted him to do it. For dignity and self-respect and confidence. I was going to use Jesse as an example. But I didn't. Jesse arrived at his destination on the back of a stork. And Josef has slipped the wrong way.

"Look, I'm happy leading an average life. I mean we're Luckoskies. There have never been any great brains in our family. We're average, maybe even below average. Why kill ourselves to be anything more?"

Why! Why do you think God went through so much trouble to give us beautiful blue eyes?

I guess Josef realized that maybe Daddy had a dream too, and look what happened to him. But Daddy isn't quite the same now. Now he doesn't bother anybody. He sits alone all the time. He's always thinking. I think he feels bad about having caused so much trouble, and I know he's hoping we'll remember him as a good father. Now he sits in view where everybody can see him. On a bench. Half way between the rusty horseshoe and the straw cross. I'm not ashamed of him anymore because he looks like someone whom you should have a great pity for. How can you hate a king who didn't succeed? It must hurt him more that it hurts me to see his black thick curly hair turning grey. And how does he feel when he puts on his trousers and he has to pull his brown thin belt one notch closer because every day he loses weight? And he knows he has no right to stop people as they pass him on the verandah and ask them where they're going and when they're coming back. Nobody thinks of stopping and telling him.

I'd like to go up and thank him but I don't know what I should thank him for. I would like to know what he thinks about. And that day when Jesse drove away from the farm in his red mini, I'd forgotten he was sitting on the verandah with his legs crossed, and his back bent, and his head hanging down. What was he thinking? Did he think that I was happy, that I had found a nice boyfriend, that I would get married, and have a good life? Did he think that all his hard labours had produced one small success? Maybe I should have told him that even if there was a wedding there would be no dancing.

*　　*　　*

There have been too many summers in my life. Bad, depressing summers. Lonely, forgotten summers. Summers when I almost died. Now there was the summer of Jesse's letter.

> *Dear Genia,*
>   *I'm having difficulty getting enthusiastic about our relationship. I have decided I want to break it up.*

I never knew how it would happen. But here it was. Words on a piece of paper. And it was over. It was the cruelty that made me cry. And I loved him so much.

> *There isn't any one reason I want to break up with you. It's for a number of reasons. You're a very difficult person to get along with. And I'm afraid that if we would have married, it would have ended in divorce. I really didn't feel all that happy with you and I don't feel at peace when I'm with you. I haven't really enjoyed that year we sort of lived together. There are other reasons too. I couldn't stand seeing you knock your head against closed doors and never get anywhere. I've noticed that since the early years at McGill you're*

slowly losing your intelligence and because of the people you associ-
ate with your mind has really degenerated. Look, I guess you can't
help the way you are, considering what sort of family you came
from, so I'm not blaming you. I don't think you're wrong. It's just
the way you were brought up. And another thing is that you should
have made more of an effort to try and get along with my parents.
And finally, I don't want you to think this had really anything to do
with another girl. I'm sorry if I hurt you. I know you always saw
life together with me, but you'll get over it. You can create a life of
your own. You just didn't fit into my world structure.

Jesse

The lump in my throat was choking me. My ears were hurt-
ing. Something was kicking me in my stomach. There was a
sharp pain in my vagina. I felt as if I had finally been ripped
open from the bottom of my feet to the top of my head. I
walked back and forth holding my breasts. I dropped to the
floor on my knees. Was nothing going to stretch out and give
me comfort?

PS: You know I'm a man of few words, so don't start calling me up
or coming to see me because I have made my decision and it's final.

Maybe he was God, because you had to wait, and then
when he said your number was up, your number was up. Now
it was someone else's turn. Somebody else is going to get everything I was to have. She is going to live in a nice house, have
nice clothes, go on nice vacations. My quick Jesse. He turned
his back on me to look after her, to make her happy, to tell her
he loves her. And me. What about me?

Like the scrap pedlar of long ago, he came, he ate, and he
left. Even if you wished you'd stepped into a better house, had
a better meal, had better company, you still should thank the
people that were there. When you break away, you should
show kindness and do it in a nice way. I would have understood. But all I wanted was five more minutes – look at him
one more time, kiss his high forehead, touch his curly hair. Did
my Jesse not realise that you can kill someone even if they
don't die?

240

Now I knew why Momma turned to stone sometimes. I know her heart must have stopped beating every time the man she loved pushed her down the basement steps, or kicked her in the leg, or punched her in the eye. She must have held her tender breasts so that they'd still be there when the cruelty was over. On a farm full of people there was no one to stretch out their arms to give her comfort.

My cardboard box with my upper-class cut-outs is gone now. I don't think I'll ever find it. But Momma still has her cedar chest. With her wedding presents. I'm going to make her open it. I'm going to make her take out the white Kenwood blanket and sleep in it. I'm going to make her use the silver tea-pot. And the dried up corsage, I'm going to make her take it out and frame it. It's important proof that she would always be there to protect the young even when there was no protection for her. I just wonder if I'll be strong enough and good enough and generous enough to give the blood in my veins as many times as she has.

The four little children have grown up. All their lives they watched me with their young eyes. Their sad eyes. Worried eyes. Wondering. Now, I will go back and tell them what they saw. But I'm not going back like Father Anotskie did. When I walk around Jasno Gora, I'll damn well know where I am. I don't want to pull anyone down. I want my suffering to redeem them. Mine will be a holy mission. A mission of encouragement. Because they're all a part of me, or I might be a part of them.

First, I'll advise August to become a doctor. He could use his fine brain to discover a cure for alcoholism. I'll tell him how to apply to university, how to cope with all the people around him, how not to let the professors put him down, how to get on with the job, how not to let it defeat you. August is sensitive and gentle. He would need advice and answers and encouragement. He'll fail if I don't help him. He thinks he isn't smart, that he hasn't got enough money to go to university, that he can't take out girls because they won't look at him. Well I'll help August. All he needs is a few answers. I have to tell him that nobody can stop him and that the person next to him is stupider than he thinks. If only August wasn't so scrupulous. Yes, he is scrupulous. I think that's how I'd have to sum him up. I must hurry and tell him about how many cheats and hypocrites there are in the world and that in the end you can't put your faith in anybody, not even God.

And Honey. Baby Honey. Princess Honey. It was worth having eight children to end up having someone as beautiful as Honey. She has huge blue eyes, pink lips, fine blonde hair, nice straight legs. It was no mistake for Momma to name her after Mrs. Montgonery-Jones. Everyone who came to the farm could see that Honey was meant to be wined, dined, courted, and castled. I'd like to make sure that Honey gets everything. There'll be real clothes for her every time a new catalogue comes out. When she walks into a dance hall she shall be the envy of every girl in the world. But I would have to protect Honey. I can't let her work hard. I don't want anyone to make her scrub floors and carry a wash pail. And I'll tell her to hum all she wants. And one day, she will learn to play the piano. I am going to make sure that she gets a good education, that she develops a sound judgement and a quick intelligence. There'll be an engagement ring on her precious little finger before any man possesses her. Nobody is going to take her for four years, turn her apartment into a dog house, leave her alone every summer, make her feel stupid, and then in the end throw her over because she doesn't fit into his world structure. Nobody, but nobody, is going to break Honey's heart.

Bernadette is going to be harder to look after. I don't see how I'll be able to spare Bernadette the cruelty of the world. Bernadette isn't growing. She is small and vulnerable and everything makes her nervous. Bernadette is too curious about sex, and she has no talents and everybody hates her. You can't help it. As soon as you see her, you want to pick on her. Bernadette is always running around cleaning the house, washing the dishes, peeling the potatoes. The more she does for people, the worse they treat her. But she is always there when you want something done. Why was Bernadette born? Nobody in the world cares for her. She is so unwanted and so unloved. And that day at Montgomery-Joneses, when she was just a baby, she already knew what hardship was. She cried so hard her belly button pushed forward, and the doctor to this very day can't figure out how to put it back to normal.

Still somehow I'll have to help her. First she'll have to stop the day-dreaming, now when she's young. She probably has a cardboard box somewhere that nobody knows about. I have to get angry at her sometimes. It's the only way I can teach her. It's the only way I can knock the day-dreams out of her. Bernadette lives too much for the future. When I see Bernadette sitting with her legs crossed, I have to yell at her. She thinks she's an old woman already. But it's no use telling her not to wear her glasses, because she's so short-sighted she walks around in such a daze you feel sorry for her. Poor Bernadette.

Why wasn't everyone like Ignacy? Even when Ignacy was small he was always standing in the middle of a room. You'd wonder how a child with such torn underpants and innocent blue eyes could become so famous. But if you were quiet and waited you could almost see a glow around him as if he came from heaven. I knew he was God's child, he was blessed in every way. He'd open up his hand and there would always be candies in it. He'd stand there with his hand open and everyone would walk by and take as much as they wanted. Doesn't matter how much he'd give away, there was always more. It seemed as if his hands were always full. It was like a miracle. We never knew where those candies came from. I want to tell Ignacy to be careful and close his hands now that he's grown up. But gifts of character don't change and Ignacy has grown to be more generous and more miraculous and more of a provider.

He's decided he won't leave Jasno Gora because Daddy needs him and someone has to look after things. He wants to settle on the farm, restore it, and make it grow something. He works like a bull and never complains. At the end of a hard day he never has to yell at God. God is always helping his little miracle worker. How peaceful Ignacy must feel to know that God is on his side. He wants to marry a little blue-eyed girl from the next farm. What a joy to live in the same place your heart is. And what a good life he'll have. He fixed the fences that had fallen down. He cut the long hay and weeds, and the land sparkled it was so green. He bought cattle and put them in the open fields. They don't seem lost at all on our farm, they run around those stones as if they thought it was always home. He got the old trucks going and they buzzed and squeaked trying to prove they were still alive.

I am so proud. Ignacy wants to preserve everything. He won't let anything be destroyed, replaced, polluted, sold out. And in one hundred years time there'll still be a Luckoskie and there'll still be a Polackville.

"Genia, you don't think it's necessary for everyone to go to university do you?"

"No, Ignacy."

I told him he was already a professor. A true professor. I should have stayed at home and taken lessons from him. Where did he get all that wisdom?

And me. I'm learning that it's not so bad if you can talk to people. If people tell you things, and you tell them things. I could sit down and think about it for the rest of my life, but I know it really couldn't have happened any other way. I was Genia. I had a troubled spirit because God had played games with me.